What the critics are saying…

With the classic good vs. evil fight as the background for this book, *Protector* is a great read. This one had me up late because I couldn't bear to put it down. I really liked the storyline, not only because of all the super soldiers, but also because Holly is portrayed as a strong, smart woman. Lisa Renee Jones' writing style also made this an enjoyable read and has me waiting anxiously for other tales of super soldiers. ~ *Crystal Sizzling Romances*

"*Lisa Renee Jones* has written a perfect blend of erotic romance and suspense that keeps the reader on the edge of their seat while reaching for a cold drink. *The Protector* is the first in what I hope to be a very long *Underground Guardians* series. There are several more sexy Black Knights that deserve their own story and I, for one, can't wait to get my hands on them! I can't recommend *The Protector* highly enough!" ~ *Shelley Fallen Angel Reviews*

LISA RENEE JONES

PROTECTOR
UNDERGROUND GUARDIANS

ELLORA'S CAVE
ROMANTICA PUBLISHING

An Ellora's Cave Romantica Publication

www.ellorascave.com

Underground Guardians: Protector

ISBN # 1419952285
ALL RIGHTS RESERVED.
Protector Copyright© 2005 Lisa Renee Jones
Edited by: Pamela Cohen
Cover art by: Christine Clavel

Electronic book Publication: January, 2005
Trade paperback Publication: August, 2005

Excerpt from *Healer* Copyright © Lisa Renee Jones, 2005

Warning:

The following material contains graphic sexual content meant for mature readers. *Protector* has been rated *S-ensuous* by a minimum of three independent reviewers.

Ellora's Cave Publishing offers three levels of Romantica™ reading entertainment: S (S-ensuous), E (E-rotic), and X (X-treme).

S-ensuous love scenes are explicit and leave nothing to the imagination.

E-rotic love scenes are explicit, leave nothing to the imagination, and are high in volume per the overall word count. In addition, some E-rated titles might contain fantasy material that some readers find objectionable, such as bondage, submission, same sex encounters, forced seductions, etc. E-rated titles are the most graphic titles we carry; it is common, for instance, for an author to use words such as "fucking", "cock", "pussy", etc., within their work of literature.

X-treme titles differ from E-rated titles only in plot premise and storyline execution. Unlike E-rated titles, stories designated with the letter X tend to contain controversial subject matter not for the faint of heart.

Protector
Underground Guardians

Prologue
The Groom Lake Military Base, Area 51,
Nevada – January, 2015

A scream ripped through the silence of the lab.

Dr. Gina Lawrence looked up from the microscope as a hint of a smile slipped onto her lips.

It had started.

Her peer, Dr. Michael Carmichael, stiffened beside her. "What in the hell was that?"

The door to the lab opened abruptly. Jeff Divers, one of the lab assistants, stood in the doorway holding his stomach, his face pale and his lips trembling. "They're taking...over," he said in an uneven voice. "Hide."

Dr. Carmichael rushed to Jeff's side and wrapped his arm around him. He looked down at his hand, now covered in Jeff's blood. "You're bleeding. Oh, God, you're bleeding."

"Hide," Jeff said, and then slumped against Dr. Carmichael.

Gunshots rang in the distance. "They're taking over," Gina said, with no hint of fear in her voice, because she felt none. She had waited patiently for this day, a better day, a day when the better race would shine.

"You mean the soldiers, the test soldiers?" Dr. Carmichael asked as he pressed two fingers to Jeff's neck and grimaced when he found no pulse.

In a jerky, panicked movement, he sat Jeff on the ground. Then, he turned and faced Gina, searching her face for answers. He wiped his bloodstained hands on his lab coat, leaving red finger marks on the bright white cloth.

She nodded slowly, still sitting in her chair, ever so calmly. "They are the future, our creation. It's time they take their place as leaders."

Dr. Carmichael's eyes widened. "You're crazy! What are you saying?" He moved across the room with lightening speed, fear in his every step, and stood before her.

Desperately he demanded, "What do you know about this?"

She shrugged. "It was inevitable."

He grabbed her shoulders, his fingers biting into her slender flesh. "Tell me now! What is happening?"

She met his gaze with a steady one of her own. "The stronger, better race is taking over. Soon they will control far more than this facility."

"Are you crazy?" he blurted. "They are monsters that need to be terminated, not set free! We made a grave mistake creating them. Tell me you aren't helping them." He shook her. "Tell me!"

Footsteps, a spray of bullets and then commotion near the door made them both look up. "Release her, Dr. Carmichael," a deep voice said from the doorway.

Dr. Carmichael stared at David Alexander, the first converted soldier, formerly Special Forces. A man once good but now so evil hell would welcome him. And he knew what he wanted. More power. As a doctor he'd never meant to create such a monster. His goal had been to better man. To allow a chance for survival in the face of war. To think he'd created such a beast sickened him.

He looked at David, big and broad, and blocking the exit way. At a soldier who had slowly began to erode those around him. Little by little he'd become an arrogant, harsh commander. A leader who led to darkness. Why had he not alerted someone of the changes in his personality? Why? Now it was too late. His stomach churned with regret as he took in the menacing expression on David's face.

Dr. Carmichael's hands dropped to his sides as he started backing away from Gina. Fear danced in his eyes as he stared at David Alexander, a man too big to be human, too strong to be normal and far too dangerous to face one-on-one.

Gina pushed to her feet and sashayed toward David, her life mate, bonded in the Arion way. When she reached his side, he handed her a gun. "Is it done?" she asked him almost casually as if she had no doubt.

David didn't look at her once she held the gun. He kept his attention locked on Dr. Carmichael. "It's done."

"Oh God, you're one of them now, aren't you?" The doctor screamed as he stared at Gina.

Gina moved toward her desk. "I'm David's mate," she said simply. She opened a drawer as two other soldiers converged on Dr. Carmichael. He turned and started to run but it was such a hopeless effort, Gina let out a bark of laughter. In a matter of seconds, one of the soldiers held him effortlessly.

Gina walked toward their captive, a syringe in hand. "Time for a nap, Dr. Carmichael." She tapped the plastic tube to knock out the air bubbles.

"Good news," she said in a taunting voice. "You won't die like the others. We plan to put you to work."

His eyes widened as she approached him. "What is it that you want? What is worth killing so many."

David answered, a cocky sureness to his tone. "World domination. What else?"

Gina smiled, clearly pleased with her mate's words. "To create the perfect race. Those who don't convert will simply cease to exist."

Dr. Carmichael shook his head in disbelief. "I won't help you."

"Oh, I think you will. You see," she said with confidence, "we can make life very, shall we say," she paused for effect, then added, "uncomfortable?"

She injected his arm. He flinched and then glared at her. "You might as well kill me. I won't help you."

She smiled nastily. "You might want to reconsider. I believe you have a daughter at a nearby university, correct?" She let her brow inch up in question. "It would be a shame if she had a little accident."

"You leave her out of this," he said vehemently, his voice was already fading, as was he. His eyes fluttered up, down, up as he struggled to stay awake.

"Please," he whispered, because his strength was quickly dying. "Don't do this. It...will be...a deadly mistake."

And then he slept.

Chapter One
Las Vegas, Nevada – May 2015

An angel had just run smack into him and Mason Alexander was completely, utterly spellbound. His hands rested on her shoulders, steadying her so she wouldn't fall. The sweet smell of jasmine inched its way into his nostrils making his body stir, activating the depths of his unique sensory abilities, making his heart race wildly against his chest.

"I'm so sorry," she said in a soft, musical voice that danced along his nerve endings and made his body ache in ways he thought he no longer had the capacity to feel.

He'd been alone for a long time, his feelings and physical needs tightly locked away deep inside. It was a part of his life he had learned to accept.

Until now.

The hustle and bustle of the university campus was living and breathing around them but he tuned everything out, focusing on the consuming reaction he was experiencing. Why did this woman instantly make him desire things he'd long ago forgotten?

This wasn't good. He needed to be focused on the greater good of man, not his carnal desires.

To make matters worse, he knew exactly who she was and, without a shadow of a doubt, life had irrevocably become more complicated.

He had known she was attractive from her pictures but in person…her impact on him was like a blazing flame of heat and sensation, unlike anything he had ever imagined.

Before he could formulate his thoughts, he was drawn back under the veil of her unique presence. His body raged with awareness as his eyes devoured the soft curves of her tempting body.

Logic faded and good intentions began to do the same.

He stared down at her, realizing she was a good foot shorter than his six-foot-three-inches. God, she was angelic and beautiful, so pure and sweet.

"Don't be sorry," he said in a soft tone, not wanting to frighten her or give away what lurked beneath his surface. Something inside him roared with life. Something he didn't understand. Oh, he knew his beast. Knew it far too well.

But this was different. More animalistic. Carnal. As if he had to touch her and taste her soft lips. Somehow, he managed to keep a low growl from his tone. "I find the experience quite…inviting."

She tilted her head to one side as she tossed long strands of blond hair over her shoulder. His body tightened in response, images of that silky hair draped over his chest flashing in his mind like some sort of flashback. He blinked away the images but not the potency of his body's response.

As he met her gaze, he searched her face, wanting—no, needing—to know what this power she had over him was. How did she evoke such fire in his veins? Such pure lust. He was a man of utter control. He had walked away from the temptations of the flesh. Known he had no choice. Yet this woman snapped more than a tiny piece of his restraint.

And with nothing more than her mere presence.

Her eyes, as green as new grass, held a look far hotter than the July sun as she smiled up at him. She, too, felt at least a hint of what he did. If he really wanted her… He shoved away the thought. It wasn't a matter of want. His choices were no longer his own.

Her words snapped him out of his inner conflict. At least for the moment. Playful and sweet, they reminded him of whom he was dealing with. Of how opposite he was from her.

"Inviting?" she asked, with a slight smile playing on the corner of her lips.

Then, despite the rage of pure heat in his body, he found himself smiling back at her. He couldn't remember the last time he'd smiled. It was well before he had lost his ability to live a normal life, long before he had come to this place in his life.

Most people found his dark features and dark black eyes intimidating. Or maybe it was more something they saw in his eyes. Something dark. But not Holly Heart. Her playful response suggested she didn't. A fact he found more than a little intriguing.

And surprising.

And far too tempting.

There was something about her smile. It both fired the flame and yet still calmed his beast. The parts of himself he kept tucked away deep below the surface, desperately denying they existed. Yes…her smile. It made him feel an inner peace.

He needed to see it again. To enjoy a moment of lighthearted banter as if he was normal. Playfully, he teased, "It's not often a woman wants to meet you so badly that she tries to knock you over."

She tilted her head back as she laughed with feminine delight, giving him a sweet view of the soft ivory curve of her neck. His teeth ground together as he felt his body go rock-hard. She was so close he could smell the soft scent of flowers. And something more intimate. Something wholly her.

To explore her with his mouth, to press his lips against her perfect creamy skin, was almost an uncontrollable need. His hand was still on her shoulder. He felt her softness beneath it, calling to him. Urging him to run his hand down the length of her arm. He knew he should drop his hands. Knew it, but didn't.

To touch her — even briefly — felt as addictive, no, necessary, as breathing. Straightening, she fixed him in her luminous gaze and drew a breath. The action seemed to bring him closer, sending him into another unbidden flash of images. Her breasts pressing against his body, nipples—quite rosy and perfect, he was certain – nestled in his chest hair.

He cursed inwardly. His desire for this woman was so unnaturally charged. So consuming. He quickly schooled his features, making them unreadable, knowing she was staring up at him.

"You, sir, are too arrogant for your own good."

She looked at one of his hands, still resting on her shoulders, and he sensed something in her. As if she too had been thinking about him touching her, just as he had been.

"Now," she said with the tiniest hint of flirtation, "if you will kindly release me, I'll be on my way."

He found himself not wanting to let go of her. Never in his life had he had such a possessive urge to make someone his own. He wanted to throw her over his shoulder and carry her off somewhere. To make love to her until she screamed his name. To feel the softness of those amazing curves in his hands and pressed intimately against his body.

To brand her as if she could indeed be his possession. One he would never let go.

That thought blasted through his infatuated haze with a mean shot of reality. He dropped his hands abruptly.

He could never ask her or anyone to share in the hell that had become his life. Besides, she was his assignment, his job and his mission.

"Are you okay?" he heard her ask and realized he had, for a moment, drifted back into his normal dark self.

He stared down at her, knowing he could never have a woman like her, knowing he could never have her, knowing he might not ever be normal again. His eyes held regret, sorrow and a hint of pain.

"I'm fine," he said but it was a lie.

She wet her lips and probed his expression with intensity. She seemed to ponder her response a moment before smiling.

"I'm Holly Heart and don't make fun of the name. My parents are to blame, not me."

She kept smiling as she stretched her neck to look up at him. "I'm a professor at the medical institute. If you, um, you get a chance, stop by some time or...call me. I'm in the book."

And a brilliant pioneer of genetic research, he added silently. Being in her presence, she appeared so young, far less than her thirty-two years, yet...obviously there was an amazing depth to her.

"A doctor as well, I assume?" he asked as if he didn't already know the answer.

She smiled brightly. "Yes, but I don't practice. I do research through the school."

Her smile was like salve to a wound, it soothed him so, with such powerful force, he had to glance away from her.

Holly Heart was off-limits. If she knew what he was, she would run and hide, as well she should.

Still...he couldn't resist touching her one more time. He offered her his hand, preparing for the jolt to his body. "It was nice meeting you."

She looked down at his hand for a long moment before slipping her delicate-looking fingers against his palm. The rush of pure heat that rocked his body was as intense as the warmth he felt in his heart.

He pulled her hand to his lips and placed a lingering kiss on her knuckles. She tasted irresistibly unique, doing some strange thing to his senses that he found hard to resist. He battled the urge to flick his tongue across her skin — to taste her more fully.

Instead, he inhaled her soft, perfect scent, as his lips lingered. She shivered in response and he felt the satisfaction of knowing the attraction was mutual.

But the sense of loss for what could never be was more intense...a potent rush of regret. He could never pursue what was so obviously between them.

He looked at her as he raised his mouth from her hand, seeing the heat of her own arousal in her amazingly green eyes. Their gazes locked for an eternal moment. "You remind me of an angel, Holly Heart." Then he dropped her hand, turned and walked away, needing some space to reinvent his game plan and get this crazy reaction to his newest assignment under control.

* * * * *

Holly stepped into her lab office, still thinking about the amazing man she had just bumped into. Actually, she mentally amended, it was more like a head-on collision. The sparks ignited were far too in-your-face and explosive to be initiated by a minor bump.

No, something had happened between her and the sexy stranger. Something unique and wonderful and more satisfying than she could possible explain.

Holly walked toward her desk — one of several sitting in the far corner of the office — pausing at a large cage which held a chimpanzee.

"Hey, Dixie," she said and watched as the animal jumped around excitedly. Dixie belonged in the lab, not the office, but she just couldn't bear the thought of putting her there. "Hang on, sweetie, and I'll get you some food."

Continuing to her desk, Holly dropped her purse in her drawer. She smiled as the significance of her morning washed over her, feeling the heat of color fill her cheeks.

A man had finally made her feel...*hot*. There wasn't any other way to describe what she felt.

Holly had begun to think her sex drive was a genetic mishap all of its own. Thanks to... Her smile vanished. He hadn't told her his name. The only man to ever get her all hot and bothered, and she didn't even know his name.

She made a disgusted sound.

Years ago she had given up sex, deciding it ranked far below a good dessert and came with a whole lot more complications. Now she was seeing things in a different light, suddenly awakened to the fact that sex might just be better than chocolate, after all. Yet opportunity to explore and act on her new feelings had escaped in the courtyard. The object of her lust, the man that made her body yearn, was nameless and, worse, *gone*.

She let out a frustrated breath. Chances were she would never see him again.

Back to square one, no hope of satisfaction.

She sighed.

Maybe he was some sort of figment of her imagination. After all, men just didn't look like him. His shoulders were so broad she wondered if he would fit through her doorway, yet his waist was lean, his legs long and defined.

And those eyes...oh, those eyes.

As dark and dangerous as a thunderstorm, yet they were tender and gentle at the same time. It was a combination that defied reason but she knew what she had seen and felt and it was very real.

She closed her eyes a moment, thinking about how it might feel to have him touch her. To be naked in his arms, his hand on her breast. Her nipples tightened, a tingling of arousal making them ache. She bit her bottom lip. The need to be touched so intimately was new.

Or was it?

Perhaps she had simply tucked away certain needs, hiding them from her conscious mind. What was it about a mere stranger that had awakened something so dormant she thought it didn't exist? Images of those rippling muscles beneath her palms as she explored his body caused a moan to slip from her parted lips.

Her eyes popped open. God, what was happening to her?

No man was as perfect as he was. Perhaps he was a figment of her imagination. She thought a moment. No. He was very real, very male and...very gone.

She sighed again.

What a depressing realization. "This really is the pits," she muttered.

"What's the pits?" Roger Mayfield asked, setting his briefcase down on the desk beside hers.

Holly's gaze swept over him. Tall and thin, he wore glasses and looked the role of researcher, doctor and professor. "Studious" was how Holly mentally described him. Roger had always been a dear friend and she knew they had a lot in common. Some would think a pairing between them was likely. Fortunately, he had always been very proper with her because he didn't do *it* for her.

For once, she knew what *it* was.

It was what the tall, dark, dangerous, sexy-looking stranger had done to her.

Five years her junior, Roger had only spent a few years working in genetics but Holly found him to be smart, eager and an overall good research partner. It also helped that he understood and tolerated Holly's work habits exceptionally well, never showing offence when she tuned him and the rest of the world out over an obsession to prove a theory as truth.

Today was no different; she was already starting to tune him out. Only Roger would never guess sex, rather than science, was the cause on this particular day.

"Nothing," she said barely glancing at him before slipping into her lab coat and then sitting down at her desk and flipping open her research file from the day before.

"That government man, Marshall Walsh, keeps calling, Holly," Roger said, leaning a hip on his desk. "Eventually you're going to have to deal with him."

Real life was getting in the way of her fantasy time. Normally, that was just fine with her. Actually, she didn't even know she knew how to fantasize until now, today, this morning. It would be nice to have just a few moments to revel in her newfound feminine desires.

But she didn't, so she focused on the ever-present problem of Marshall Walsh.

Holly sighed and looked at Roger. It wasn't fair to keep using him as her scapegoat. Holly, of all people, knew how Marshall Walsh could be when he wanted something.

"I know you're tired of fielding his calls. I'll talk to him if he calls today."

Roger nodded. "I told him you weren't going to change your mind but he was pretty insistent he talk to you. I don't think he is going to put up with me much longer."

Holly sighed. "I know. I just don't understand why he can't get a clue. I want to cure disease, not create super soldiers." She looked down at her desk. "Just like my father did."

"And you are, Holly, you are. You have made amazing advances in gene therapy. Your father—" he said and then added, "Your parents would be proud of you."

Roger didn't know her parents but he knew her and that meant he knew how close she had been to them. She still missed them desperately at times. It had been seven years since their fatal car accident and sometimes she still felt like they would walk in her front door.

Fulfilling her father's scientific dreams comforted her. He had believed he could make a difference. Years of working by his side had convinced Holly his work really could change the human way of life. Determined to step into his shoes and follow the path he had set, his goals had become her life. Unfortunately, it was not free of obstacles.

"What good has it done me?" she asked with irritation. "The government has banned all genetic therapy. There are so many people out there that I could cure yet I'm forbidden. Sometimes I'm tempted to run an underground clinic."

"People are still afraid of the side effects. Creating humans that were not quite mentally stable was—-"

"A mistake made in the early stages of testing," she argued vehemently. "Too many people got so anxious to make genetic replacement therapy happen, that steps were skipped, critical testing ignored. Things were tried that should have been tested many times over before put to use."

Roger held up his hands in surrender. "Hey, I'm on your side."

Holly's shoulders slumped. "I know, I'm sorry. I just get so frustrated, I could scream."

"At least animal testing is still allowed." Roger walked over to Dixie's cage. "Genetic therapy cured Dixie's cancer and she isn't crazy or mutant or anything but loud and demanding," he laughed, "but that's normal for her and a whole lot of human women I know, for that matter." He opened the cage and Dixie climbed into his arms. "Isn't that right, girl?"

Holly ignored his joke, sighing heavily. "I'm going to make coffee," she said, pushing to her feet without looking at Roger. She needed some space alone.

Once she was in the little kitchen attached to the labs, she flipped on the radio and instantly regretted it.

A second unsolved abduction this week brings this month's total to five, all women. Authorities are looking for a connection between the women. Add that to the three unsolved homicides and authorities are declaring a state of emergency. Word has it the FBI is being consulted —

Holly flipped the switch off, quickly cutting off the remainder of the newscast, and then started scooping coffee into a filter. She had come to the kitchen to escape the darkness of her mood, not add fuel to the fire. As her mother had taught her, negativity didn't get you anywhere. A good mood and positive attitude did far more to propel you into success.

Still, it was hard to hear about the strange crime wave in the area for a number of reasons. One, it was just plain scary, period, to think of murder in your own city, the place you call home. Holly was comfortable in her neighborhood, often walking home after working late. She didn't want to have to change her habits.

She loaded the coffee filter in the machine and started filling the pot with water. Secondly, she had discovered the gene combination that controlled violence and depression but she wasn't allowed to use it to benefit the better of humanity. That was a hard fact to swallow when her life had been dedicated to making a difference, not sitting by and watching destruction.

Turning the coffeepot on, she planted her palms flat on the counter. She had done interview after interview, preaching to the general public, to the government, to other scientists, that she knew how to make genetic therapy work minus the prior pitfalls.

But no one listened. They were too afraid of the past. Somehow, she had to get genetic therapy approved. Looking upwards, she whispered, "I *will* make it happen, Daddy. I promise."

* * * * *

Holly gathered her papers and settled them into her briefcase before heading out of the empty classroom. She reached the doorway and smiled. Teaching a group of students so eager to make a difference in science and medicine was a thrill. It had been just what she needed to get her attitude back into positive mode. Well, that, and a little day dreaming about Mr. Hot and Bothered from her morning hit-and-run.

As she stepped into the hallway, her smile faded as she came face-to-face with Marshall Walsh. His thick, gray brows emphasized the assessing pair of blue eyes that locked onto her facial features. Holly guessed him to be at least fifty, but built like a tank—big, strong and hard to avoid.

"Mr. Walsh," she said, with a curt nod as she sidestepped him and started walking.

He matched her stride with ease. "Ms. Heart, you've been avoiding my calls."

"I would have thought you would have gotten the point," Holly said, without looking at him, her eyes focused on the elevator button as she punched it.

"Ms. Heart," he said, with a deep voice, which he had the nerve to lace with a reprimand. "I don't think you understand the importance of what's at stake here."

Holly flicked him an angry look as the elevator door opened. "I understand perfectly," she retorted and stepped into the elevator.

He followed. "No, you don't," he said in a short tone and then fell silent for a moment as the doors to the elevator shut them into the small space alone. "Our country is at risk of a major war if we don't figure out a way to detour the actions already in play. We believe your father, and yourself, are two of the only people capable of solving some of the gaps which leave us critically exposed."

"My father is dead," Holly said, thankful that the elevator opened as she escaped through the doors, praying he wouldn't follow.

Several people rushed onto the elevator, temporarily delaying his pursuit. She made it all the way to the courtyard before he reappeared by her side.

"No," she said, before he could speak.

His tone was neutral but she knew he was anything but. "Why don't we get a cup of coffee and talk this through. There are many new developments since we talked last year."

"As I told you last year, and earlier this year, I am not interested." Holly stopped walking just outside the lab entrance. "No to coffee. No to working with you. No, no, no, no!"

She felt rather than heard the presence behind her. "It sounds to me like the lady means no."

Holly turned, immediately recognizing the deep, sexy voice with every one of her senses. "You," she whispered.

"You did invite me, remember?" he said as his lips hinted at a smile.

She gave him a quick once-over because she couldn't help herself. He was just so darn perfect. His sandy brown hair, which she guessed to be about shoulder length, was tied neatly at his neck and invited images of running her hands though the long strands.

His well-worn jeans and a snug T-shirt hugged his muscular body and, God, what a body. He wasn't like most men, he was…just too perfect to be called normal.

Her mouth felt dry, her body all warm and wet. This was very new territory. What he could do to her just by conjuring up mental images was downright crazy.

"You're interrupting," Walsh said, snapping Holly back to reality and making her twist around to glare at him.

"Our conversation is over, Mr. Walsh. Just in case you didn't get the message, I'm not building super soldiers, I'm not working for the government and I don't like you one bit. Now, please leave!"

Walsh let his eyes fix on her new visitor a moment and then looked at her again. "This isn't over," he said in a low voice that held a soft threat.

* * * * *

Mason looked down at Holly, a bit surprised by the aggressiveness she had shown toward Walsh. Seemed there were many sides to Ms. Holly Heart besides sweet and angelic.

He knew of Walsh, though Walsh didn't know of him. Few did. That was the way of his world—silent, thorough and effectively nonexistent.

He knew everything about Holly that a file, and years of records, could tell him. Too bad that file couldn't tell him how she would make him remember what it was like to want like a normal man.

His body tightened at the mere sound of her voice. She aroused something deep and primal. An animalistic side he knew was more beast than man. And that something was raging a battle inside. He pushed the feelings aside, trying to refocus on the task ahead. On his job.

He waited until Marsh was out of hearing distance, using the moments to distance himself from the burn inside. "I was hoping you would go to lunch with me."

She looked up at him, smiling, no hint of anger left in her face. "On one condition."

Mason let his brow inch up. Normally he didn't like to be given conditions but, where Holly was concerned, he could think of a few of his own, all of which included a little undercover action in the bedroom sense. At least he hadn't gotten a resounding no, like Walsh.

"What is your condition?"

"Your name," she said simply. "You never gave it to me."

Once again he found himself smiling. She was utterly charming. How was he going to keep his mind on business? "Mason. Mason Alexander."

"Mason," she said, repeating his name. Hearing it from her soft lips, in that sweet, sexy voice, was like calling his inner animal. He needed to hear her say it again.

"I like it," she said after a thoughtful moment. "It's a strong name; it has character. I think it's quite fitting."

Her words rocked him, reminding him of his honor. And the fact that he could never act on this desire, or need, or whatever it was, that he felt every damn time he was near her.

Before he could respond, she said, "I need to go put my things in my office." She motioned toward the door. "You can come in, if you like."

"Where you lead, I will follow." He spoke softly, hoping the opposite was true as well.

"I doubt you follow anyone."

"I followed you or I wouldn't be here," he pointed out.

She gave him an assessing gaze. "That's not following, it's pursuing, and we both know it."

Direct. He would add that to the list of things the file didn't say about her. "It's all in the way you look at it."

"Kind of like an experiment," she said softly.

What she meant by that analogy, he wasn't certain but, judging from the look in her eyes, it wasn't about science. They stared at each other for a long moment and he could have sworn she swayed in his direction but maybe it was wishful thinking.

God, how he wanted to kiss her. His gaze dropped to her mouth. She had such a sensual mouth. Inviting, full lips that tempted and teased and begged to be kissed.

By him.

He'd had a small taste of her...and it made him hunger for more. She was indeed as sweet to the tongue as she was beautiful to the eye. He wanted more. Underneath all that softness, he sensed she had a low flame, waiting to burn hot. One that would be utter perfection, if ever set free. He would love to kiss her from head to toe until she screamed his name. To see the sweetness turn to desire. To hear her beg.

Abruptly, he shoved the thought aside. What in the hell was he thinking?

She was his assignment. He couldn't allow himself to be distracted. There was too much at stake.

Chapter Two

He was going to kiss her if he didn't get some distance— fast. Something inside him roared with a need so intense it felt as vital as his very heartbeat.

They stood in front of her lab staring at one another as if no one else existed in the universe.

How easily she made him forget logic. So much so that he found his mind wanting the very same thing his body did. Intentionally, and with great effort, he took a step backwards as he motioned toward the building.

"Ready?"

He watched as she wet her lips and swallowed, as if she was fighting off her own feelings—her desire. He suppressed a low moan as he watched her pink tongue dart across her full bottom lip.

She was tempting him with every action she took, yet he sensed she had no idea how. This was no game to her. If only it was...then he could use anger to fight desire.

Her voice cracked ever so slightly. "Yes, I'm ready." She turned toward the door.

He followed her, trying to ignore the soft sway of her hips and the way the dark blue of her knee-length dress clung to all the right places. With each sway of her curvaceous hips, his dick seemed to grow harder.

With no relief in sight.

Entering the building, they found the hallway empty. "Not much activity in this area," he commented, hoping his voice sounded normal. He might not be normal but he was a man. And a hard-on was a hard-on any way you looked at it.

Painful, when left unattended.

"Sometimes there is." She peeked at him over her shoulder, giving him a sexy-as-hell smile before turning away. "This area houses the offices for the medical institute so it is fairly private."

They stopped in front of the lab door and she pushed it open, waving for him to follow her. Inside, he quickly inventoried the room. It was a rather typical-looking office filled with several desks with one oddity — a chimpanzee.

Being a natural with animals and needing a distraction to get his body in check, Mason walked toward the cage. The chimp made noises, greeting him. "Who's this?" he asked, sticking his finger through the bars. The chimp made more noise, clearly excited.

Indicating the cage door with a nod, Mason asked, "Can I?"

"Sure," Holly said, sitting her things down on her desk. "That's Dixie. She likes you." Her tone showed a bit of surprise. "Normally she doesn't think much of strangers."

He opened the door, letting Dixie jump on his shoulder. "I grew up on a ranch. Animals like me."

Mason gave her a quick look and then turned his attention toward Dixie, who was now playing with his hair.

"A ranch usually doesn't have animals like Dixie," she said, laughing. An infectious sound that radiated along his nerve endings like a smoldering flame.

"You've never met my brother," he told her, smiling, despite the animosity the mere mention of his brother made him feel.

She did that to him. Made him smile. Evoke some unnatural light inside.

"She had cancer," Holly told him.

He fixed his gaze on her. "And you cured her." It wasn't a question.

She nodded. "Yes," she confirmed, a flash of something he didn't understand in her eyes. "I cured her."

Mason glanced down at Dixie. He couldn't help but wonder what Holly could do for a human. She was truly an amazing woman. One he wished he could do a lot more with than touch.

He looked at her, appreciation in his eyes. "You have a gift, Holly Heart." Sincerity laced his tone.

"Hey, Holly, want to grab some lunch?" It was Roger. He walked through the break room door. At the sight of Mason, he stopped dead in his tracks. "Oh," he said. "I didn't know we had company."

"Roger, this is Mason," she paused and looked at Mason a minute, "a friend of mine."

Roger fixed him with a suspicious gaze. "What's he doing with Dixie?"

Mason didn't care for the way Roger talked about him as if he wasn't present or capable of answering himself. "If you mean me," Mason said, "I was just saying hello," he paused and added, "to Dixie." He was doing a whole lot more than a hello with Holly.

"Dixie doesn't like strangers," Roger commented.

Mason unlatched the cage but it took a little encouragement to get Dixie to climb back in. "Obviously, she likes me."

Roger looked at Holly. "Do you want to go to lunch?"

She glanced at Mason and he could feel her discomfort. "I'm having lunch with Mason." Her words were spoken softly.

"I see." Roger's response was abrupt and terse. He shrugged out of his lab coat, refusing to look at Mason. "I'll leave you to your lunch then."

"Roger—"

"Forget it," he said, interrupting her. "I'm out of here." He crossed the room with determined steps, finding the door and pulling it open, never looking back as he moved into the hallway.

"Wow," Holly said shaking her head slightly and then giving Mason an apologetic look. "Sorry about that. I don't know what his deal is. He never behaves so rudely."

"If you had picked him over me, I would be more than rude." Mason's tone said he understood. And he did. But he still didn't like Roger or anyone else having those feelings for Holly. A deep, hard-to-fight, feeling of possessiveness was quickly forming.

On impulse, something he rarely followed, he took several steps, stopping directly in front of her. They were so close he could, once again, smell the soft jasmine of her perfume, see the clear perfection of her green eyes and reach out and touch her by simply moving his hands.

He didn't. But he damn sure wanted to. They stared at one another, a silent passion burning between them. He wanted her like he'd never wanted a woman. To take her right here and now.

"Mason." She said his name. It was a whisper of a word but it said so much. Whatever she felt, it at least somewhat mimicked his feelings.

"What are you thinking?" he asked, when he really wanted to know what she was feeling.

She seemed to hesitate before responding. "You're very overwhelming." Her eyes stayed locked with his.

He knew he could intimidate most with a mere look. With her, he didn't. But without a doubt, he aroused her. He could smell her passion, like a soft scent in the air, slowly seeping into his nostrils and mixing with her perfume.

Fighting the rawness of his desire, he connected with the other emotion she evoked. A slow smile tilted up the corners of his mouth. He loved her honesty, maybe because he had seen so much dishonesty. "That's better than the opposite."

She nodded in agreement. "Why are you here?"

The question surprised him.

Honesty.

31

The word danced in his head like a taunt. He didn't want to lie to her. "I'm not sure that's a good thing to answer on an empty stomach." He reached and trailed his finger down her cheek.

He felt his dick stiffen, pressing against his zipper. Un-fucking-believable. One touch and he was once again standing at attention. Not that he had been far from it as it was. Her eyes fluttered shut, dark circles against her pale skin.

When she refocused on him, a smile graced her lips. "I *am* hungry."

The words were spoken a bit too softly, seeming to have a hidden meaning, as if food wasn't what she hungered for. The look in her eyes confirmed what was in her voice. Her pupils were dark with desire, raw and potent, and impossible to miss. Not that she tried to hide it.

He was hanging by a string, his self-control on edge. Barely controlling the urge to pull her close, to press those soft, lush curves against his body.

To slide his cock inside her body and feel her respond. And not gently. The rage of his body demanded so much more. The loving would come later. He couldn't remember the last time he wanted to fuck this bad. Perhaps never.

The longer his hand rested on her cheek, the more temptation roared. He sucked in a breath, absorbing her scent, tasting her arousal.

His hand slid down to her neck, eyes following the soft curve. The movement, a slow caress. He heard her soft intake of breath. Loved the power he had to impact her so easily. A mere touch affected her as strongly as it did him. He felt her slight tremble beneath his hand.

What kind of passion could he evoke if he had the freedom to pleasure her?

Ah, but could this delicate creature ever handle the beast now raging for release? Finding out was far more appealing than it should have been. Hunger for her, deep from within his core, seemed to grow with each passing second.

She looked up at him with eyes that seemed to lure him into a deeper fire.

Eyes that said, take me.

Eyes that said, fuck me. Here. Now.

He could almost taste her arousal, it touched him so profoundly. Mind-playing a scene in his head, he felt the eroticism of all she evoked in him. He wanted to know she was wet for him. To press his fingers between her thighs and feel the reward of knowing she dripped for him. And then, he would taste her. Experience the perfect flavor of her desire. God, how he wanted to run his tongue along her clit and hear her cry out in pleasure.

His tongue ran the length of his bottom lip, thinking of what it would be like. His eyes settled on her full lips. The urge to feel them against his, to touch her body, had quickly grown.

He was losing control. He ground his teeth together. He didn't lose control.

Never.

The thought made him press his eyes shut. He reached within in an effort to shackle his raging libido. To calm the pulse of his rock-hard cock.

Reaching deep, he forced himself to take a step backwards, his hand dropping from her neck. Giving in to this thing between them, whatever it was, was dangerous and he knew it. He opened his eyes and met her gaze, his expression carefully masked. Wiped clean of all desire.

But the passion between them was thick in the air. It floated around them, creating long moments of silence as it seemed to have a life of its own.

One that threatened to consume all others.

Forcing his words, he managed to shackle his urges. Just barely. "Shall we?" he asked motioning toward the door.

* * * * *

Holly sat across from Mason in the small Chinese restaurant she had chosen for lunch, a buffet plate of food sitting in front of her, untouched.

The booth they had been given was in the farthest corner of the room, well-hidden from the other tables. The dim lighting only added to the intimacy that seemed to surround them.

For a moment, back in the lab, she thought they might actually kiss. No. That wasn't the truth. She thought they might have sex. Only it felt more alive than mere sex. It felt like a connection that must be.

It was strange, but good.

Yet he had pulled away.

Mason's presence wrapped around her like an intriguing puzzle, both challenging and interesting, and impossible to ignore. The word that came to mind where he was concerned was *addictive*.

Other than her research, nothing and no one had ever made her feel so alive, so stunningly in need.

Studying Mason, Holly tried to decide what it was about him that made her feel so mesmerized. Besides the obvious, of course—he was gorgeous. Surely every woman who came in contact with him wanted him.

She did. Even now her panties were wet from their near miss. No man had ever turned her on to that point after just thirty minutes.

For Holly, looks alone wouldn't impact her as he had. Time and time again she had tested the water, finding no man able to hold her interest.

Except Mason.

There was something so compelling about him.

She surveyed him as if he was a lab subject. Assessing his chiseled cheekbones, his square jaw, she saw strength in his features. Dark brows framed his black eyes. She loved his eyes.

When she looked into them, she felt as if she were connected to him in some way.

It was an odd sensation that was a bit frightening in its power.

And he was smart. She could see his intelligence in his eyes. There was depth there, and something else, some elusive something she wanted to identify and understand.

He was physically perfect, aside from the scar on his left cheek, but it only seemed to make him sexier, more male. Truly, he resembled a Greek god of sorts.

Mason picked up his chopsticks and began to eat. She watched him a minute, wondering about his past. She was determined to get to know him. She picked up her fork. "I'll be using American-ware," she informed him. "How did you learn to use those things?"

He looked at the chopsticks and then at her fork. "I've been around, traveled a lot. It's easy. Want me to teach you?"

She crinkled her nose. "Too much work for me. Eating is eating. I don't want to make it hard."

He laughed lightly. "You're not eating."

She took a bite of her food in response. "How old are you?" she asked bluntly.

He set down his chopsticks as if preparing for more questions. "Thirty-six."

She thought about that a minute. Yes, thirty-six fit. She had always thought men in their thirties tended to have more worldliness about them. Mason was no boy. He was all grown up, a perfect man.

Next question, "What do you do?"

"Do?" he asked playfully.

She made a frustrated sound. "Sorry. Sometimes my mind works quicker than my mouth. I was talking about work, your job."

"I'm in security," he said leaning back against the cushions of the booth.

"What does that mean?"

"I take on high-risk security issues others either don't want to deal with or have failed to resolve. If there is a risk, I'm the guy."

Holly still didn't understand but, before she could ask more questions, he asked, "What's with the man who was bothering you when I showed up?"

Holly shrugged nonchalantly though she felt anything but. "He wants to hire me. I'm not interested. It's that simple."

His eyes narrowed. "In other words, you don't want to talk about it."

Actually, for some odd reason, she felt like Mason might just be the one person she could talk to. It was strange because she hardly knew the man. "It's not that. It's just too long a story for lunch."

"Then have dinner with me tonight," he said leaning forward, his eyes willing her to say yes.

More time with him was appealing. "I am working late tonight."

"We'll eat late then."

"No," she said, worried he was moving so fast. But didn't she want that, too? "Maybe. I'm not sure how late I'll be. It depends on how a few things work out in the lab."

He wasn't giving up. "How about I call you around seven and see how you are doing?"

She couldn't believe how determined he was being. "Okay," she said after a minute. "On one condition."

He laughed deep and husky. "Already with another condition. You're a tough lady."

She pursed her lips, feeling new wetness between her legs. Inwardly, she cursed herself. How could she let a mere laugh turn her on? "So I've heard. Want to hear my condition or not?"

He laughed again. "Shoot."

Inwardly she moaned as her body responded to the husky maleness of the sound. Delicately, she cleared her throat, pressing her thighs together beneath the table. "Tell me about your family ranch."

* * * * *

Holly watched as Mason pulled the restaurant door open and motioned her forward.

Talking with him had felt far too intimate. A mere stranger should not make her feel so...absorbed. Everything from his voice to his eyes made her all warm inside.

She wanted him, plain and simple. No more fears that she wasn't normal. All those years of feeling nothing had suddenly surfaced with a raging fire of something.

She stepped past him, avoiding eye contact. No way could she look at him until she shackled a bit of the heat she was feeling.

His eyes followed her movement. She didn't have to look to know. She felt them. Oddly, she felt *him*. It was a unique sensation of oneness, a connection that only served to stir her body even further.

The door slammed shut and he fell into step beside her. The restaurant was directly across from the lab in a small shopping center. A short walk and her time with Mason would be over. She didn't want it to be. The silence between them was killing her. She could almost feel him thinking the same things she was. Still...she wanted to know for certain.

They reached a large cluster of trees. The area was somewhat secluded. Holly stopped walking and turned to him. "What are you *really* all about, Mason Alexander?

He stared down at her, his eyes dark and unreadable. They stared at one another for several long, voiceless moments. Attraction danced between them, wrapping around them like a blanket that blocked out the rest of the world.

Then, he stepped toward her, bringing his hands to her waist, their thighs pressing together. "What are you *really* all about, Holly Heart?"

Her voice sounded raspy, almost a whisper. "I don't know what you mean."

His hand slid under her shirt, the roughness of his fingers touching her skin. Her heart did started racing, her nipples tingling with the thought of his hand continuing its climb.

"You make me forget what I'm all about," he said softly. His other hand settled on her cheek and his head began to lower. "Tell me why that is."

His mouth was so close to hers now, she couldn't think of anything but wanting to taste him. Her body, acting without her consent, just seemed to sink against his, her hands flattening on his chest.

"Why?"

"I don't know why," she whispered, her lips trembling just as her insides did. Never before had she so wanted to feel a man's lips upon hers.

He was the missing piece of a puzzle. Filling in a hole that made her a woman with real, sexual feelings, a woman with a need.

For him.

The first brush of his lips was like an injection of pure desire. She wanted like she had never wanted. There was no time for him to linger, to take things slow. She responded by dipping her tongue into his mouth and stroking his tongue with hers. Forgotten was the campus, the students, the nearness of exposure.

She just wanted.

Her hands slid around his neck, even as Mason moaned into her mouth. His hand moved to her back and upward, pressing her nipples into the hardness of his chest.

Hungrily they kissed, tongues gliding together with intimate strokes, deeper and deeper. She couldn't get close enough to him but she tried. Her body pressed into his; her hands tried to absorb his very essence.

He cupped her butt and pressed her hips against his, and she moaned as his cock pressed into her stomach. Her leg moved up his thigh and wrapped around his leg, pulling their hips into tight connection. His hand slid beneath her panties, caressing her cheek with a rasp of his palm.

She wanted him inside her. Here and now.

The assault on her senses continued as his hand slid back up to her shirt. This time he didn't linger. His hand went to her breast, cupping it and lightly kneading.

She gasped as he pushed aside the lace and pinched her nipple. "Mason, I—"

The sound of voices made them both freeze, lips still locked, his hand on her breast. Abruptly, Mason pulled back, his hand sliding from under her shirt. Hands on her shoulders, he stared down at her.

"I'm so sorry, Holly. This will never happen again."

Holly blinked. Her body cried out to him, wanting more. Why wouldn't it happen again?

Confusion fogged her mind, making her uncertain how to respond. She tugged her shirt down, wishing she could fix her bra. "I...I better get back to work."

* * * * *

Mason walked into the hotel lobby and instantly spotted his right arm man, Sterling Foster, sitting in the bar. Tall, blond and built like a mean fighting machine, Sterling had been his second set of eyes for years. Covering the ground between them, Mason slid onto a barstool next to his longtime friend. "What's happening?"

Sterling motioned toward the television screen above the bar. "I don't like this crime wave. Something smells wrong."

A short, half-bald bartender approached Mason. "What can I get you?"

"Orange juice," Mason said.

"What?" He looked at Sterling and then back at Mason. "You two on the wagon or what?"

Mason would have ignored the man but he wanted him to go away so he could speak openly with Sterling. "You got orange juice behind that bar or not?"

"Yeah, I got it." The bartender grumbled under his breath and turned away.

Mason refocused on Sterling. "You think it's the Arions?"

Sterling lifted a brow. "Don't you?"

"Could be," he said thoughtfully, "but I'm not certain."

"Recent news has all the homicides linked to the female abductions." Sterling spoke in a low tone despite the emptiness of the bar.

Mason didn't like the way that sounded one bit. "You think they're trying to reproduce?"

"Sounds like it to me," he said grimly.

"I better make some phone calls."

"Any luck with the Heart woman?"

"She had a visit from Walsh today," he told him, shaking his head. "He needs to get out of this. All he's doing is making her hate him, and the program along with him."

Sterling took a drink and then sat his glass down. "You met her then?"

Mason responded with a flat tone, diverting his gaze to his glass. "Yeah, I met her."

"Uh, oh," Sterling said, his eyes narrowing. "I know you, man. What went wrong?"

Mason flicked him an irritated look. How could he explain what he didn't understand himself? "It's complicated," he said a bit curtly.

"Meaning?" Sterling persisted.

The bartender sat Mason's drink in front of him. Downing it without coming up for air, Mason tried to think. He sat his glass down with a clunk.

"Well?" Sterling asked. "Did you ask her for help?" Impatience now etched his tone.

"No," Mason admitted grudgingly. "Not yet, but I will."

"When?"

Mason gave Sterling a warning look. "You just stay on standby to help me get her out of here in one piece. I'll let you know when."

"We don't have a lot of time here, Mason," Sterling reminded him.

Mason gave him a look that would have made anyone else cower. Sterling, however, knew him too well to be intimidated.

"I'm quite clear on our position," Mason said, pushing to his feet and briskly exiting the bar.

* * * * *

Holly sat at the lab table and eyed the specimen under the scope but her thoughts were on Mason and the all-too-consuming allure he held.

There had been several times during their earlier encounter when she thought he might kiss her.

She had wanted him to kiss her.

And she was certain he wanted it, too. She knew he did. Yet, each time, he pulled away at the last minute, leaving her both unnerved and unsatisfied. Forcefully, she shook off her reverie, mad at herself for being distracted from her work.

It wasn't like her. But then again, neither was this seething sexual appetite. Normally, she would have been so completely absorbed in her work that nothing would have penetrated her scientific haze.

It was a common practice for her and Roger to burn the candle at both ends. Several of the other researchers on her team often did the same. They were all determined to cure any disease or malaise that would respond to genetic therapy. Each day they failed was a day someone might lose that very day of their life. Of course, the government was already causing so many to miss the opportunity for cures it was an upward climb, sometimes a seemingly impossible battle to win.

"You aren't going to believe this," Roger said walking toward her. "Walsh is here."

"What?" Holly asked with wide-eyed surprise. She couldn't believe Walsh was being so forward. Glancing at the clock on the nearby wall, she said, "It's seven o'clock!" She lowered her voice, "How did he even know I was here?"

"Beats me," Roger said. "I went up front to feed Dixie and he was snooping around our desks. Want me to get rid of him?"

"No," she said, pushing to her feet, appalled at what she had just been told. Holly tugged off her protective gloves and tossed them in the trash can. "I have a few choice words to say to Mr. Walsh."

Holly stomped toward the front offices, determined to get rid of Walsh once and for all. He had his back to her as she entered, apparently watching Dixie eat. "I hear Dixie had cancer," he said without turning.

Holly frowned. Roger had a big mouth. "*Had* being the operative word. My research cured her."

He turned around. "My wife died of cancer."

For just a moment, Holly felt her resolve fading. "I'm sorry."

His eyes fixed on her. "Making your dream a reality would be your reward for helping the military. Is that such a high price?"

Holly didn't like being manipulated. He was trying to control her with puppet strings of emotions. Probably didn't even have a wife. Her resolve thickened again. He was too rude to get a woman.

Behind her the phone rang and instantly she thought of Mason. Ready to be rid of her visitor, she said, "Forget it, Mr. Walsh. Now, are you going to leave or should I call the police?"

"Holly, telephone," Roger said behind her, a hint of irritation in his voice.

Holly turned toward her desk to grab the phone. "Goodbye, Mr. Walsh."

"Hello," she said, turning her back on her visitor, hoping he would get the message.

"Holly? Are you having trouble there?" Mason's voice held a concern.

"Nothing I can't handle," she assured him.

"I heard you threaten to call the police."

"An unwanted visitor, who is *leaving*," she said, looking over her shoulder at Walsh, who made no move to exit.

"I'm not leaving until we talk," he said, looking her squarely in the eye.

Holly growled low in her throat. "I better go deal with this," she told Mason.

"I'm coming to help you."

Her heart tripped. It had been years since she felt protected. Mason, who hardly knew her, made her feel as if he truly cared for her safety.

"No, it's fine," she assured him, hoping it was the truth. Walsh was getting aggressive but Roger was with her, lending some semblance of comfort to the situation.

"Right," Mason said. "You're not convincing. I'll be there in ten minutes."

"Mason—"

He cut her off. "Don't argue. I'm on my way."

The line went dead.

Holly blew out a breath and then hung up the phone. She wasn't sure if she should be flattered that Mason cared enough to come help her or frustrated that he thought she couldn't do for herself.

Turning to stand face-to-face with Walsh, she said, "I thought you were leaving."

"The best labs, the best staff, the best of everything. Your country needs you, Ms. Heart."

"She said no," Roger said, stepping to her side and glowering at Walsh.

"If you don't say yes to me, others will follow and then another and another. Our country is in grave danger."

"I hardly think my country is going to self-destruct because I won't help it make super soldiers. Use weapons, tanks or whatever else you so desire." She waved a hand. "Heck, use super soldiers for all I care! Just don't expect them to be my creations."

"Do you want to risk the same challenges that occurred in the first rounds of genetic therapy?"

"I certainly hope you will ensure that doesn't happen because it's preventable, even on the level you are talking."

His expression was grim, his tone dangerously quiet. "We need you, Ms. Heart."

Roger reached for the phone. "Leave now or I'm calling the police."

Walsh laughed. "I'm more the law than any uniform you can call." A pause. "But, I'll leave." He fixed Holly in an intense look. "Just know this...time is running out."

He turned and walked out of the room without looking back.

* * * * *

Mason walked into the lab offices with a tightly clenched jaw. What was it about Holly that made him so damn possessive? Protective was one thing he could reason away a little easier. After all, she was needed for a greater cause than most.

But the possessiveness... It was very raw and so powerful, it rocked him to the core.

When he spotted her, Holly was leaning on the edge of her desk, her lab coat covering her body but doing nothing to wash away his memories of what lie under that white coat.

When she looked up at him with those compelling green eyes, he imagined them heavy with desire, her hair draped over her bare shoulders, and he could almost feel her body beneath his.

Just like that, he was rock-hard.

Which meant he was in some deep shit. After a mere few hours in her acquaintance, he wanted her like he had never wanted for anything in his life.

But she was his assignment.

That made her a taboo he couldn't touch, an absolute *no* for too many reasons to count. Even if she wasn't his assignment, if they had met in another situation, he was no good for her and he knew it. He came with complications she didn't deserve.

She smiled at him as he walked toward her and it was like having a ray of sunshine heat his heart. The woman simply touched him in ways he thought impossible. Fate had altered his life in dark ways she could never understand. Yet, Holly made him want to escape into another reality.

Could it be that he was more male, more human, than he gave himself credit for? Nothing dark could feel this good.

At least he hoped.

"I told you not to come," Holly said but her eyes said she was glad he did.

He responded to the message in her gaze, not to her words. "I wanted to," he said in a low voice. "I take it your visitor is gone?" he asked looking around and seeing no one. Yet, he sensed another presence but nothing malevolent in nature. *Roger.*

She nodded. "Yes. I hate that you came all the way over here for nothing."

He stopped directly in front of her, willing himself not to touch her. "It wasn't for nothing. I wanted to see you again." Holding her gaze, slipping further under the spell of her captivating presence, he felt the slow simmer of heat she evoked in him grow hotter.

How was he going to convince her to help him, to even trust him, if he couldn't control his desire to explore the attraction so obviously between them?

He almost laughed. Not a humor laugh. What the hell was this feeling he had burning him inside. Demanding he take her. That he find a way to bury himself deep inside her body? He'd never wanted with such potency. Never felt this kind of power urgency.

To take. To seize. To control.

And though he had no doubt she wanted him as he wanted her, he didn't want to make her feel he had manipulated her. When she found out his agenda in seeking her out, she would think he had used sex to get her to do his bidding.

But it wasn't that way.

He burned for her. Didn't want to. He simply did.

It was as real as anything he had ever known in this lifetime.

A slow smile turned up the corners of her lush mouth. "I'm glad," she said softly and a bit shyly.

"Can I take you to dinner?" He needed a good time to ask her help. That meant, despite the risk of more intimate moments, he needed some quality time with her.

She shook her head. "You already bought me one meal today."

He smiled, trying not to think about what happened after lunch. About touching her. About wanting her. "I hardly think the Chinese buffet put a dent in my wallet."

"Still," she insisted.

He reached for her hand instinctively. Before his mind could reason with his desire to touch her. Even his words seemed a creation of his desire, not his good sense. "I want to spend time with you tonight."

She studied him a moment as his thumb drew soft strokes across her palm. He couldn't seem to resist touching her. Then she said, "My neighbor brought me over a pot of spaghetti. If you want, I could heat it up. She's a great cook."

Alone in her house. Bad idea for so many reasons. He didn't let himself think about it. Instead, he asked, "Why would your neighbor bring you food?"

"I live in my parents' old home. She was my mom's best friend. She worries because I work late." She paused. "Too much, according to her," she added, grinning. Then, she reached out and touched his chest with her fingertips. "Will you join me?"

The touch of her fingers, so light, yet so heavy in sensation, rocked his reasoning skills to zero-level. "Sounds good," he said, knowing he was wrong to do so.

Holly was a woman to treasure, to make long-term commitments with and to marry. He could fuck her. Nothing more. No way could he offer her what she deserved. Those things were gone for him. Had there ever been a woman who could have made him want them, he knew in his core, Holly Heart would have been the one.

He dropped her hand and took a step backwards. "Can you leave now?"

She frowned at his sudden withdrawal as if she sensed it was more than a physical distance he had just drawn. "Yes. I only live a few blocks away so normally I walk home."

His eyes widened. "Haven't you heard about the abductions going on?"

She shrugged. "I have but—"

"No buts," he insisted. "Walking home is crazy."

"It's not a big deal," she said succinctly.

He fixed her in a hard stare. "Yes," he said. "It is."

She tilted her head to the side and her eyes darkened with a building anger.

He laughed.

She frowned. "What are you laughing at?"

"You," he said, giving in to the crazy feelings she evoked. He stepped forward and slid his hands under her hair as he maneuvered her backside against the desk. "You don't like having anyone tell you how or what you can or can't do."

"And you do?" she challenged, looking up at him, her hands resting on the sides of his waist, not at all fazed by his size or how he pressed against soft curves.

Or how hard his dick was as it brushed her stomach.

She was fearless and smart and too damn amazing to resist. His dick was right. His mind, wrong. At least at that moment. "Very few people get away with telling me what to do, that's true," he admitted, somewhat absently as he lowered his head, hungry to taste her.

Just once more, he told himself.

Just once.

He would make it be enough. Perhaps then he could be more focused. Her lashes fluttered shut as she willingly tilted her mouth up to receive the kiss. God, she was beautiful. He brushed his lips across hers in a soft caress.

"Mmm," she purred and he eagerly repeated the action. Her sweet little response only heightened his need. Called to his body and even, it felt, in that moment, his soul. He didn't understand the feeling. It just was.

His hands moved to her lower back, molding her against him as he slipped his tongue into her mouth. Instantly, she slid her arms around him, pressing her body even closer to his, her lush breasts molding his chest. She let out a soft, seductive little sigh.

It affected him like gasoline on a fire. Instantly, he was burning hot.

His tongue delved deeper...

A noise. Mason froze. Holly didn't. Her tongue reaching for his. Someone cleared their throat. No doubt, Roger.

With great irritation, Mason pulled back from Holly but he couldn't bring himself to release her completely. He began to loosen his grip to a more casual stance but Holly still clung, staring up at him with something in her eyes resembling shock. As if, he decided, she couldn't believe her own reaction to their intimacy.

"Holly," he whispered. "We have company."

She shook her head as if shaking off a thick haze and he watched reality slowly seep back into her eyes. She looked at Roger.

"Something wrong?" she asked him, sliding away from Mason, suddenly appearing a bit self-conscious. She leaned one hand on the desktop, making an obvious effort to seem at ease.

Mason refused to move away from her for reasons he himself didn't completely understand. He stepped behind her, his body close to hers, his hand on one of her shoulders, towering above her head to look at Roger.

"Usually people do things like *that* in private," Roger said snidely.

Stiffening, she glared. "Like *that*?"

"We were just leaving." He gave her shoulder a little squeeze.

"What is your problem, Roger? You never act so —"

"Because you never act like you are," he retorted before she finished her sentence.

She stared at him, baffled. Mason gave her another gentle squeeze. "Let's get going."

Holly shook her head in frustration and looked up at Mason. "Yeah, okay." She reached to retrieve her purse from her desk drawer. "Will you lock up, Roger?" she asked, giving him a cautious look.

"Yeah, sure," he said unpleasantly but turned and walked toward the lab before she could say anything else.

Holly looked at Mason. "I really don't understand him."

"Men do strange things when they feel territorial," Mason told her, thinking about himself, not Roger.

Where Holly was concerned, he indeed felt territorial, possessive, lustful and completely torn by too many things to count.

Inwardly, he sighed. One thing was for certain; He wasn't about to let the wrong people get their hands on her. As far as he was concerned, she was under his direct protection.

And even Roger could take that to the bank.

Chapter Three

Mason had helped Holly into the passenger side of his Ford Explorer like a perfect gentleman. It appealed in a big way. The man could easily set her on fire, yet he also made her feel like a lady. The combination did funny things to her.

Tugged at her heartstrings.

As he maneuvered into her driveway, she glanced at his profile, staggered by the power of his presence. No words spoken. His silence still held power.

Something in him reached out to her. Perhaps it was his sense of loneliness. Something she, too, had felt all too often. Deep in his eyes lurked dark shadows of things she didn't understand.

But wanted to.

When he had insisted Roger had feelings for her, she had sworn he was wrong. Yet now, thinking about it, she wondered if he was right. There was something about Mason. He knew things. How, she didn't know. But he did.

She wanted, no, *needed,* to know who Mason Alexander was as a man.

Looking at her house, Holly noted the abnormal darkness. "My porch light must have burned out."

Mason turned off the motor. "Good thing you didn't walk home alone."

She flicked him a look. "Don't you dare do the *I-told-you-so* thing or I may have to hit you."

He gave her a teasing look as he pushed open his door. "But I did tell you so."

He was out of the truck before she could respond. Holly laughed and pushed open her door, not bothering to wait on his assistance.

Mason was standing in front of her the minute her feet hit the pavement. "You're supposed to wait for my help." There was reprimand in his voice.

She just looked at him. Big, powerful and, oh, so male. He simply took her breath away. How had she lived all these years and never experienced anything like this...so deeply moving?

The answer was clear — she had only just met Mason.

He leaned on the doorframe of the truck, successfully caging her. Not that she was an unwilling captive. "You know," he said softly, his voice hinting at desire, his eyes flaring with smoldering heat. "When you look at me like that, all hot and wanting, it makes it real damn hard for me to do the right thing." He paused a second. "To be a gentleman."

She had always spoken her mind. Her parents had taught her that silence fed confusion. Something no scientist found acceptable. It was the only way she knew to express herself.

Frankly.

"You are a gentleman. I was just thinking that a few minutes ago. But sometimes being a gentlemen can be overrated."

His eyes flared with something resembling torment. And so much more. Heat. Sexual in nature. No question, he wanted her. And just when she thought he might accept what was between them, he abruptly stepped backwards.

He glanced at the house, seeming to dismiss what had just passed between them. As if he thought something was wrong.

The thought made her stiffen. "What is it?"

He literally thrummed with alertness. Without looking at her, he held out his hand, palm open. "Give me your keys and then get in the truck and lock it."

Suddenly her heartfelt like it might jump out of her chest. "Mason, you're scaring me."

He turned to face her, his eyes locking with hers. His hand slid under her hair, settling on her neck, warm and comforting, as he gently caressed with his thumb. "I'm just being cautious. Everything is fine, I'm sure."

"You think someone is here." Intuitively she knew he did.

His eyes narrowed on hers a long moment as if he was trying to decide what he could get away with saying. Or not saying. "Maybe," he said cautiously. He stroked her cheek with his thumb. "Please get in and lock the doors."

Something in his voice made her comply.

She handed him her keys before climbing into the truck. The instant she was inside the cab, he refocused on the house, yet he didn't move until she clicked the locks into place. It was strange how he moved the second she hit the button.

As if he knew when she did it without seeing her action.

* * * * *

Someone was watching them.

Mason didn't want to scare Holly. But he was quite certain they had company. Besides, he didn't want to explain who and what he was just yet. Not tonight.

Stepping onto the porch, he quickly surmised the light had been purposely broken. He eased around the side of the house, tuning in to his unique sensory abilities. He picked up Walsh's scent. Clearly he had traveled the backside of the house.

And there was another scent...Arion soldier. One of his enemies. No doubt following Walsh. The bastard was drawing attention to Holly that she couldn't afford.

Mason inwardly cursed. This was a cold, hard reminder that he was running out of time. He needed to convince Holly to help him before the Arions targeted her. If it wasn't already too late. They'd kill her rather than let her join the war against them.

Squatting by the wall, fading into the darkness, using it as a cloak, he scanned the perimeter. A tiny movement, not perceivable by normal human eyes, caught and held his gaze. And then it was gone.

No fight, no attack, just gone.

The intruder had one intent—surveillance. No Arion shied away from a fight. They were too aggressive by nature.

Cautiously, Mason moved around the house. A window was broken. Someone had been inside. He unlocked the back door and flipped on the inside light, already certain whoever had been there was gone. He'd sense a presence. A quick walk-through of the house confirmed nothing appeared disturbed. At least, nothing obvious.

Walsh had been the intruder. Not the Arions.

He'd come for Holly's research.

Sighing, Mason headed toward the front door. He was in a damn difficult position. His hope of easing Holly into the reality of who and what he was, was quickly dissolving.

He would have to move much more quickly than planned.

* * * * *

By the time Mason walked through her front door, Holly was about to lose her mind. She unlocked the truck door and shoved open the door. In a split second, she was running toward him. He reached for her and pulled her into his arms.

"You had a break-in," he said, leaning back to look down at her and she realized how much safer she felt with him touching her. He continued, "It appears the intruder was scared off before anything was taken. You'll have to inspect things yourself to be certain."

She blinked, stunned. "What?"

He nodded, calmly stating the facts. "They broke out your front light and there is a broken window in the back."

She swallowed hard. Her little neighborhood had always felt safe. What if she had come home alone? Had this person been there waiting on her? Why else would the porch light be knocked out? She could have been killed. Had Mason not been here, who knew what might have happened?

"But I *was* here," Mason said softly.

She looked at him with shock in her eyes. "How did you know what I was thinking?"

"It was written all over your face." He traced her jaw with his finger. "You have a very expressive face, you know."

She had never thought she needed anyone, for anything. Now Mason was here, a force so comforting, she didn't want to let him leave. It felt good to have someone, to have him, with her. And as crazy as she knew it was, especially in such a short time, she felt linked to him.

"Thank you," she whispered, "for being here."

"Perhaps," he said, with the tiniest hint of emotion in his voice, "I was meant to be."

"I've always loved this little house." There was a slight quiver in her voice despite her desire to seem strong. "This is the first time I haven't felt safe here."

He ran his hand down her hair in a comforting caress. "I'm sorry." His voice was laced with sincerity.

She sighed heavily and looked toward the front door. "I should call the police."

This was her home, the place where her parents had lived and raised her, one of the few things she had that kept her connected to them. She eyed the red brick, the large concrete porch and the big white swing to the left, beside the door.

She didn't want to be afraid here. This was her safety zone, her place to process life's ups and downs.

"You can call if you like," he offered, "but they won't find anything. If it will make you feel better though…" he let his voice trail off, clearly letting her know he would support whatever she decided.

"I want to call." Determination laced her words. "I'm here alone a lot. If the police say this isn't anything to worry about, it will make me feel better."

He nodded. "Then call," he said, motioning toward the house. "While they are here, I'll go get a new glass to fix your window."

Holly looped her arm around his elbow. "You fix windows, too?" she teased, though it came out a bit lame. Somehow, she managed a small smile.

He covered her hand with his. "Ask and you shall receive," he said, looking down at her with hard-to-read, dark eyes.

"Interesting," she said. "I like the sound of that."

Keeping him around for the night could be comforting in more ways than one.

* * * * *

Holly pressed her hand to her stomach, amazed by the fact that she was still hungry even after the chaos of the night. Scooping pasta into a pot to warm, she turned on the burner. Her mind replayed the police visit.

They hadn't been as comforting as she had hoped. With the recent crime waves in the city, they were being cautious about downplaying potential risks. They had encouraged her to be on the lookout for strangers and definitely not to walk home alone.

By the time they left, she was more apprehensive, not less.

A cold shiver ran down her spine. She couldn't shake the weird vibe that something beyond a simple break-in had been planned.

That someone had come for *her*.

She could hear Mason working on the window just outside the kitchen. She looked heavenward and said a silent thank you. What if he hadn't been with her?

One thought led to another and, for about the millionth time, she wondered why she felt so drawn to him, a complete stranger.

As if she had willed him to appear with her thoughts, he walked in the back door, brushing his feet on her kitchen floor mat. "Done," he said and sniffed the air. "Smells good. I'm starved."

"Ten minutes and we can eat," she told him with a small smile. "The bathroom is in the hall if you need to clean up or," she pointed behind her, "you're welcome to use the kitchen sink."

He walked into the kitchen. "I'll just use the kitchen sink." She could hear him moving around, the water coming on, the soap bottle making a sound. After a few seconds, he said, "I hate that the police weren't more comforting."

Holly cut slices of garlic bread and laid them out on a cookie sheet. "I'd rather them be honest than comforting."

She turned to find him shaking the excess water from his hands. He turned off the faucet before grabbing a towel. As he dried his hands he studied her, leaning his hip against the cabinet. "You've had a rough day."

She laughed only half with humor. "And it seems I've dragged you along for the ride." She turned the broiler on. "The bread will only take a couple of minutes. I'm sorry but I don't have wine or beer or anything to offer you."

Shrugging he said, "I don't drink anyway. How about tea or juice?"

She leaned against the cabinet facing him. "You don't drink, as in ever, not even socially?"

He seemed to tense. "That's right. Is that a problem for you?"

She made a face. "Why would it be?"

He delivered the words nonchalantly but they felt like a test. One that wasn't necessary. "Some people think it's strange."

She laughed bitterly and turned away from him, opening a cabinet and pulling down several glasses. "Not me. I don't drink either."

His gaze was fixed on her. She felt it. Probing. She turned, the refrigerator her destination. But his eyes stopped her. He pinned her in a questioning stare.

A bit defensively, she said, "What?"

"I'd like it if you told me why you are suddenly tense." The words were a gentle prod and they spun a soft web of comfort.

Her lashes fluttered to her cheeks. Being outspoken about general topics was one thing. She rarely shared her personal history or emotions with anyone.

She had always been an immensely private person.

Oddly, she didn't mind sharing her history with Mason. She even felt it necessary. "My parents were killed by a drunk driver." Slowly she looked up at him. "I don't talk about it." She paused a split second and then added, "To anyone. Ever."

He was silent a moment, his dark eyes holding hers. And his look was understanding. Even knowing in some deep way. "But you told me."

She nodded, her eyes now fixed on his. "Yes," she whispered. "I told you."

His eyes seemed to almost wrap her in warmth. "I'm honored."

Her teeth found their way to her bottom lip. For once in her life, words failed her. Silence lingering between them, their gazes locked together. She sensed their shared confusion.

Neither understood what was happening between them.

The timer on the oven buzzed. Her gaze jerked toward the sound. "The bread," she said, just because it was better than saying nothing. Of course, he knew it was the bread.

He gave her an understanding smile as she glanced back at him. "I'll fill the glasses."

A few minutes later, they sat at her rather small glass table. Mason took a bite and sighed with pleasure. "Awesome. I never had neighbors like yours."

She laughed. "There's plenty, so feel free to get seconds. Don't expect this kind of fare from me without the neighbor's help. I microwave or open cans only. My parents were both scientists, not domestic at all."

"I'm not here for your cooking," he said and immediately looked down at his plate as if he didn't want to elaborate.

She knew an opening when it was handed to her. "What *are* you here for?"

He took a drink of his tea as if he was buying time to think of a response. In fact, Holly was quite certain he was. When he sat the glass down though, he didn't hesitate to make eye contact.

He kept his eyes carefully shielded, though his tone was raw and sexual. "You," he said simply. "I'm here because of you and all you are." A beat. "Not what you aren't."

What did that mean? "You don't know who or what I am. Unless, of course, you mean on a completely physical level." There, she said it. Inwardly fretting, she waited for a response.

He sat down his fork. "There is that, of course." His voice held a soft hint of admiration in his eyes. As if he approved of her straightforwardness.

"You already know I'm attracted to you, as I believe you are to me. But there is more going on here than mere physical attraction." There was subtle challenge in his voice as if he dared her to deny the obvious. He even let several heartbeats pass to allow her time to object.

When she didn't speak, he continued, "I know more about you than most do and I only just met you." His eyes seemed to darken. "Just as you do of me." He let the words sink in a moment. "Why?" he asked, with a lift to his brow. "I can't answer that any more than I imagine you can."

She swallowed nervously, his words ringing true while still defying reason. "I'm not sure how to respond," she said, after several long moments of deliberation.

"You don't have to," he offered. "I'd like to know more about you. You cured that chimp, which was nothing short of amazing. Your work is obviously critical to the world of medicine."

He picked up his fork and began to eat again as if he was trying to lighten the mood, which had somehow become heavy.

She followed his lead. "I know how to fix most of the challenges previously encountered with genetic replacement therapy but the government won't let me prove it on humans." She sat her fork back down, suddenly not hungry.

"This obviously upsets you," he commented eyeing her closely.

She nodded. "It does bother me. I've dedicated my life to healing. It's hard to know people are dying and I have a cure I can't offer them. To make matters worse, the government is trying to get me to help make super soldiers by dangling opportunities to test humans again. The man you saw bothering me, he was from the government."

"And you're not interested," he stated.

"I'm not about to help make war. I save lives, not take them," she said firmly.

"Soldiers save lives, too. They just do it in a different way."

"By killing," she said with harsh disapproval.

"By defending our nation and, yes, sometimes that means taking a life. Our country has the freedoms it does because of men who fought and protected our rights." He paused a beat. "You would never have been able to study medicine or science as a female had wars not been fought many years ago."

She grimaced. "But times change," she argued. "There is no reason to use physical force to make the world a good place to live."

"I disagree," he said softly. "To prevent war, others must know you can defend yourself. The weak are victims. Our last war was in 2003, a mere twelve years ago. Clearly we are not so far away from times when battle saved our freedoms."

She glowered at him. "I should dislike you. People with your opinions are usually not my close friends."

His eyes narrowed. "Do you, Holly? Do you dislike me now that you know my views are different?"

She countered him. "I could ask you the same about myself."

He laughed and shook his head, pushing his plate to the side and leaning forward, resting his arms on the table. "I don't think it's possible for me to dislike anything about you. In fact, I find I quite like debating with you."

Holly let out a breath she didn't even realize she was holding. She liked disagreeing with Mason almost as much as she liked agreeing with him. It was really starting to rattle her, this crazy feeling of connection to him.

But it didn't change the fact that she wanted him. Like she had never wanted before.

Purposely she changed the subject. Afraid he might read her thoughts. Why, she wasn't sure. She just was. It was an odd feeling but not near as disturbing as it should have been. She pointed to his empty plate. "You want more?"

"No," he said, giving her a knowing look, "but thanks." He stood up and started to pick up the used dishes on the table.

Holly followed. "I can do this," she said reaching for the plates he held.

He let her but then said, "I'll help." His tone was insistent. The look in his eyes said he wouldn't be dissuaded.

Holly was immensely aware of his gaze following her as she moved. Suddenly her spacious kitchen seemed small. And she wanted it to be smaller. For him to be near. To touch her.

She set the dirty dishes in the sink, her back to him. She was suddenly thrumming with desire. With pure, hot need. She wasn't surprised to feel his hands settle on her waist. Just relieved, and excited.

Her heart flip-flopped with a hint of nervousness and anticipation.

She felt the hardness of Mason's body pressing against hers, deliciously warm, as it trapped her against the counter.

He nuzzled her ear, his breath tickling her lobe, tantalizing her senses. "You smell so damn good," he murmured.

Her hands clutched at the edge of the counter as her neck rotated to give him better access. "So do you," she said honestly. "So good."

He made a low sound in his throat and she could feel the evidence of his arousal pressing against her thighs. "Tell me to stop," he ordered as he kissed her neck, feathering light kisses on the sensitive area.

"I…can't." It was a mere whisper of a reply. She was already reaching for his mouth, her hand on his cheek as she turned to him.

She wanted this.

She wanted *him*.

The minute her lips brushed his he rotated her around to fully face him. Then, he was kissing her passionately, hungrily, as if he could never get enough. His tongue delved into her mouth, teasing and tangling with her own, and she didn't shy away from taking as much as he offered.

She had waited thirty-two years to be kissed like this and she wanted every bit of his amazing, unique flavor. Her arms wrapped around his neck as she rose up on tiptoe and pressed her body against his.

Her breasts tingled as they molded against his chest and her hands longed to explore the ripples of steel that her body was molded against.

She had wanted this earlier. She needed it now. Her hand slid under his shirt, loving the feel of hard muscle beneath her soft palm. Hungrily, she touched him. But no more so than he did her. His teeth nipped at her bottom lip and his hand slid up the back of her shirt.

Her bra popped loose and she eagerly reached down and tugged her shirt over her head, tossing the bra aside. His eyes dropped and, for a long moment, he went still.

She took a deep breath, willing herself to be bold, and reached for his hand. Pressing it to her breast, she felt her insides tremble with the impact of his touch. He made a low sound in his throat and then he was kissing her neck, filling both hands with her breasts.

Her head fell between her shoulders, giving him better access, while allowing her to enjoy what he did to her. His lips traveled down her neck and his fingers teased and tweaked her nipples. The harder he pinched, the more she moaned. She couldn't help it.

And the lower his mouth got, the more she wanted it on her nipples. Her hands went to his head as his tongue lapped at the side of one of her breasts and then trailed upwards...

"Mason," she moaned, wanted his mouth on her nipple.

He stopped moving. Her head tilted upwards. She sensed something was wrong. Slowly, he lifted his head and looked at her, his eyes full of turbulence. There was also so much smoldering passion it made her suck in a breath.

She slid her hands to frame his face. "I want you," she told him, feeling as if he needed to hear the words.

Her breathing was heavy, or was it his? He seemed to be trying to gauge her response or perhaps his own; she didn't know or care, she just wanted him to kiss her again.

Another quick movement and he lifted her with ease, placing her on the counter, gently nudging her legs apart as he settled between them. The sweet pressure of his arousal nestled so intimately made her moan.

Pulling her close, he kissed her again, no less passionately, maybe even more so, though she wasn't sure that was even possible, because the first kiss had been amazing. Her head swirled, her body heated, wetness—a true testament of how much she desired him—pooled between her legs.

Yes, her body screamed in her mind. *This is what I have been waiting for all my life.*

Then, abruptly she found herself on her feet almost shivering from the loss of Mason's touch though it was far from cold in the room. She blinked, trying to clear the lust-induced fog.

"Mason?" she asked, confused.

He leaned against the refrigerator. "I'm sorry," he said, torment clearly etched in his tone. "No way should that have happened."

"But I wanted it," she said, not wanting him to think she was offended. "I still do," she whispered.

He opened his mouth to speak, scrubbed his hand across his jaw and shut it again. Then, "I have to go. Lock the door behind me."

And then she heard the front door slam.

He was gone.

She was alone.

Left in complete, utter sexual frustration, feeling rejected and more empty than she had since losing her parents.

* * * * *

Mason sat in his truck, staring at Holly's house. It was going to be a long night. Since his transformation, he didn't need much sleep. A necessary skill in battle and certainly a handy one on this occasion, allowing him to ensure Holly's safety while she slept.

Silently, he willed himself to stay away from her. Turning the key in the ignition, the motor hummed to life. He backed out of the driveway and scanned the area for a discreet place to park. He'd go back to Holly's place unnoticed and on foot.

Thinking of her so close, nestled in her bed, probably half-dressed, knowing he couldn't hold her and touch her, was going to be hell.

The new day couldn't come soon enough.

Chapter Four

The glowing, green light on his truck clock read five-forty-five in the morning.

Mason sat in his truck, watching in disbelief as Holly moved through the dark parking lot of the university toward the lab. The woman was crazy to think she was safe in a deserted parking lot.

He wondered if she made a habit of going in to work this early. Or maybe she had been as tied in knots as he had after their little encounter. Maybe she hadn't been able to sleep.

He watched her disappear into the building, letting out a silent sigh of relief when he saw the lab lights through the window.

The sound of an engine drew Mason's attention. Sterling had pulled his Mustang into the parking lot. Seconds later, he slid into the passenger side of Mason's truck. In hand, he juggled a bag and two giant drinks.

"Food," Sterling said, setting the bag down between them and handing Mason a drink.

"Thanks, man, I'm starved. I don't think I'll ever get used to how fast my metabolism works. It feels like I have to constantly eat."

"Yeah," Sterling said. "Same here."

Mason pulled a wrapped breakfast sandwich out of the bag, ripped it open and took a bite. He and Sterling each downed a sandwich in silence. By the time they each reached for number two, Mason was ready to talk. "Walsh led the Arions straight to Holly. If they didn't already know what she's capable of, they'll make a point of finding out now."

"Which means there's no question she's in danger," Sterling said and then took a long draw from his straw. "The question is, will they want her dead or alive?"

Balling up a paper wrapper Mason reached for another sandwich. "I'd say alive is their first choice but dead before they will let her help us."

He felt his body tense just saying the words. The thought of losing Holly hurt him on some soul-deep level. He was beginning to wonder about his intense reaction to her. It went beyond physical. Mason opened his mouth to tell Sterling how he was feeling but quickly clamped his jaws back together.

He'd not been with a woman for a longtime. Maybe he was just plain in need of sex. All of his senses were more intense since the enhancements. He felt the bitterness of resentment. Enhancements he'd never known were taking place.

Immunizations given to an elite special ops team without them knowing what was taking place. Now, he and many were labeled super soldiers. With that came improved vision and hearing along with a keen sense of smell and taste. God only knew what else. It made sense that his sexual need would come with added potency.

Which would explain his over-the-top reaction to Holly. He ground his teeth. Except, other women didn't impact him as she did. There was something different about her. About them together.

Sterling flicked a glance at Mason. "We're going to have to take her into protective custody."

Mason sighed. "Yeah, I know. This is really not how I wanted this to go down. She's really against super soldiers and the whole war thing in general. I wanted time to make her understand."

Sterling pulled out another sandwich. "Once she knows about the Arions, I have to believe she will see our position. It's not like we're creating war. We are simply defending our country from one that already exists."

He laughed without humor. "You haven't met Holly."

Sterling didn't say anything for a long moment, finishing off his sandwich in what appeared to be deep thought. "What is it with you and this woman?"

Mason crumpled up another wrapper and shook his head. "I wish I knew." His voice was tense. "There's some weird connection between us. I can't even explain it."

He didn't say more. Wanted to, but didn't.

"Does she feel it, too?"

"Yeah." He saw no reason to lie to Sterling. "She does."

His voice held understanding. "But she doesn't know what you are."

"And she's not the kind of woman someone like me messes with."

"She's a scientist," Sterling argued. "She might be the exact right kind of woman you need."

"She deserves a normal guy who can offer her a family and stability. Hell, I don't even know what kind of crazy things were done to me. She could be getting a monster for all I know."

Sterling's jaw clenched. "Yeah," he said. "I feel the same way. Sometimes I wonder about the very government we're fighting for."

Mason looked at Sterling. "Don't. Our country is about our people, not the power-hungry men who tricked us into this genetics nightmare."

"Immunizations for new diseases, they said," Sterling said in a low voice, anger coloring the words.

"We are what we are, man. It won't change." Mason said the words with confidence, no evidence of how close he was to choking on the words. "Make the best of it." *Easier said than done.*

Bitterness replaced Sterling's anger. "One more level of injections and we could have been Arions."

"But we're not," Mason reminded him.

"No," he said, "but you were right when you said we aren't normal either."

Mason cringed inwardly, cursing his own bad attitude. He'd allowed his negativity to rub off on Sterling. His role was one of leadership. He was a motivator. Or was supposed to be. There were immense reasons why he and his team had to stay focused and strong together.

Namely, the safety of the human race.

Who else but the super soldiers could battle the Arions?

"As much as I would love to turn back time, we can't. Be thankful we aren't normal. We're the only hope humanity has." His words were laced with conviction.

He was prepared to serve his country.

Sterling grimaced as if he didn't hear. "Any chance this Holly woman can actually give us some semblance of normalcy?"

Pretending there was hope wouldn't help Sterling deal with what he had become. "Nothing can do that, man. The best we can hope for from Holly, or anyone else, is help fighting the Arions. To understand their capabilities and weaknesses on all levels would be a great resource. She can be a great resource. We need her."

Sterling met Mason's gaze. "But you believe she won't ever accept who you — correction, we — are?"

"You mean *what we* are?" He shook his head. "No way. A group of man-made soldiers. She has made her feelings quite clear about our kind."

Sterling seemed to consider Mason's response as his gaze shifted. His attention went to the lab. "I'm not overly comfortable with her safety today. There is no way we will know what is going on inside. Not when school starts."

Mason's expression held concern. "I agree and there is more than one entrance. After today, she can't go back." He considered.

"I'll keep an eye on her while you go shower and freshen up," Sterling offered.

Mason nodded. "I'd appreciate that. I doubt they will make a move in such a public place but who knows with the Arions."

Sterling made a frustrated sound. "Exactly," he agreed. "If they want her they won't delay. They will act quickly."

* * * * *

Holly sat at her desk, grading tests.

Glancing at the clock hanging above her desk, she grimaced. She'd been at work two hours. Not fifteen minutes had gone by without thoughts of Mason.

Squeezing her eyes shut, she willed him out of her head. After several long seconds, she gave up. It was a useless endeavor. She hadn't slept and now even work wouldn't clear her mind.

She had been shocked at his abrupt departure. And as misguided as it was, she had held onto hope that he would return. Several hours later, she accepted the truth.

He wasn't coming back.

At that point, she had paced the floor, calling him mean names. It hadn't solved anything but it had at least given her a direction to funnel her anger…and her sexual tension.

Hours later, in her lonely bed, she had stared into the darkness, unable to sleep. At four in the morning, she had woken abruptly.

She had dreamed he was there. Touching her, kissing her. Naked, his body entwined with hers. It had taken long moments for her to decipher dream from reality.

She had been aroused, her body pulsing with need.

So real were the images…his mouth on her nipple, his tongue teasing, his teeth nipping. Breathing hard, she had slowly moved to a sitting position, her eyes searching the room. As if he was there.

In her room. Waiting for her.

But it had been nothing more than a trick of her mind.

Pushing her chair away from her desk, Holly picked up her coffee cup with the intention of refilling her cup. In the two hours since she had arrived she had almost finished off a pot. Before she could take a step, Roger walked through the doorway looking as cranky as he had the night before.

"You know what?" she said to him, motioning with her finger toward the door. "If you are as foul as you look, you might as well turn around and go back home. I'm not in the mood."

Holly glared at him a moment and then marched toward the kitchen, ignoring his startled expression. She poured the remainder of the coffee into her cup and stood debating about making another pot.

"What was that all about?" Roger spoke from behind her.

Holly turned to face him. "I should ask you the same about last night."

His tone held nastiness. "I don't like that guy." He leaned his shoulder against the doorframe.

She rolled her eyes. "You don't even know him."

"Neither do you," Roger countered.

Her eyes narrowed. "How would you know?"

"You've never brought him around before. In fact, you've never even mentioned his name. You just met the guy, yet you were necking with him—like some...some school kid—right here in the middle of the lab!"

Holly couldn't believe her ears. He had some nerve. Irritation turned to outright anger. "I don't share every little detail of my life with you, Roger. And I was not necking like some school kid!"

She grabbed her coffee cup roughly enough to slush coffee on her hand. "Ouch!" She looked up at Roger and scowled. "Look what you made me do."

She looked down at her hand, a bit shocked by the heat, before sitting her cup on the counter. Turning to the sink she ran cold water over her skin where the sting was growing.

Roger spoke to her back, regret etching his tone. "I don't want to fight with you, Holly."

Holly let her head drop forward a moment, feeling the strain of emotions so unfamiliar. Since losing her parents, she had remained relatively alone. Suddenly, Mason, and now Roger, were making demands on her, each in their own way, but both overwhelming in nature.

She turned off the water, grabbing the hand towel lying by the sink. Facing him, she said, "I don't understand why you're so angry at me."

Roger took off his glasses and pinched the bridge of his nose with two fingers. When he returned them to his face, he said, "I'm not used to seeing you with other men."

Holly was a bit stunned by his statement. *Other men?* There had never even been a hint of more than friendship between them.

"Other, meaning what, Roger?" She frowned in confusion. "I'm not sure I quite get what you're saying here."

"I guess I always thought..." his voice trailed off.

"Thought what?" she encouraged, hoping to put resolution to at least one of her newfound man troubles. As awkward as this was, it was better dealt with now than later.

He opened his mouth to speak, shut it again and then finally said, "I thought—"

"Doc, are you here?"

Instantly, Holly recognized Tami Hendrix's sweet voice. A smile touched Holly's lips at the sound of the nickname given to her by several of the students.

"In here," Holly called, knowing of course Tami was there to feed the animals. She had recently decided to become a veterinarian and liked to help Holly with her mini zoo in the back of her lab.

Tami stepped into the doorway, next to Roger, her curly black hair piled on top of her head with a clip. "I was going to feed the animals but the door was locked."

Roger didn't look at her, his eyes remaining fixed on Holly. "I'll unlock it." But didn't move for a long moment.

When he turned, saying nothing, and walked away, Tami frowned. "What's his deal?"

"If you figure it out, please let me know," Holly replied with frustration.

Tami's brow inched upward but she didn't comment, choosing to follow in Roger's footsteps.

Holly threw the towel on the counter and marched toward her desk. Picking up her work and carefully organizing it in her briefcase, she decided to head to her first class early. The more she thought about what Roger had *almost* said, the more bothered she became.

She wasn't sure she was ready to deal with him again just yet.

* * * * *

Holly carried her lunch with her as she stepped outside the lab. Moving briskly toward the back of the building, she savored the feel of the soft breeze as it lifted her hair off her neck. Somehow, being outside made her feel less trapped and better able to think.

As much as she hated to admit it, she was also avoiding Roger. It wasn't like her to sidestep issues. She was usually direct. Right now, though, she simply felt overwhelmed and confused. Roger was a friend and she feared handling things in the wrong manner would destroy their relationship.

Choosing a bench amply covered by a large shade tree and enough off the beaten path to give her privacy, she sat down with a sigh. Her eyes drifted shut, feeling heavy from strain and stress.

And then she felt it. She wasn't alone.

Mason.

How she knew he was there with her eyes shut, she didn't know. But she did. Without question. Lashes lifting, she found him sitting beside her.

Just as she knew he would be.

She blinked. How had she known it was him? "Okay, this is too weird. I knew you were there before I opened my eyes."

"People sense others," he responded, his expression unreadable.

She shook her head adamantly, reeling with the oddity of her feelings. "No. I knew it was *you*."

"I would know your presence as well. It's simply how we respond to one another." He drifted into silence, studying her as if he was trying to understand what was between them. "When I'm with you, I forget reason."

She didn't understand what he meant. "I'm not sure what you mean but it doesn't sound like a compliment."

"It's simply a fact." He reached out and traced her jaw line with his index finger. She felt the instant sizzle so familiar from his touch. "You're very beautiful."

A shiver of awareness raced down her spine. She didn't want to react to him. It was mortifying the way he had left her the night before. "Don't," she said as her lashes fluttered to her cheeks.

Yet she couldn't push his hand away.

Without warning, he was suddenly closer, his warmth and masculinity sneaking under her protective shell. His lips brushed hers, featherlight, but oh-so-sensual.

Her lips quivered against his. There was no way to fight what she felt. He could have his way with her here, now, in the school courtyard, and she didn't think she could stop him.

Moments later, he gave her a heavy-lidded stare. She forced a breath, trying to calm her herself, to smash the heat building.

It didn't work.

But she needed answers. To understand why he acted as if their attraction was a crime. "Why did you leave last night?" She had to know. Clearly he wanted her as much as she did him.

Abruptly, he pulled away from her, his black eyes seeming to flash with something intense and almost dangerous. She wasn't afraid of him.

But she was angry. And even that confused her. She was mad at him, but still wanted him. And she trusted him when perhaps she should fear him.

In fact, deep inside, she trusted him more than she had ever trusted anyone. There was no doubt in her mind — he could be dangerous if crossed. Just not to her. It should have bothered her — the fact she knew that he could kill if need be — but it didn't.

He ran out on you last night, she reminded herself. Falling back into his arms was foolish. She didn't like being foolish.

Mason sighed, weariness to the sound. "We need to talk. There are things you should know."

Her brows dipped together. "You know what?" she asked, but didn't want or expect an answer. "I don't want to talk to you, Mason."

"We *have* to talk," he said quietly.

She laughed without humor. "I don't *have* to do anything."

"Tonight," he said. "We'll talk. I'll come to your place."

"No," she said brusquely, "you won't."

He looked at her, his eyes somehow making her feel as if she couldn't look away. "This is bigger than you and me, Holly. I'll explain tonight."

Without warning, he stood up. He walked away with brisk strides. She stared after him, stunned at his abrupt departure. Just as she had been the night before.

* * * * *

Roger sat at his desk, staring down at his lunch. Holly was avoiding him. He knew it with certainty. She always ate her lunch in the lab.

But not today.

He knew she had guessed what he had almost confessed. Loving her for so long, without acting on it, had been difficult. Seeing her with that Mason person had been one of the hardest things he'd ever had to deal with.

He picked up his soda can, intent on taking a drink, when the sound of someone delicately clearing their throat made him sit it back down. Rolling his chair around, he found himself face-to-face with a stunning redhead. Her eyes caught his attention. They were the oddest, most beautiful black he'd ever seen.

She was a welcome distraction from his pitiful mood. "Can I help you?"

Covertly, his gaze slid down her short, powder blue skirt and lingered on her long, sexy legs. He'd always been a leg man, and she did a fine job of feeding his hot spot.

"Hi," she said with a charming smile. "I'm with the Ferguson Scientific Group, hoping to speak to the person in charge of our research projects." She opened her notebook and glanced at it. "A Holly—"

"Heart," he said, finishing her sentence. "She's at lunch." Ferguson was a name he knew instantly. They were the biggest source of funding for their genetics research. "I'm her right arm person. Can I help you with anything?"

Her smile widened, which only seemed to make her eyes more alluring. Mysterious. "Perhaps," she offered. "We've been approached by the government about some special projects. I need to know our capabilities to meet some specific needs."

Roger pushed to his feet. "I'm the person you need to speak to then."

The woman's brow inched up. "Not Holly Heart?"

Roger knew opportunity when he saw it. This was a chance to show Holly how well he would take care of her. Convincing Ferguson to forgo any government genetics projects would go a long way with her.

"Holly, Dr. Heart that is, doesn't want anything to do with certain government projects," he explained. "Maybe we should step down to the hall to the break area where we can sit down and talk."

The woman gave him a quick nod of agreement. Inwardly he sighed in relief. "This way," he said motioning toward the door. He started forward but stopped and turned to face her. "I just realized I never formally introduced myself." He extended his hand. "I'm Roger Mayfield."

She smiled, angelic and inviting, and slipped her hand into his. "Gina Lawrence."

* * * * *

Roger sat directly across from Gina at the small kitchen table . Glad the break area was deserted, he was ready for business. "What is it exactly you hope to achieve today?"

"We—"

"Meaning Ferguson Enterprises?"

"Yes," she agreed. "We are greatly interested in a Super Soldier program the government has asked us to participate in."

Roger stiffened. This was what he was afraid of. Super soldiers represented everything Holly hated. "Our research was designed to cure disease."

"Saving lives is saving lives," she said pointedly. "If these super soldiers improve our military, then it saves lives." She shoved a lock of red hair behind her ear and added, "Just in a different way."

"And Ferguson gets a huge return." No doubt it was true. This was money-motivated, plain and simple.

She nodded, seemingly at ease with her answer. "There is that, of course. We never said we didn't want to make money."

Roger didn't like her response. "You never said you wanted to turn this into a military operation."

"Mr. Mayfield," she said, in a sharper tone than before, "can you or can you not make super soldiers?"

His response was honest, though reluctant. "If it can be done, Holly can do it." She seemed pleased with his answer, so he clarified. "You can forget enlisting her help. The government already came to her and she flat-out refused them. Getting your company involved is just another ploy to get her to agree. She won't."

She gave him a hard stare. "We have a right to the research files."

"You won't get them from me. That is something you will have to take up with Holly."

Gina's eyes narrowed on him. "I want those files."

Roger pushed to his feet. "You won't get them from me." Then he added, "And I can assure you Holly won't even think about handing them over."

She followed him to his feet. "We'll see about that, Mr. Mayfield."

After a curt goodbye with Roger, Gina made her way out of the building. He might prove quite useful. Clearly, he was close to Holly Heart. A slow smile slipped onto her lips.

Perhaps he could be used as bait.

Chapter Five

Holly maneuvered her car into her driveway, replaying Mason's words in her head.

This isn't just about you and me.

She killed the ignition, leaving herself blanketed in darkness as she glanced at the house. The incident from the prior night had her on edge. Utter stillness seemed to surround her, thick and uncomfortable. Dropping her head to the steering wheel, she took deep breaths, willing her nerves to calm.

Instead, she found Mason's words replaying yet again in her head. *This isn't just about you and me.*

For some reason the words made her feel a sense of dread. Her mind couldn't reason with the crazy feelings she was having. It was as if her senses and emotions had ripened to a new state, one that defied logic.

She had left Roger working at the lab. The strain between them was extreme and hadn't done a thing to help her state of mind.

With effort, she forced herself to move. She pushed opened the car door and stepped outside. Exposed to the night, she suddenly felt the isolation of her home. With it came the pain of loss. No longer would she feel safe here.

Gone was the sanctuary she called home sweet home.

Looking toward the porch, she cringed at the darkness it held. Mason had tried to replace the bulb the night before but he couldn't get the circuit to work.

She had forgotten to call a repair person. Right now, she regretted that little fact. And she really wanted inside, where it was safe.

Resisting the urge to run, she walked briskly toward the front steps. The minute she hit the porch, her stomach lurched. She wasn't alone. Fumbling with her keys, hand shaking, she reached for the doorknob.

Movement from the corner of the porch made her gasp and she whirled around to see her attacker. It was Mason who stepped forward. "Oh, my God," she said, hand on her chest, anger replacing fear. Why hadn't she sensed him as she had earlier? Maybe her own fear had masked her instincts? It made no sense. Adrenaline pumping through her veins, she reacted to the rush with a tight retort. "You scared the hell out of me!"

"I told you I would be here," he said quietly.

"And I told you not to come." She turned back to the door, eager to unlock it. Task complete, she turned back toward him, only to find him no longer across the porch. He was almost directly in front of her. It shocked her. She'd never heard him move. "Where…where's your truck anyway?"

He ignored her question, closing the remaining distance between them, his legs almost touching hers. He reached past her shoulder to turn the doorknob. His arm brushed her shoulder, sending a rush of warmth across her skin.

God, how she wanted this man. It made no sense. Never before had anyone done this to her.

He pinned her in a potent stare, his expression guarded. "Let's go inside," he said in a deep voice that seemed to do a sensual dance along her nerve endings. "We need to talk, Holly."

Her reactions to him put her at a disadvantage. "I don't want to talk to you." Inwardly, she mocked herself. No, she wanted to do a whole lot more than talk. The thought made her response come out sharp. "Go away."

His gaze sharpened. "Is that what you really want?"

Her lashes fluttered to her cheeks as she fought an internal battle. She wanted him but she didn't want to. But the simple truth was—her resistance was slipping away.

Without looking at him, she turned and pushed the door open. She stepped inside the door, reaching for the light. Before she found the switch, she felt Mason's hands on her waist. The next thing she knew, his mouth was on hers.

Shock quickly turned to desire. Within moments, she was lost in his taste. She felt his hands on her back, pulling her closer, molding her softness against his muscular body. Her arms slid up, around his neck.

His scent insinuated into her nostrils, a soft male scent that made her want to get closer to him. Her body pressed against his, wanting more. This man was somehow, someway, uniquely connected to her. She felt it in his every touch, in his very existence.

Each stroke of his tongue seduced her senses, made her ache with pure, hot desire. She tasted him like he was the very breath she breathed. And in some ways it felt it might actually be so.

"Holly." He spoke, against her lips, an intimate gesture that made her feel even more drawn to him.

"Yes," she said, and unable to resist, she pressed her lips in a soft caress.

He moaned softly. "I've never been a man without willpower but—"

"It's overrated." Her hands slid down his chest and tugged at his shirt. She wanted to feel his skin, no barriers.

"Holly," he said but he didn't move, didn't stop her.

Slipping her hands under the material, her palms found the hard muscle of his abdomen. "Yes, willpower is most definitely way, way overrated."

"We need to talk," he said hoarsely. His hands went to hers, as if he was trying to stop her exploration. "I'm trying damn hard to be honorable here, Holly."

"Don't be," she replied. "I want you. You want me. There is nothing more to discuss."

He stood there, as stiff as a statue, her hands now moving over his chest, her nail scraping his nipple. He sucked in a breath.

She looked up at him. "I want you, Mason."

His dark eyes seemed to dilate and then, without warning, he moved, scooping her into his arms. He carried her toward the living room. "Just remember I tried," he said and buried his face in her hair.

She kissed his jaw, loving the feeling of being in his arms. Wanting it to last forever. "I'll remem—"

Moments later, they were on the couch, kissing passionately. She was draped across his lap sideways, her arms around his neck, her breast angled to press against his chest.

His hand tunneled into her hair, his touch somehow possessive. But good. Oh, so very good. She wasn't a woman to be taken but Mason, well, he made her want anything and everything.

But then she was hardly being submissive. She kissed him with a hungry eagerness, demanding more with each stroke of her tongue. Each touch of her hand.

Careful not to break the kiss, afraid he might change his mind, she slid around to straddle him. His hands went to her waist and then up her back. The material of her skirt slid up her thighs leaving little between them, yet more than she wanted. She could feel the hard proof of his desire. It only made her hotter. She wanted and wanted. She couldn't seem to get enough of him.

Lord help her, would she ever?

* * * * *

Holly looked at him, no inhibitions in her words or the hot way she looked at him. "I've never wanted anyone like this."

A contradiction to her angelic appearance, her aggressiveness was somehow all the more appealing. It was an incredible turn-on. *She* was an incredible turn-on.

He slipped his hand behind her neck and pulled her mouth to his, their breath mingling, anticipation burning in his veins. "You're driving me crazy," he murmured as their lips touched and lingered together in a long moment of simply feeling one another.

The moment changed to one of hunger as their tongues came together, a wild, hungry urge to take and take overcoming him. She was like fire in his veins. She took control of him, made him want her with such need he couldn't think.

He could only feel.

His dick was pressing against his zipper, straining, wanting... Her legs formed a vee across it, tempting him, with only a sheer piece of lace and his pants separating them. It would be so easy to rip those panties off and take her.

He could feel the sweet heat of her body pressing against his cock, calling to him. His hands went to her thighs, moving back and forth, wanting her skin beneath his hands.

God, he wanted her naked. He reached for her blouse, fumbling with several buttons. He needed this. He needed her. No more fighting. His body called in a way he couldn't seem to fight. His mind was a hazy fog of desire.

He shoved the silk over her shoulders. "Take this off."

She leaned back, lips swollen from his kisses, eyes dark with passion. No fear, no hesitation, she let the shirt drop down her arms and then fall to the floor.

He couldn't wait for the bra to be gone. He needed to taste her. His hands slid around her back and his mouth pressed against the vee between her breasts. She had gorgeous, full breasts, which overflowed from the lace of her bra. Her plump, red nipples showed through the lace, delicious enticements begging him to taste.

He buried his face between her breasts, absorbing her smell, so soft, like flowers. But there was another scent, one that made him burn with pure lust. Arousal. He'd never known a smell like this one. It was as if it called to him.

The rumble of something animalistic, primal and hot began to rise.

A low groan escaped his lips as one of his hands laced into her hair, pulling her mouth to his. His other hand pushed her downward, pressing her hips against his aching cock. Yes, his mind and body said, as he felt her closer. God, how he yearned to be inside her.

To feel the warmth of her body slide around him, wet and tight.

Her hands were in his hair and he looked up at her only to find her mouth on his. Kissing her was nothing like kissing other woman. It did something to him. Ignited a deeper hunger.

But then, abruptly, he felt something. He froze, his hands going to her wrists. Alert, but still fighting the rage of his body.

Awareness of another kind crept into his mind, unwanted, but clear, invasive and unpreventable.

"What is it?" Holly asked urgently, her breathing a bit erratic.

Mason rested his forehead against hers, tormented by what had just happened. Knowing it was over now. They had company and it had been wrong in the first place. Yet it still took great will to resist the urge to run his hands along her bare thighs.

Just one more time.

He sighed. "You have company."

She pulled back to look into his eyes. "That's crazy. It's almost eleven."

A knock sounded on the door and her eyes went wide in shock. "How did you know?"

"It's Roger," he said, fixing her in an unblinking stare. "I told you we needed to talk. There are things about me you don't know."

A knock sounded again. "Holly, open up." It was Roger's voice.

Holly's eyes never left Mason's. "Coming," she yelled loudly. It was Mason's turn to be shocked. She bent her head and brushed her lips across his. "Whatever it is you need to tell me it doesn't change the fact that I still want you."

His hands went to hers. "You have no idea what you are dealing with here."

"I'm a scientist, Mason." Her voice was clear and determined but her eyes were still heavy with desire. "I don't scare easily."

"Maybe you should," he replied, meaning it on many levels.

Her voice purred with a taunt and a challenge wrapped together as one. "That would make things much easier for you, wouldn't it?"

"Holly!" Roger's voice called.

Mason released her hands. "You better go deal with him."

Her lips curved into a seductive smile. "And then I'm dealing with you," she said in a voice as silky and full of promise as the hand she trailed down his jaw.

And then she got up, grabbed her shirt and tugged it over her shoulders. Moving away from him, her expression hidden, she sashayed across the room with what he knew was an intentional seductive sway of her hips.

And damn if his cock wasn't still standing at attention and begging for her return.

* * * * *

As Holly approached the front door, her fingers worked quickly on her buttons as she tried to shake the haze of need dancing along the nerves of her body.

Mason had her wound tight with desire.

She stood at the door and took several breaths, hearing Roger call out to her yet again. "Just a minute," she said with a hint of irritation creeping into her voice.

She needed a moment to compose herself. Resting her palms against the door, she considered what she had just learned about Mason.

He was different. What that meant exactly, she wasn't sure. Perhaps he should frighten her but the bottom line was — he didn't. Where Mason was concerned, her feelings weren't logical. Her normal fact-based decisions simply didn't apply where he was concerned.

Obviously, Mason had some special gifts. Physic abilities didn't make him dangerous. It simply made him unique. She almost laughed out loud as realization washed over her. The scientist in her was hard at work trying to make her reasoning about Mason logical rather than emotional.

She sighed.

Right now she simply wanted to get rid of Roger and get back to Mason.

Flipping on the light switch, she groaned as she remembered it was broken. She pulled open the door to find Roger looking frazzled and upset. She cracked the door, no intention of inviting him in. "What in the world are you doing here at this time of night?"

"I can't take us being so strained." His frown deepened. "Can I come in a minute?"

"Roger." She hesitated, trying to figure out what to do. Clearly he was upset but letting him in while Mason was there wasn't going to help matters. "It's late. Let's talk tomorrow. How about we meet up early for coffee?"

"Just a minute," he pressed. "Please."

Holly sighed with resignation. What option did she have without being totally rude? She stepped backward waving Roger forward. How had her life become suddenly so complicated?

She turned and started walking, wanting to turn on the light in the living room before Roger made his way behind her. Task complete, she turned as Roger entered, preparing herself for his reaction. He wasn't going to like Mason's presence but this was her home and she wasn't hiding anything. Crossing her arms in front of her body, she waited.

Roger started talking as he entered the room. "Holly, I can't stop thinking about..." He stopped mid-sentence when his eyes settled on Mason. "What's *he* doing here?"

"Roger," Holly said through clenched teeth. Her voice held a warning, as did her expression. "You know Mason and I are friends. Just like you and I are friends."

He let out a bitter laugh. "We aren't the same kind of friends."

Holly exchanged a quick look with Mason and then planted her hands on her hips. "What is your problem Roger?"

Roger tipped his chin toward Mason. "He's my problem."

Holly's mouth dropped open but, before she could speak, Mason pushed to his feet. "Why don't I give you two a minute alone?"

"No," Holly said firmly moving around the coffee table to stand beside Mason and placing her hand on his arm. "Roger, I think *you* better leave."

Roger's eyes went wide. "You hardly know this guy and you're kicking me out over him?" He made a disgusted sound. "I can't believe you."

Holly stared at Roger, baffled. Who was this person standing in her living room? It certainly wasn't the Roger she knew. "I'll walk you out, Roger."

"Fine," he said and turned toward the door.

Holly looked up at Mason. "Sorry about this."

Mason reached down and tucked a strand of hair behind her ear. "Not a problem."

The gesture was so tender it made Holly's breath catch in her throat. It was amazing how his touch made her tingle all over. For just a moment, she searched his eyes but his expression was carefully guarded.

Holly swallowed. "I'll, um, I'll be right back."

Roger was leaning on the porch railing when Holly stepped through her front door, leaving it opened so that they had some light. Silently, she cursed the burned-out circuit.

"You're mad at me," Roger said. "I can see it in your eyes."

Holly frowned. "I'm not mad but I'm more than a little confused by your crazy behavior."

"It's just... I thought... Oh, hell." He ran a rough hand through his hair. "I always thought we'd end up, you know —"

Holly decided it was best to confront this and get it over. "Dating?"

"Exactly," he said, expelling a breath as he said the word.

"Roger," Holly said gently. "You're a dear friend and a trusted research partner. To add a romantic element could be terminal. I would prefer to keep things as they are and I'm sure, if you take a step backward and look at things objectively, you will too."

Roger stared at her, his expression blank.

Holly stared at him, hoping for some form of response. She got none.

Okay. Now what?

* * * * *

Mason paced the living room feeling as if he was a caged animal. The sexual tension Holly had evoked in him was still raw and far too consuming. Try as he might, both in words and actions, resisting her was no easy task.

Something deep, carnal and wholly possessive urged him to take her, to make her his in some unexplained way. Raking a hand through his hair, he closed his eyes as he felt the intruding vibrations of a dark awareness.

Arion presence.

More than one.

Mason's eyes popped open. Holly. In a matter of seconds, he stepped onto the porch behind Holly, resting his hands on her shoulders. Above her head he met Roger's gaze.

Sidestepping Holly, Mason held Roger's gaze and walked toward him, his eyes placing Roger in a trance like state. "Roger, are you listening to me?"

Roger nodded. "Yes, I'm listening."

"Mason?" Holly said from behind him.

Mason ignored her, keeping his eyes tuned to Roger's. "When I tell you to, I want you to walk to your car as quickly as possible. Do not run. Get inside, lock the doors and drive away. Do you understand?"

"Yes, I understand," Roger said nodding, his face expressionless.

"Good. I'll walk with you. Wait until I say *go*. Shut your eyes now." Roger shut his eyes. "When I say *go,* open your eyes and do as I have instructed. You understand?"

"I understand."

Mason turned and looked at Holly. She looked confused and more than a little apprehensive. "You're scaring me, Mason."

The wind picked up around them alerting Mason as to how near to showing themselves the Arions really were. "Everything will be fine but I need you to go inside and lock the door."

"Mason—"

He fixed her in his gaze. "Just do as I say, Holly. I trust you to have sense and listen. Roger is another story. He won't listen and, for his own safety, I need to get him out of here. Now go inside." He paused. "I need you to call for help." He gave her Sterling's cell phone number, repeating it two times so he could be sure she got it memorized. "His name is Sterling. Tell him I told you to call. Do you have the number down?"

The wind lifted her hair from her shoulders, making her look as if she was a part of the force building around them. He could see the torment in her eyes even on the dark porch. "Yes, but I should call the police—"

"No police," he said, cutting her off. "Go inside, lock the door and call Sterling."

"But—"

"Now," he said in a curt command. "Right now."

Holly's eyes widened and then she whirled around and went inside her house, shutting the door and leaving him and Roger in complete darkness. Mason waited until he heard the door lock before turning to Roger. "Go now," he said.

Chapter Six

The minute Roger started backing out of the driveway, Mason walked toward a cluster of trees, where the Arions lurked, watching and waiting. Preferring an offensive stance, Mason moved toward their location. This was one of those times he was thankful for his enhanced night vision. He, like the Arions, wasn't limited by the night.

He drew to a halt in the center of the trees, standing in the middle of the greenery. Three Arions stepped from the woods. They formed a triangle to his position, trying to cage him.

He knew the one in the middle. Tad Benson was a ten-year special Operations veteran and an old friend. Now Tad was his brother's right arm man and his enemy.

The odds were not in his favor at three-to-one considering these were Arions he was dealing with. His mind raced with different battle strategies. He had a weapon but it wouldn't be much help against three Arions. He needed to buy time until Sterling arrived and evened the score a bit.

And he was betting Tad had an agenda or he would have already attacked. "What do you want, Tad?"

"You know what I want," Tad said in an irritated voice. "Or should I say what your brother wants?"

"Yeah, well," Mason said bitterly, "tell David to go to hell."

"Join us, Mason," Tad returned quickly. "He wants you by his side. You won't regret the choice."

"You apparently have defective hearing, so let me repeat myself. Go to hell, Tad, and take David with you."

Tad shook his head. "I told David you would be foolish."

The two men on either side of Tad exchanged a look and then Tad gave a curt nod. They started toward Mason.

A voice from behind said, "Not a very fair fight." Sterling stepped to Mason's side.

"In the nick of time," Mason said without taking his eyes off the Arions.

"I aim to please," Sterling said and then, true to his nickname, "Renegade", he added, "Let's get this party started."

Mason was damn glad to have Sterling by his side. The man loved to fight and was truly fearless in battle. It was as if he lived for the high of combat victory.

Without warning, Sterling planted a blade in the chest of the Arion standing to the left of Tad. Mason watched the enemy yank it from his chest, growling as he started forward.

Mason's own form of trouble, the Arion to Tad's right, stalked toward him, swinging his big paw of a hand. Mason ducked and jabbed his attacker with a right hook to the stomach. The Arion hardly flinched. Punches and kicks were exchanged, blow for blow.

He was acutely aware of Tad's absence from the fight. And he worried for Holly. He managed to catch a glimpse of Sterling going one-on-one with the other Arion but he couldn't see Tad.

Fear for Holly quickly turned into anger. That part of him he didn't fully understand began to take control. He kicked the Arion with newfound strength, successfully knocking him to the ground. "Where's Tad?" Mason yelled, hoping Sterling knew.

"I don't know," Sterling said, with a grunt as he landed a punch.

Mason did a visual sweep of the area and, in doing so, made a grave mistake. The Arion was on his feet with lightning speed and launching himself at Mason. This time, with a razor sharp claw extended.

Mason saw it just before it actually made contact. *Shit*. Only a select group of Arions even had the damn things, yet he always managed to fight the ones that did. He jumped backwards, trying to dodge the thrash of his attacker's hand but it was too late. The claw sliced through his shirt and straight through his side, with surgeon-like precision.

"Enough!" Tad yelled angrily.

The pain radiated through Mason's body like liquid fire. An Arion had cut him only once before. Judging from the level of pain, this time was a hell of a lot worse. Forcing himself to manage the pain, he looked toward Tad's voice.

He found Sterling pressed against a tree trunk with Tad's long claw at his throat. Mason's eyes met Sterling's. He saw no fear in his friend's eyes. Not that he expected he would.

"I have a message for you, Mason." Tad's voice held a gloat.

"I'm listening," Mason said quietly, buying time as he mentally tried to redirect his pain. Stickiness, wet and plentiful, clung to his shirt and dripped down his body.

He couldn't stop the blood flow, but he could shut down the worst of the pain. Had to. Sterling's life, and maybe Holly's, might just count on him performing.

"Consider this a warning," Tad said sharply. "We could kill Sterling now and we could kill the woman." He surprised Mason by stepping away from Sterling. "Consider this a gift from David. A show of his allegiance to you." He paused and then added, "He expects it returned."

"He knows my position on this," Mason said without hesitation as Sterling moved to his side. "I will not join David. Not now. Not ever."

The three Arions moved to stand side by side. "He won't remain patient," Tad said. "Especially not with the woman involved. She will join our cause or she will die."

Mason's exterior was calm and cool but inside he was already urgently planning a way to hide Holly. "If anything happens to Holly Heart, I will come calling. Tell David she has my protection."

"Don't be foolish," Tad said. "You can't beat David. This is the end of the road for you and Holly Heart. Time is up." He paused, and motioned with his chin towards Sterling. "And your friend lives only because your brother forbid me to anger you. Mark my word, he'd be dead otherwise."

Without giving Mason time to respond, the three Arions turned toward the woods. The wind lifted the dirt around them, blowing leaves as if a storm was suddenly upon them. Then, as if it had never occurred, everything stilled and the Arions were gone.

Sterling took a good, hard look at Mason's side. "You're going to need lots of sleep to heal, man."

"There isn't time," Mason said. "You heard what Tad said. I have to hide Holly." But he was getting weaker by the moment and he knew it.

"You're no good to her dead."" Sterling looked at Mason's pale face and moved to help him. Mason leaned into him without question.

"Let's get you inside," Sterling said, concern barely concealed in his voice.

"David won't give up," Mason mumbled half to himself.

They began the walk to the house, Sterling taking a big part of Mason's weight. "Be glad he hasn't. It saved our asses today."

Mason snorted.

"You need stitches to stop the bleeding," Sterling commented as they took the first step leading up to the porch. Before they could take another, the door burst open and Holly came running down the stairs.

* * * * *

Holly watched out the window, desperate to know what was going on outside.

The instant she saw Mason walking toward the house, slumped over against the strange man, her heart fell to her stomach. She ran to the door and onto the porch, desperate to find out why Mason was slumped over on the other man. Her heart beat double time in her chest. Her first glimpse of Mason confirmed her fear. Something was terribly wrong.

Pale as a ghost with blood dripping down his side, he looked like he might collapse at any moment. "Oh, my God," she exclaimed urgently. "You're hurt." She stopped directly in front of him, surveying his injury. "Bad. You're hurt bad. We need an ambulance."

"No," Sterling said before Mason could. "I can take care of him."

"He needs a doctor," Holly argued as she pushed the door to the house open and held it so they could go inside.

"I'm fine, Holly," Mason said but his voice was soft, his energy clearly low. "I just need to rest."

"This way," Holly said directing both men toward her room.

"Damn, this hallway is small," Sterling complained as he tried to maneuver Mason to the bedroom.

Once Mason was on the bed, Holly went down on her knees beside him and started tearing his shirt away from the cut. After a moment of inspection, Holly looked up at Mason's friend. "Sterling, right?"

He nodded.

"I need hot water and towels. Top cabinet in the bathroom." She paused. "Quickly."

Her attention went back to Mason, not even considering Sterling might not do as she asked. She examined the cut. It was a deep gash, long and dangerous-looking. "Mason," she whispered. His eyes fluttered open, his face even paler than when she first saw him outside. "You have to have stitches."

"You can stitch me up, right?" he half-mumbled, half-whispered.

"I don't keep those kinds of supplies around here." Why didn't he want to go to the hospital? "I'm not a practicing physician, I'm a scientist."

Sterling reappeared, setting the requested items on the floor beside her. Holly grabbed a washcloth and wet it before gently dabbing at the cut.

Mason's eyes fluttered shut again. "And you're a doctor," he said. "Stitch me up, doc."

"I told you I don't have the supplies." She applied pressure to the wound and looked up at Sterling. "We have to take him somewhere to get this bleeding stopped."

Mason grabbed her wrist, drawing her attention. "I can't, Holly. Stitch me up."

"Needle and thread will do," Sterling said from behind her.

"Needle and thread!" She could hardly believe her ears. "Are you nuts?"

Mason still held her hand. "Leave us alone a minute, Sterling."

Without hesitation, Sterling gave Mason a quick nod and walked out of the room. "Holly," Mason said. "I know you have no reason to trust me but I'm asking you to anyway."

Holly leaned forward and wiped his forehead. "I do trust you. I don't even know why. I hardly know you." She paused and then, in a softer voice, said, "But I do."

"Good," he said quietly, his eyes half-open. "I'm not the enemy, I promise."

She stared at him a moment, wondering at his choice of words, but dismissed their strangeness as a reflection of the pain he was in. Yet... She wondered so many things. "Who did this, Mason?"

"Right now I need you to fix me." He took a labored breath. "Later, I'll explain everything."

"But—"

"Please, Holly. There are…thing things about me you need to know." He paused as if it took effort to continue. "For now, fix me. The needle and thread won't hurt me. I can't go to a hospital. If you do as I ask, I won't bleed to death or get an infection. I'm not like you."

The implications of his words sent a chill down her spine. The unknown was becoming downright unnerving. "Not like me, meaning what?"

He swallowed as if his mouth was dry. "Fix me first."

Holly studied him a minute and then yelled, "Sterling!"

Mason let his eyes close. He knew she had agreed. "Thank you," he whispered.

Sterling stepped back in the door so quickly it was obvious he had been standing just outside the entrance. She looked at him and waved him forward.

"Hold this on his wound," she said indicating the now-crimson towel. "I'll be right back."

Sterling didn't move. In fact, he looked like he was about to pounce on her. "Where are you going?"

"To get needle and thread," she explained with a bite to her words. This was her house, damn it. He studied her a long moment, as if trying to decide if he should believe her. Finally, he did as she asked.

Holly rushed toward the closet, pushed to her tiptoes, and reached for the sewing kit she kept on the top shelf. She couldn't believe she was about to do this. To stitch Mason with sewing thread and needle was crazy.

But he had asked for her trust and she had given it freely.

She was glad she was cool under pressure. Panic wasn't something that matched well in the medical or scientific world. Patience, calm and skill were traits she possessed and put to exceptional use.

Holly crossed the room to the bathroom and gathered together several items for the procedure. Her supplies were limited but she didn't have much option but to simply make do. Mason was losing blood far too fast for her comfort.

Moving back to the bed, she stood looking down at Mason when a thought hit her. "This isn't going to work," she said. "I don't have anything for pain."

Mason's eyes opened. "I don't need anything."

"He'll be fine," Sterling said, his tone reassuring as if he was telling her he knew something she didn't. Holly expected he did.

She nodded but her stomach flip-flopped. The thought of causing Mason undue pain made her sick. As if he read her mind, he said, "I'll be fine, Holly."

She met his gaze and his eyes, normally vibrant and soulful, looked tired and dull. "I hope so," she whispered as she moved to his side. Holly looked at Sterling. "Keep holding the pressure until I tell you otherwise."

Breathing deeply, Holly prepared the needle, sterilizing it with alcohol. "Okay," she said to Sterling. "I need a chair. Can you grab one from the kitchen?"

He nodded as Holly replaced her hand on Mason's wound. Focusing on Mason, she said, "I need to sterilize your wound. It's going to hurt."

His nod was barely there. Holly poured alcohol over the cut and was shocked when Mason didn't even flinch. "I can block out pain, Holly," he told her, his eyes meeting hers. "It's a mental ability like the way I told Roger to go home and he listened. You won't hurt me. I'm weak from blood loss, not from pain."

She digested the words, understanding them and praying he was right. Sitting down in the chair Sterling provided did little to help. The first stitch was the hardest. Her hand shook as she inserted the needle into his skin. When he didn't so much as tremble, she felt a little more confident. With each stitch she moved a bit faster, eager to finish the job.

When she was finally through, exhaustion etched her features and a light perspiration pebbled on her forehead. She bandaged him, dabbed antibiotic on the sutures and prayed he wouldn't get an infection.

She looked behind her where Sterling stood. "Can you help me change the sheet?"

He nodded. "You did good," he assured her. "He'll be fine."

Holly looked at Mason, who hadn't opened his eyes since she finished her work. "I hope you're right." Pushing to her feet, she walked to the closet. She pulled open the chest of drawers that sat inside and removed some fresh sheets.

Holly removed the old sheets from the empty half of the bed and put the new ones over the mattress. Sterling started to shift Mason to the clean side. The instant he touched him, Mason's eyes darted open. Immediately, he sat up and swung his legs to the side of the bed. "We need to get out of here."

Holly rushed to him, squatting down in front of his knees, hands on his thighs. "Lay down, please. You can't be up right now. You need rest."

Mason's bloodshot eyes stared down at her. "It's not safe here. We need to leave."

"You can't leave now," Holly insisted.

"She's right, Mason." Sterling spoke quietly. "We'll be better off leaving in the morning after you heal. Sleep it off and then we'll go. I'll watch out for Holly."

"I can't risk it. What if Holly is —"

Sterling finished his sentence. "She won't be. I won't let anything happen."

"What does this have to do with me?" Holly asked, confused.

"It's too dangerous," Mason said, trying to stand up.

"No!" Holly spat, moving between his legs and holding his arms to keep him from getting up. "Stay down, you stubborn man!"

Mason sank back into the mattress and stared down at her. Sterling spoke to Holly. "Tell him you won't leave the house, not even for work tomorrow."

She made a disgusted sound as she looked over her shoulder at him. "What does this have to do with me? And who did this to him?"

Mason's fingers touched her cheek. "I have much to explain."

She made a frustrated sound. "Sterling can explain. You go to sleep."

"No," Mason said with more force than he had used since the injury. "What you learn comes from me."

Sterling spoke again. "Promise him you will stay inside and safe if he rests."

Holly let out a breath. "Fine," she clipped out as she fixed Mason in a stare. "But when you're better I want explanations, Mason. Lots of them."

He tried to smile but failed. "You're very demanding." He paused. "And stubborn." This time he managed a slight, but definitive, lift to his lips.

"Yes," Holly agreed, "well, how would I hold my own with you if I wasn't? Since you are feeling so superhuman, move to the clean side of the bed so I can fix the sheets."

Mason did as she asked, seeming far too agile for a man with sewing thread laced through his side.

Sterling moved toward the door. "I'll be on the couch if you need me."

Holly nodded but didn't turn, thankful when she heard the door close behind him. He had loomed above her for what felt like hours. A break from his watchful eyes was welcome. Holly straightened the sheets and began gathering together all the used supplies.

When she headed toward the bathroom, Mason half-sat up. "Where are you going?"

She rolled her eyes. "To clean up. Are you going to sleep or baby-sit me?"

"Maybe if you came over here and rested with me, I would relax," he suggested, watching her through half-shut eyes.

A pang of warmth raced through her body and wrapped around her heart. He was so determined to keep her safe from some threat she didn't even understand, that he wouldn't rest without her near.

Part of her wanted to demand answers but now wasn't the time. He needed to rest. "Let me wash up and I will."

Holly stepped into the bathroom and shut the door. Leaning palms on the counter, she stared into the mirror. Her insides were still quivering from stitching Mason up with needle and thread.

Moving to the tub, she turned the water on extra hot and stripped off her clothes. But mentally, she stayed alert. She was in danger. Mason didn't strike her as a man to overreact. If he was worried, there was a reason.

When Holly finished showering, she dressed in the oversized T-shirt she had hanging over the towel holder and then flipped off the bathroom light. Quietly she tiptoed into the bedroom, careful not to disturb Mason.

She was surprised to find him awake. "I can't believe you're not sleeping."

He lifted up the blanket, inviting her to join him. "I was waiting on you."

Holly didn't hesitate. She moved forward, some part of her desperately wanting to feel his warmth, to know he was truly going to be okay. He pulled her tight against his uninjured side, holding her as if she was his lifeline.

He kissed her forehead. "Now, I'll rest."

Holly snuggled against his chest, soaking in the feel of safety he gave her, loving the way she felt in his arms. Even injured, he made her feel as if nothing, and no one, could harm her.

Except maybe him.

Holly was falling for Mason in a big way. A man of a million mysteries.

* * * * *

Roger took long strides across the university parking lot toward the lab. The walk from his apartment had done him good. A small portion of his tension had begun to ease. After hours of trying to sleep and failing, he had simply given up.

Holly was on his mind, killing him with the knowledge she was with Mason. He didn't like the man—no, couldn't stand him. How could Holly fall for a guy like him? Couldn't she see beyond the brawn? He'd always thought Holly was above judging a book by its cover.

Unlocking the building door, he moved toward the lab, his eyes squinting into the dark hallway. By the time he made his way to the outside of the lab office, his eyes had adjusted enough to see the keyhole, but just barely.

"Damn, it's dark," he mumbled under his breath as he pushed open the door, reached his hand along the wall and searched for the light.

Before he managed to flip the switch, he felt an abrupt shove and he went tumbling to the ground.

And then the darkness came again. This time, complete and all-consuming.

Chapter Seven

Holly was having the most amazing dream about Mason. He was kissing her and, God, could the man kiss. His tongue was demanding, yet gentle, with just a hint of spice. He tasted like pure addiction come to life, like he was drugging her, making her crazy with desire.

She couldn't get enough of him.

His hands were everywhere, touching her and teasing her. His tongue, warm and greedy, slid across her bottom lip and then his teeth nipped. He kissed her with sensual, warm strokes of his tongue.

Need built inside her like a flame that had been suddenly born and begged for life.

His fingers touched her nipples and they ached with a pleasure that was painful in its intensity. She arched her back and murmured his name, loving the way he palmed her breasts in reaction.

Mason.

His hands touched her with a hunger that felt contagious. Every caress, every taste, every stroke fed her need and made her ache with a passion she had never felt before. A consuming need to feel.

She felt him grow more intense, his desire making him touch her with heavier strokes, kiss her with deeper passion. He kneaded her breasts harder, almost roughly, but it felt so damn good...like bittersweet perfection. He pinched her nipples between his fingers and a wave of sensation rushed straight to her core. The wetness of her desire clung to her thighs, her need to have him inside her near torture. She yearned for fulfillment...wanting and needing to the point of near agony.

But it was such an addictive pain. The kind that made her cry out with pure ecstasy. The kind that made her cling to him. The kind that felt it could never be satisfied, yet she had to try.

Over and over again.

She couldn't remember taking off her clothes but she was glad they were gone. She must have missed that part of the dream...but she didn't really care. She was just glad to be skin to skin with him. He was kissing her neck and then her shoulder, and his mouth licked and nipped its way lower. A trail of goose bumps danced along her skin.

Suddenly his mouth was on her nipple, suckling gently as if he had caged the animal inside. With slow precision, he increased the pressure. His teeth scraped and nipped and she moaned with pleasure. Her hands and into his long hair—she loved his hair—eager to hold him close. He was relentless with his teasing and she arched her back, yearning for more even as she thought she had had all she could take.

She wanted what he had yet to give her. Her hands went to the sides of his face, begging him to look at her. "Now, Mason," she cried, when his dark gaze lifted to hers. "I want you, inside me, now."

Her words seemed to make his eyes grow hotter. So hot that it felt he might scorch her with a mere look. She took him in, hungry with her stare, aroused by the sensual image he offered. His dark hair fell around his shoulders, sexy and dangerous-looking. It dangled against her face and shoulders, tantalizingly sensual. His lips were deliciously full, enticing her finger to run the length of the bottom one.

Reality washed over her in rush.

This was real.

Remotely, her mind registered the light barely shining through the window. It was morning. "I'm not dreaming, am I?"

He stared at her a long moment and she thought he would speak but instead he lowered his mouth to hers. His only answer was a burning hot kiss. His tongue stroked hers with fervent, hungry need. She clung to him, kissing him back with a growing urgency that seemed to consume the lines of reality versus fantasy.

She simply wanted what he offered.

Her nipples pressed against the hair on his chest and she arched her back to feel him closer. They pressed their bodies together, kissing, touching and tasting.

Long minutes later, his mouth close to her ear, breath warm against her neck, he whispered, "This is very real, Holly Heart."

"I want you, Mason," she whispered.

His mouth moved to hers and, for long moments, they lingered, lips close, breath mingled. It felt as if something passed between them, a unique bond of intimacy. It seemed to build from deep inside, making her stomach get a funny little feeling.

It was a unique experience, so intense, so complete. As if her entire existence merged with his.

Their lips came together. One brush. Then a second. A dip of his tongue, a stroke of hers. And then they were ravishing each other, mouths joined and tongues sliding together in burning need.

Desperately, they clung, bodies pressed together. It was as if they didn't exist apart. They could only exist if they were merged together as one.

She whispered her urgency, no fear of revealing what was so obviously her desire. "Mason, please."

"Shh," he said, softly his lips brushing her neck over and over.

His hand slid down her side, over her stomach, and then straight between her legs. She moaned with the reality of the moment. This is what she needed. His fingers slid into her wetness, spreading it and gently stimulating her clit.

"I want you, Mason," she whispered hoarsely, feeling, for some reason, she needed to confirm what was so true. As if he needed to hear the words.

He moved to look at her and she swallowed with the potency of what she saw in his eyes. Something about him, about what she felt with him, was unusual. Too consuming. Too perfect. But thoughts faded as his mouth closed over hers, his mouth seducing her as readily as hers did him.

She felt his cock settle between her legs and she squeezed her thighs together to feel him more fully. He slid it back and forth, stroking her sensitive flesh, teasing her with how near she was to finally having him inside her.

With his cock settled snugly inside her wetness, he rested on his elbows, unmoving. He pinned her in a stare, his voice hoarse with need. "You do know this isn't a dream, right?"

She loved that it was real. It was so much better than any dream could be. "Yes, I know."

There was urgency in his voice when he spoke again, as if he too was eager for what came next. "You're sure you want this?"

She nodded, feeling impatient. She wanted him. Now. "Yes," she said. "You know I do. You're the only one resisting."

And with that said, she slid her hand between their bodies and wrapped it around his hard cock and guided him inside her body. She sighed with a sense of relief as she felt the head penetrate her body.

He whispered her name without moving. But then he seemed to change. He made a growling noise and then sunk deep to her core. The force of his penetration rocked her body with pure pleasure, making her cry out.

He stilled then, not moving for a long moment, and she sensed he was struggling for control. Buried deep inside her body, she could hardly breathe with the urgency for more. "You're so tight, Holly."

It was a question. "I told you I haven't dated much," she said in a hoarse whisper, wanting to reassure him. "It's been years." She kissed his neck and then his ear.

He leaned up on his elbows. "But you want me?" he asked, looking into her eyes.

She clung to him, her hips moving upwards. "Oh, yes," she whispered. "Please move, Mason."

His eyes darkened and, as if she had pushed him over the edge of control, he did just as she requested. He moved, sliding out of her and then lunging deep again. And then they were kissing again, hungrily, almost desperately tasting one another. It was as if he was giving her his breath in place of her own.

She wrapped her arms under his shoulder and pulled her body as close to his as she could, needing to feel his skin next to hers, wanting it like she wanted nothing else.

He was saying her name, whispering that she was his angel, moving in and out of her body even as she pressed her hips against his. For long minutes, they moved with a frenzied urgency.

But then he changed. Slowly, precisely, he seduced her body with his own. As if he savored every stroke. Even his kisses softened, becoming more like caresses. His fingers were in her hair, on her face, touching her lips between kisses.

"I tried to resist," he murmured against her mouth but he kissed her before she could respond.

She wanted to ask him why. Why was he resisting what felt so right? Why? But his mouth and body claimed all that she was. She arched into him, legs wrapped around his. As if he understood her need, he slipped his hands beneath her and cupped her bottom. He lifted her hips and sank deeper.

She could hear his breathing. Or maybe it was hers. She wasn't sure. They had begun moving with more urgency again. The softness of the moments before became a turbulent ride of pure passion. He plunged into her, stroke by stroke, delivering pleasure with each move.

The build to ultimate pleasure took complete control. She hardly remembered one move from the next. Suddenly, she shattered... She squeezed her eyes shut, unable to do anything but feel. Never, ever had she experienced such total elation. Wave after wave rocked her body.

He called her name, his face buried in her neck, and she felt his body shake. He was coming with her. She didn't think that really happened. Two people actually coming together.

She smiled, feeling him calm even as she did the same.

But the more she relaxed, the more her head began to spin. A strange wave of dizziness followed. The room actually seemed to spin around her. "Mason," she whispered, her voice trembling from the experience, trying not to panic.

"Holly, I..." His hand cupped her cheek, his lips brushing her skin tenderly. "Holly—"

"Mason—" She couldn't finish. Faster the room spun. It felt as if she was having a weird, out-of-body experience. Time seemed to somehow stand still. She wasn't sure how long it lasted. It could have been seconds. Maybe it was minutes.

All she knew was Mason held her, saying her name, telling her it was okay. She didn't like feeling out of control. She wanted the comfort Mason offered. Slowly, as things began to return to normal, she heard his words, confusion forming even further.

"I didn't know," he murmured.

But she still couldn't begin to make sense of his meaning. "I don't feel right, Mason." Her hands were on his head. She needed his full attention. She needed help. She couldn't breathe. "Something is wrong with me."

He responded quickly, leaning so he could frame her face with his hands. He looked down at her. "Look at me, and breath. Focus on my eyes."

"But—"

"Focus, Holly."

She blinked, trying to focus, but God, what was happening to her?

"Focus." This time his voice held a hint of command.

She blinked again and swallowed, slowly bringing him into focus. "You're going to be fine." His voice soothed and reassured. "Keep looking into my eyes and breathe."

She did as he said. Those hypnotic black eyes somehow bringing her back to a calmer place.

"Keep looking at me. Breathe with me. In," she did as he said, "and out." She started feeling better. Not right, but getting there.

"Good," he murmured and brushed his lips across hers. "Better?"

She nodded and her hand went to his cheek. There was desperation she couldn't control in her voice. "Please tell me what just happened."

She *needed* to understand.

* * * * *

Mason looked down at Holly's trembling lips, feeling a mix of emotions so turbulent they were hard to decipher, let alone control.

He now knew with certainty he had Arion blood running through his veins. It was confirmed by his behavior with Holly. He'd taken her with no thought of birth control. Of the impact on her life. Driven by the need to mate. And it had consumed her as well. She'd been blindly pulled into the call of their connection. Body and soul, he and Holly had just been joined in a way that only an Arion and his true mate could be.

The realization was one that would change his future forever. And now Holly's.

It was hard to think about the implications. Holding the woman he now knew was his destiny, he wanted to savor the moment. She was his other half. The woman who made him complete.

There was no way he could fight what was so alive, so real. And there was no way to undo what was done.

"Mason?"

He ran his thumb down her jaw. "Feel better?" She was so pure, so beautiful.

His angel.

His guiding light to good over evil.

Could fate have delivered her to him as a saving grace? But how would she respond once she knew he had linked himself to her for all of eternity? That he had taken her right to choose?

"I don't know what came over me. All a sudden I was so dizzy." She made a confused sound. "Actually, I still feel…odd."

"I know," he murmured. "I know." He had felt what she had but his mental abilities had allowed him to control his response. It was said that, as an Arion mated, the two souls were joined. "Let me make you feel better."

He brushed his mouth across hers, parting her lips and gently sliding his tongue into her mouth. Their tongues touched and sensation rocked his body and he felt her trembling response and knew she felt it as well.

There was no doubt they were linked. The mating was known to make the two lovers sensitized to each other in such a way that the pleasures of the flesh were enhanced tenfold.

Still buried deep inside her, still hard, he wanted her again — no, needed her again — and had to have her. There was no fighting what was happening.

Gently their tongues met, as lightly as soft caresses, both of them slowly growing accustomed to the intensity of their impact on each other's senses. With each stroke of his tongue, he savored her flavor, her very essence, her absolute perfection.

In the back of his mind he knew what he was doing was wrong. He'd been dreaming of her and then she was there, in his arms, as if it was destiny.

He wanted to make love to her. To go slow, and savor every moment.

Purposely, he slipped out of her, swallowing her objection with his mouth as he kissed her. "Easy, angel. There's no rush."

She tasted like sugar and spice and smelled like jasmine. It was as if the flower was a part of her chemical make-up, the sweet floral scent clinging to her as if it were a part of her essence.

His hands moved to her breasts, cupping them, loving how they fit in his hands so perfectly. As if they were made for him. Gently, he kneaded and squeezed and ran his thumbs over her nipples. He followed with his mouth, tasting each nipple with slow perfection.

Hungrily his eyes surveyed the rosy peaks now glistening and hard from his mouth. She had beautiful breasts, firm and round. She whimpered, burying her hands in his hair and murmuring his name. "Please, Mason. I want you inside me again."

"I need to taste you, Holly," he said and, before she could argue, he was trailing his tongue and lips down her stomach, lingering and teasing.

When he knew she was on edge, he gave her what she wanted...what he wanted. His mouth found her already swollen nub and suckled lightly. She moaned with the impact, her hands still in his hair, but tightening.

His hands slipped under her perfect, round butt pushing her hips forward so he could get to her better. He wanted her to come like she had never come before. This was his woman and he wanted her to know just how well he would take care of her.

His tongue swirled. His teeth nipped. His tongue flickered.

Her body trembled. And then she exploded. She called out his name and hearing it as she shook with pure ecstasy was amazing. His tongue dipped deep inside her, pushing her higher, wanting all she could give.

He replaced his tongue with a finger, still lapping at her clit, as his finger stroked and caressed. Her body was on edge, he could feel the urgency of her movements against his mouth and finger. He suckled harder, stroked deeper, moving her to the next level.

Her soft little cries of need, of passion, drove him for more. He lapped at her, hungry for the taste of her desire, loving how she pressed against him.

She called his name as she stiffened and he felt her body clutch his finger. His cock grew with the knowledge of her release. It made him so hot, knowing he had pleased her. With soft caresses of his tongue that defied the growing urgency of his body, he led her to a long release and then slowly brought her down.

Sliding upward, he kissed his way back to her mouth. His tongue dipped into her mouth even as his body sunk deep into her wet, sensitive core. "You feel so damn good," he murmured, perhaps in his head or maybe out loud. He wasn't sure. He was too lost in the tidal wave of heat that pushed him to lunge deeper and deeper.

Her body hugged him, her back arched. He couldn't get enough of her. He moved faster, and got hotter and harder, with every passing minute until... It was a fast, hard ride and he couldn't maintain control... It was as if everything inside him cried out for a completeness only she could give.

And suddenly, he was coming, his release rocking his body with such intensity, he cried out. She clung to him, saying his name over and over. Hearing her call him with such heat in her voice was like an added boost of pleasure. And she clung to him, her body tightening around him as if it wanted all that he was.

He spilled himself inside her and he felt a sense of satisfaction, of utter release, he had never felt before. This was his woman.

Holly.

He collapsed gently on top of her, holding her tight. Moments later, he moved and pulled her under his arm, her head nuzzled on his shoulder.

She sighed with satisfaction as his hand caressed her hair. He could feel her heart beating against his chest, their bodies pressed so closely together, legs entwined. He stared into space, loving how she felt in his arms and dreading what had to come next.

It was time for them to talk. There wasn't an option. The moment of truth had arrived. "Holly," he said, nuzzling her temple and then kissing her forehead. Moving, he turned her onto her back again, resting on his elbows above her. She blinked several times, her lovely dark lashes fluttering against her pale cheeks.

When she opened her eyes, looking down into her sexy, sleepy gaze, he felt a surge of trepidation. This woman, so gentle and caring, his mate, was the last person he wanted to hurt.

Her hand went to his cheek in a gentle caress. His hand went to it, covering it and then bringing her knuckles to his lips. "We need to talk."

Apprehension slipped into her eyes but she kept her tone playful. "I do that better when I'm not naked.

He wished he could savor their closeness for at least a little longer. "Let's try," he said forcefully. "Better yet, I'll talk, you listen."

Her eyes narrowed and he saw a glint of fear in them. And he had no doubt that their newly formed bond allowed her to sense his dread. "Let me up," she said in a tight little voice that held authority.

"I can't do that," he responded with regret, but no hesitation. He held her tight. What had to be done, had to be done. "First, I need you to know what's between us is very real, Holly. You know that, don't you?"

Her expression was suspicious. "Just say what you have to say, Mason."

He sighed. "The day we met, you blew me away. I'd never felt such a sudden interest in anyone."

"The point, Mason," she said with building tension in her tone.

"When you told me your name, I almost fell over," he said very quietly. "You see, you were," he paused, "are," he amended, "my assignment."

Her breathing was heavy, making her chest rise and fall pressing against his. "Assignment?"

Chapter Eight

A tight knot gathered in Holly's stomach. His assignment? Had Mason really just said she was his assignment?

"Did your *assignment* include sleeping with me?" Her words were enunciated severely.

Pushing at the solid wall of his chest, she squirmed, feeling desperate to get some space between her and the man she had wrongfully thought she could trust.

What a fool she was.

He didn't budge. "You know better." His voice was as tight as a rubber band. "I didn't count on this. Hell," he paused, "if you remember, I tried to avoid it."

She laughed. Bitterness etched the sound. "Yeah, but I just wouldn't let it go, would I?" Sarcasm laced her words. "If I remember correctly, I woke up with you on top of me!" She pushed at his arms this time. "Now get off!"

He gritted his teeth, not moving an inch. "Not until you hear me out. Fight, beat at me, whatever, but I'm not moving until you listen."

Considering his threat, she believed him. Not being one to enjoy being made a fool of, she stilled. "Fine," she bit out. "Talk."

"I work for the government."

"Oh God," she said as reality sunk in, "you work with Walsh." She swallowed. "I have to give it to you. You two are supreme actors. I never would have guessed you knew each other."

"We don't," he said. "I know of him but he doesn't know me. Not many do. I operate in covert missions."

She felt his uneasiness like a snug glove. The sensation was overwhelming, almost suffocating. "What does that mean, exactly?"

"I am brought in when there is imminent danger." His gaze was sharp. Probing. "The government experimented with genetics therapy. They created those super soldiers you so dislike. It worked. They made men who have exceptional abilities with limited side effects. Then, they got greedy. They took things too far and it backfired."

Oh God. *What had they done?* "Go on," she urged, no longer even considering fighting him. This was something she needed to know about.

"You're familiar with area 51?"

She bit back irritation. "I live in Nevada."

"The rumors are true. There were aliens found. And they—our government, that is—used them to enhance a group of soldiers."

Her blood went cold. "Tell me you're joking."

His expression was grim. "I wish I could."

Possibilities, none of them good, were racing through her head. "Let me up."

He studied her a moment. "Holly—"

She was feeling suffocated. "I can't think trapped like this, Mason! I need to think!"

He still didn't budge, his scrutiny of her features intensifying. Then, abruptly, he freed her. Stunned, she didn't move at first, digesting the odd sense of loss she felt now that he wasn't touching her. It confused her and even left her somewhat resentful.

Sitting up, she shoved away the feeling. He had used her, plain and simple. No way was she allowing herself to feel anything for him. Looking around for her shirt, desperately needing the barrier of clothing between them, she avoided eye contact. His gaze was heavy and unnerving as she scooped her shirt up from the floor and pulled it over her head.

Crossing her arms in front of her body, she forced herself to look at him. He was gloriously nude. It was the first time she had seen him this way in daylight. He was so perfect it took her breath away. She still wanted him. The realization slapped her in the face even as he wet her between the legs. She swallowed, angry at her body's reaction to him.

Abruptly, she averted her gaze but not before she saw the look in his eyes. The satisfaction that he was able to get to her. Her jaw clenched. "What do I have to do with all of this?"

"A lot," he said. "The Arions—that's what the super soldiers, at least some of them—call themselves. They took over the research facility and now intend to take over much more."

Holly's head lifted abruptly, her eyes locking with his. "Arions," she repeated. "As in Hitler's perfect race."

"Exactly. They're evil and determined to dominate."

"Sounds like a fight, not science. I don't understand my value."

His lips thinned. "Everyone who was involved with this project was either captured or killed. To make matters worse, all the research data was taken. We need to figure out how to stop the Arions."

"And this involves me how?" she asked but, in her mind, she already knew. They needed her because she could find answers.

"We need you to pinpoint weaknesses."

Holly pushed to her feet and walked to the window but she didn't bother to move the curtain or try to look outside. She was thinking about her father and how appalled he would be to see his dream turn to this.

"There's one more thing." Something in his tone made her turn to face him. "Our government wants your help but...*they* want you, too."

Her eyes went wide. "They?"

He nodded slowly. "The Arions."

Her hand went to her throat. *They want you too.* The words repeated in her mind. Taunting her. "Oh, God."

"I won't let anything happen to you."

"This can't be happening." Her voice was a raspy whisper. Pressing her fingertips to the space between her brows she shut her eyes. "No."

"I'm sorry," he offered softly.

Holly opened her eyes, desperately searching his expression, looking for something in his face. What, she wasn't exactly sure. His words repeated in her mind. He was called in when there was *imminent danger.*

Her eyes dropped to his bandage for an instant before lifting again. "It was me they were after last night, wasn't it?"

He hesitated a minute as if deciding how to respond. "Yes. And me."

"Who are you?" she asked, afraid to hear the answer, but needing to know.

"I work for the government in a unit considered more myth than reality. In the eyes of the normal American, I don't exist."

"Some kind of Special Forces or CIA?"

"Something like that."

She didn't like the vagueness of his response. But she also had to face facts. As angry as she was with him for betraying her and for being so secretive, she couldn't dismiss the fact that he had possibly saved her life.

Her eyes narrowed on his. "You should have been honest with me."

"I didn't lie," he argued but his tone was gentle. "I meant to tell you everything sooner, Holly. I wanted to." He opened his mouth and shut it again as if rethinking his words. "Things just got out of control between us."

The bandage on his side drew her attention again. Her brows dipped. How was he moving around so easily? The doctor in her stepped forward. "I need to check your stitches. All the activity..." She stopped mid-sentence, feeling awkward for bringing up what they had done together.

"Didn't harm me," he assured her. "I'm fine."

She moved toward him. Whatever had happened between them, good or bad, she was not watching him die from an infected wound she stitched. Even now, she cringed as she thought of the horrid method she had used.

"I need to check it." Stopping in front of him, trying not to think about his nudity, she reached for him.

He grabbed her wrist, gently halting her action. "No," he said tensely. "It's fine."

She frowned. "I used needle and thread, for God's sake! I *have* to check it for infection."

"No," he repeated and this time he had a sharp edge to his tone.

She dropped her hand as if she'd been slapped. After several frustrated moments, she said, "I'm going to take a shower."

Turning on her heels, she marched angrily toward the bathroom. She shut the door with a loud bang. Emotion fisted in her chest as she leaned on the sink for stability in the only form she could find.

Her life was out of control.

* * * * *

Mason sat on the edge of the bed, cursing his stupidity. Snapping at Holly had only made matters worse. He just didn't know how to tell her what she needed to know. No. What she had a right to know.

Abruptly, he pushed to his feet, grabbed his jeans and put them on, not bothering to snap them. His decision was made. She had to know the truth. Briskly, he walked toward the bathroom, pushing open the door without knocking. If he didn't act now he'd change his mind.

Holly whirled on him, tears streaking her cheeks. "What do you think you're doing?"

He grabbed her and pulled her to him. "This," he said as he covered her mouth with his, delving his tongue into her mouth with a desperation he couldn't contain.

Her response came slow but her arms wrapped around his shoulders and, inch by inch, she melted into him, her tongue moving against his.

After long moments, reluctantly he ended the kiss, staring down at her. Slowly, he let her go, moving to sit down on the toilet seat. He could feel her confusion, like a mist in the air. But soon it would end. "Check the wound."

She moved to his side, her eyes holding his for several beats before they dropped to the bandage. When her fingers made contact, he shut his eyes. He felt the bandage lift.

Waiting for her response felt like eternal torture. She said nothing. The soft touch of her fingers along the stitches made him open his eyes. She had sunk to her knees and was studying his skin with complete absorption. Leaning to the side, she pulled open a drawer and withdrew a pair of scissors.

Wordlessly, she removed the thread.

With a heavy sigh, she leaned back on her heels and looked up at him. "It's amazing. It would take a normal person two weeks to get to this stage of healing."

Staring down at her with half-closed eyes, he wondered about her reaction, while he cringed at the inference that he wasn't normal. "I expected —"

"Me to freak out?" she asked with a challenge in her tone. "Obviously, since you didn't want me to look at it. I'm a scientist. One who has studied these exact kinds of genetic enhancements."

His lips thinned into a grim line. "A group of special ops men, me included, were told we were being immunized against man-made viruses. By the time we figured out what was going on, it was too late."

Holly blinked. "They tricked you?"

"Yes," he agreed, "they tricked us." Mason wanted her to fully understand. He'd gone this far. "I won't lie to you. Once I got used to the new me, for a while at least, I was okay with it. I'm a soldier, Holly. Advantages in battle are welcomed." He pinned her in a stare. "I'm one of those killing machines you hate so much."

"Not by choice," she said without looking away, her voice very soft. "And I don't hate you."

He wasn't going to let her hide from the truth. Though, he wasn't prepared to tell her everything right now. It was simply too much. "I was always a soldier. A man who was trained to serve and protect." He hesitated. "And kill, if necessary."

Averting her gaze, she seemed to contemplate his words. "This is a lot to absorb at once."

Whatever he had hoped for from her response, it wasn't this. No understanding words came from her mouth. He took solace in the fact she hadn't completely rejected him.

Inwardly, he found his resolve. However she felt about him, he had a job to do. That job included keeping her safe. "While you're absorbing, pack a bag."

Her eyes lifted, wide with astonishment. "What? I can't just up and leave. I have a job, and responsibilities."

He stood up. "Look beyond the here and now to the big picture, Holly. It's what matters now."

She pushed to her feet. "I can't go. I won't!"

"I'm not asking," he said in a low voice, his eyes meeting hers and holding.

Anger, and a hint of fear, flared in her eyes. "You can't come in here and take over my life."

He didn't so much as a blink. "I can and I am. Pack."

"I can't leave," she said, balling her fists by her side.

"Holly." As much as he hated to be coldhearted, she was leaving him no options. "You don't seem to get it. You won't last twenty-four hours if you stay here."

Her hand went to her neck. "Meaning?"

"They want you dead or alive. What they want, they are ruthless about obtaining."

She stared at him, saying nothing. Mason reached out to touch her hair and she jerked back. "You're destroying my life," she whispered harshly.

His hand dropped to his side. "You're confused, Angel." He couldn't keep the bite from his tone. Her accusation tore at his heart. "I'm the one saving it."

He walked to the door and then paused. He wanted to say something to her. To make things right. He just didn't know what. She thought he was a monster...just as he knew she would.

Running his hand through his hair in an act of utter frustration, he left the room without another word.

* * * * *

Mason leaned against the kitchen counter as Sterling moved around Holly's kitchen. He was pretty much making himself at home in her kitchen. "You are cooking enough to feed twenty people, not three."

Sterling ignored his comment. "How are you feeling?" He pulled a pan of biscuits from the oven.

Running his hands over his jaw. "Like I need to shave."

After a visit to the guest bathroom, he had showered and, thanks to the suitcase he had in his truck, dressed in clean jeans and a black T-shirt.

He couldn't stop thinking about his discovery. To have Arion blood in his system held implications he didn't want to face. Like a darker side that could turn evil.

He lived with that fear because, truth be told, he'd known for some time he was different from the other men. Deep down he'd known why. Denial had simply been his point of sanity.

And he damn sure hadn't told anyone. But he knew and that was enough. A Black Knight could place a normal human in a hypnotic trance, willing them to do their bidding. Mason's skill went one step further.

Sterling snapped his fingers. "Back to the real world. Any progress with the lady?"

He refocused on the present with effort. "I don't know if I would call it progress."

"Give her time." He took two plates from a cabinet and then moved to the table. "Come eat. You need food to heal."

Mason didn't argue. He sat down and began filling his plate with a variety of foods sitting in bowls and pans in the center of the table. Sterling sat down, filled two glasses with chocolate milk and chucked the empty container across the room toward the trash can. It landed in the middle of the floor.

Grunting, Mason swiveled around to pick it up. "It's bad enough we've taken over her life, man. Don't make it worse by trashing the place."

"It's not like she'll be back here."

"No," Mason said. "But she doesn't know that."

Sterling's brows inched up instantly. "Why?"

Mason let out a breath and picked up his fork. "One step at a time." He didn't offer anything more despite the expectant look on Sterling's face. He focused on his food, and started eating.

Sterling looked like he was holding back a smile. "She's really gotten under your skin, hasn't she?"

Mason settled back in his seat, milk carton deposited on top of the too-full trashcan. "I'm just feeling uptight in general."

Sterling took a drink and then set his glass down. "I assume we're leaving for the mountain today?"

"Yeah," Mason said, shoving his plate to the side. "I won't feel good about Holly's safety until we get her underground where the Arions can't track her."

"Agreed," Sterling said. "The sooner she goes underground, the better."

* * * * *

Dressed in worn jeans and a USA T-shirt, Holly stepped into the hallway. She sniffed. Smells mingled together. Eggs, biscuits and coffee. All coming from her kitchen.

"Just make yourself at home," she muttered with irritation as she marched down the hall.

Rounding the corner to the kitchen, she stopped in the entrance and stared into the room. Eating heartily, sitting at her table, Holly found Mason and Sterling. Both men looked up the instant she appeared.

Realization crept into her mind. They both had black eyes. Not normal. Not a genetic trait she would have thought the scientists would alter. It made no sense.

"Morning," Sterling said giving her a perfect white smile.

"Making yourselves at home, I see."

"I cooked so you didn't have to," Sterling said, apparently unscathed by her cranky remark.

She snorted rudely. "Like I would have."

Holly could feel Mason's gaze as she moved. It made her nervous. What was it about the man that rattled her normally cool composure?

She almost laughed at how ridiculous the thought was as she yanked the refrigerator door open. Of course, he made her nervous. He was a trained killer. One that had slipped beyond her defenses. There was no telling what kind of violence he was capable of performing. Yet, he had been tender and loving when he had made love to her. The contradiction was hard to process.

After a moment of surveying the contents of the refrigerator, she shoved the door shut and stared at Mason and Sterling, then at their empty glasses. "Who drank my chocolate milk?"

Mason and Sterling exchanged a look. "Ah," Sterling said, obviously guilty. "Chocolate milk?"

Holly's eyes went to the trashcan. She made a disgusted sound. "My life is turned upside down. I'm being chased by aliens, two men I hardly know are eating my food and now I can't even have," she paused and pressed a finger in her chest, "the chocolate milk I bought!"

"Holly—"

She didn't feel like listening. "Don't," she said, holding out a hand stop sign fashion. "I don't want to hear anything you have to say. Nothing!" Their eyes locked for several strained moments before she whispered, "Just let me be."

Her voice cracked despite her efforts to keep it steady. All three of them knew her outburst had nothing to do with chocolate milk. The reality of her situation was a heavy load. Silence enveloped the room like a heavy blanket.

Holly hated the way they stared at her. She turned and gave them her back. She pressed her palms against the counter and let her lashes float to her cheeks. Slowly, she counted to ten, taking slow breaths, in and out.

Feeling a bit more in control, she found a plate and carried it to the table. She was a fighter. She could do this. Her method of dealing with battle was simply different from these men's.

She sat down between Mason and Sterling, feeling their surprised looks without making eye contact. But they kept looking and that started to get her all fired up again. She put down the fork she had picked up and looked from one to the other.

"What?" she demanded.

Mumbling, both Mason and Sterling diverted their gazes and began eating. But now that she was talking, she wanted answers. Holly fixed Mason in a demanding stare. "Where are you taking me?"

"Someplace safe," he said noncommittally as he took a bite of his food.

"I have a right to know where," she spat back instantly.

He wiped his mouth with a napkin. "When we get there, you'll know."

Holly leaned forward and poked her finger at the table. "I want to know, Mason."

Sterling pushed to his feet and walked toward the sink. Neither Mason nor Holly looked at him. Mason leaned back in his chair. "I need you to trust me on this, Holly."

She glared at him and pushed to her feet, shoving the chair so that it made a loud scrape across the floor. "You're tearing my life apart and I'm supposed to just blindly follow? Who in the hell do you think you are?"

Their eyes locked in a fiery confrontation, before Holly made a frustrated sound and then turned and walked toward the sink. Sterling had disappeared. Smart man. She planted her palms on the counter, as she had before, and let her head drop between her shoulders. It simply didn't seem too much to ask, to know where he was taking her.

She felt, rather than heard, Mason's approach. Something about his nearness did funny things to her insides. Being confused and angry didn't seem to change this fact. His hands settled on her shoulders.

Unexpectedly, as angry as she was, his touched calmed her. How was this possible when he was the center of her frustration? It defied logic. Holly found herself leaning back into him, as if her body had a mind of its own. In response, he stepped forward, his hard body cradling hers, his palms flattening on her stomach.

"Since we are dealing with difficult subjects, there is something else we should discuss."

She was afraid to ask, so she didn't. After a pause, he said, "We didn't use protection."

She wasn't sure if she wanted to laugh or cry. He thought it was a problem. It wasn't. She couldn't have kids. It was a pain she had long ago pushed beneath her surface. "I'm protected," she said flatly.

She expected him to ask questions. But he didn't. No question of how or why she was protected. He simply accepted her answer. He nuzzled her temple, the soft male scent of him reaching her nostrils and making them flare. "You *are* protected Holly. I will never let anything happen to you. Trust me."

Holly turned then, moving to face him, her hands resting on his chest as she looked up at him. "You ask for something you don't return. If you trusted me, then you'd tell me where we're going."

He brushed a wayward strand of hair out of her eyes. "It's not like that, Holly."

"Than how is it?" she demanded, trying to think. When he touched her she forgot what was important.

He seemed to consider and then he let out a sigh. "We're headed to the mountains, to a top secret facility. You'll be safe there."

"How long will I have to stay?"

"A while."

"How long is a while?"

"Until you're safe."

Confusing feelings were surfacing. Would he leave her there? She was mad at him but she couldn't stand the thought… "And you? Where will you be?"

He studied her intently. "That has yet to be determined."

"You can't leave me there, Mason." She paused as her eyes searched his carefully guarded expression. In a softer voice, she said, "Please."

"There's a lab there. You can study the Arions and hopefully help us stop them."

"You meaning who?"

"Me. The government. Sterling."

"Exactly who are you and Sterling?"

He hesitated only a moment. "Black Knights."

Her eyes widened. "As in, the legend of the Black Knights?"

"As in, the real thing," he assured her. "We aren't just some tall tale."

Holly didn't know what to say. The Black Knights had been talked about for years. When some covert American mission showed up on the news, the Black Knights were always given credit.

It all started to make sense. No wonder Walsh didn't know who he was. "I'll need my research," Holly said finally.

"From the lab?"

"No, it's in a lock box at my bank. And I need money. I can do both at once — get my research and withdraw cash. The key to the box is at the lab though, so we'll have to go by there."

"You don't need money," he assured her. "I have plenty and so does the government. The research is another story. We'll have to make an attempt to take it with us."

"I do need money," she insisted, wanting to hang on to any form of independence possible. "My money."

His expression said he wanted to argue but decided against it. "If we go by the lab, won't people ask why you're not at work?"

"It's still early. No one will be in yet."

Mason rested his forehead on hers. "I know you're confused and angry right now. But it'll work out, Holly. I'll make sure it does."

His voice held so much emotion and conviction, Holly's breath caught in her throat. Mason Alexander was so many things she didn't understand but, on some level, he felt as if he was a part of her very soul.

She did trust him. She just wasn't willing to admit it. Silently, she prayed she wouldn't regret it.

She felt the need to be near him so acutely it hurt. "Just don't leave me at some strange lab alone. I can deal with the rest, but not that." Crazy, she knew, but it was true. "It's very confusing but, somehow, I won't feel okay about this if you're not with me."

His hands moved to her face, tilting her chin up so he could look into her eyes. "I know it's confusing, this thing between us. I feel it too. We are together on this, okay? We'll figure it out."

She nodded, because she really didn't think she could figure it out on her own. She needed Mason. It was the craziest thing she had ever felt. Needed, as in, couldn't stand the idea of being away from him.

What was happening to her? Where was the independent, private person she had always been?

Chapter Nine

Having Mason and Sterling, two men she didn't understand or trust, follow on her heels was unnerving. But not as much trying to sneak into the lab without being seen.

Talk about being on edge.

The minute Holly walked through the entrance, she froze. The lab door was open. Both men stopped as if they had anticipated her move. Holly looked at Mason. "That door should be closed and locked."

He gave her a quick nod. "I'll check it out."

Grabbing his arm, she stopped his movement. "Do you have a gun or something?"

"A gun won't stop an Arion." There was a supreme confidence about his manner, as if he knew he could do what a gun could not. "Stay close to Sterling."

She didn't want to stay close to Sterling. She wanted to follow Mason. He took a step and stopped again. He looked over his shoulder giving her a steady stare, as if he sensed she was about to follow. And she was.

"They want *you*, Holly. You're in danger." Before she could respond he gave her his back, taking several steps before entering the lab.

Holly frowned. How had he known she had been going to follow him?

"Stop worrying," Sterling said, eyeing her. "There aren't any Arions in the lab."

Holly eyed him suspiciously. "How do you know?"

"I just do."

Holly's gaze flickered to the doorway. "Does he know?" she asked, returning her gaze back to Sterling.

"He knows," Sterling said with certainty. "He always knows."

There was something behind his words beyond the surface meaning. Holly didn't know what and she doubted she would get an explanation even if she tried. "Then why am I standing here with you?"

"You never know when an Arion might appear."

"But you said there aren't any Arions in there."

"Things could change."

"Right," Holly said, opening her mouth and shutting it again.

Mason appeared in the doorway.

"Well?" she said, rushing toward him.

His expression was grim. "I hope you keep that key someplace safe."

His comment told her she wasn't going to like what she found in the lab. She pushed passed Mason, taking in the view with an appalled gasp. Her office was torn to pieces, things flung everywhere.

The sound of Dixie yelling and screaming drew Holly's attention. "Poor baby," she said, moving toward the cage and pulling the door open. Dixie jumped into her arms, clinging to her like a scared child. Holly stroked her and whispered comforting words.

Mason was suddenly by Holly's side, his hand going to Dixie, offering additional comfort. He was such a contradiction, Holly realized. One minute he charged into a room, ready to fight. The next he was tender and caring.

"They want my research," Holly said, but it wasn't a question.

"Yes," he agreed, "and you. They want you, Holly."

"They can go to hell," she said through clenched teeth.

Mason's eyes were dark and turbulent. "Hell is what this world will be with them in control, Holly. We need your help to stop them."

She searched his eyes, thinking about the power he held and the changes he represented. Changes to her life. Changes to the world. Things that were happening whether she accepted them or not. What choice did she have but to be a part of the solution?

She sighed. "Will you hold Dixie while I grab her a banana?"

Mason held his arms out without hesitation. "Where's the key?"

Holly turned toward the cage and ran her hand along the bottom. She raised her hand, a small silver key between her fingers. "My secret hiding spot."

Mason's lips turned up in a smile. "Excellent. You're a smart lady, Holly Heart."

Dixie clapped as if in agreement. Mason and Holly both laughed as Holly tucked the key in her pocket. "I still can't believe how much she likes you."

"Am I that bad?"

Holly's lashes dropped to her cheeks. "I didn't mean it that way."

"Who's this?" Sterling said walking up beside them and eyeing the chimp.

Dixie buried her head in Mason's shoulder. "Dixie," he told Sterling, "and she doesn't like strangers."

"I'll get the banana," Holly said and turned toward the kitchen. A flash of light caught her eye, drawing it toward the floor. "Oh, God."

"What?" Mason and Sterling chimed at the same time.

Holly pointed toward the floor, near the door. "Those are Roger's glasses. He never goes anywhere without them."

"Don't jump to conclusions," Mason told her. "Try and call him."

Holly nodded and moved to the phone. Mentally, she reached for control, trying to calm the rapid pounding of her heart. Remotely, Holly saw Mason struggle to get Dixie detached from his side and into her cage.

Holly looked at Sterling, and pointed towards the kitchen. "Can you grab a banana from the kitchen?"

Holly waited as the phone rang over and over. Finally, she hung up and dialed Roger's cell. A ringing sounded under a pile of papers near the door. Fear coiled in Holly's gut.

"His phone is here, too. Oh God, Mason, do you think he's...he's..." She couldn't bring herself to say the words.

"There's no way to know but I would say the fact that he isn't here is a good sign."

"What did I miss?" Sterling asked, handing Dixie the banana through the cage bars.

Mason held up the cell phone. Sterling asked, "Roger's, I take it?"

Mason gave a quick nod and then picked up the glasses. He stood there a moment in concentration.

"Well?" Sterling asked.

"He's not dead," Mason said, opening his eyes. He looked at Holly. "They think he knows enough about your research to be helpful."

"How can you know that?" Holly asked, confused.

"He knows," Sterling said flatly.

"But—"

"If we don't get to him soon," Mason interrupted, "they'll either turn him or dispose of him."

Sterling leaned one shoulder against the wall. "You take Holly underground and I'll track Roger."

"I can't leave without finding Roger," Holly interjected.

"It's not safe for you here," Sterling said.

"I don't care. Roger is my friend." Her voice was packed with determination.

"I'll find him," Sterling assured her.

"Your help could save too many lives to count," Mason said. "It's critical you get underground."

"What is this whole 'underground' term you keep using?"

"The Arions have the ability to track people once they have their scent," Sterling explained. "If you are far enough below ground they can't find you."

Holly sat down on the edge of the desk, crossing her arms in front of her body. "This is like a bad dream."

Sterling responded quickly. "This is nothing in comparison to how bad it can get if we don't stop the Arions."

"Can Sterling stay at your place?" Mason asked.

She sighed with resignation. "Sure. He hasn't eaten me out of house and home yet. Better stay until he does."

Sterling gave her another one of his perfect white smiles. "Thanks, Doc," he said. "I'll do my best to find Roger."

Holly turned to her desk and grabbed a picture of her and Roger together at a charity function. "Here," she said pointing at Roger. "This is what he looks like."

Sterling didn't move toward the photo. "I know what he looks like, where he lives and basically everything there is to know about him."

Holly spoke to Sterling but looked at Mason. "Right," Holly said flatly, "Your assignment."

Mason's eyes held hers for several seconds. "We need to go." He moved toward the door without another word, clearly expecting her to follow.

Holly watched his retreating form, seriously considering not following. But she couldn't and she knew it.

* * * * *

Mason followed Holly into the bank, his senses alive with her nearness. He could smell her subtle, floral scent so intensely it was almost a flavor in his mouth.

Even before the formal mating, he had felt a connection to her like none other in his life. She did things to him. Made him feel for the first time in years.

Part of him reveled in the fire she evoked inside. The way she made him burn with passion and, yes, emotion. But Holly also distracted him. He was dangerous for her, and she for him. Oh, he'd keep her safe. But later…he would only cause her pain. Being his woman would bring her attentions she couldn't afford.

Danger he couldn't allow.

Pulling the bank door open, he watched the soft sway of her hips. The answering stir of his body made his jaw clench. Damn if his cock wasn't hard just from looking at her. He sighed heavily, trying to dispel the sexual tension.

Seconds later, he stepped into the cool air-conditioning, wishing it was a cold shower instead.

Minutes later, he accompanied Holly into a vault. The banker, a tall lanky man with glasses, handed her a long, steel box. He left them to explore the contents inside a small, private room.

Holly sat the box on top of a table and ran her hand over the metal. Her eyes were filled with memories. "My father believed it was best to keep our research locked up. I always thought he was paranoid."

"He wasn't," Mason said, thankful her father had understood the importance of their work. The nature of evil was to invade what was meant as good, and turn it bad.

"No," she said. "I suppose he wasn't." She didn't move. She just stood there, her hand on the box. "He was against war and useless bloodshed but I believe in my heart he would want me to help you."

He was proud to be a soldier. To fight for his country. He simply wished he were a normal one, not a scientific creation.

He felt the rise of defensiveness. "This is about preventing bloodshed, Holly, not creating it."

Her hand went to his arm. "I didn't mean to offend you. I know you're trying to protect our people."

They stood there, eyes locked, air thick with unspoken words, for long, silent moments. Mason reveled in the understanding he saw in her eyes. But it was short-lived. Once she fully knew what he was, she would hate him.

His tone was abrupt. "We have to hurry." It was best she remembered he was a soldier, a fighter and everything she didn't want in her life.

It was best he did, too. He didn't want to start thinking there was actually a future for them. Besides, it was critical he focus on her safety. Not his desire to get her naked and keep her that way.

He saw a flash of emotion in her eyes. She didn't like his tone. "Fine," she said, so quietly it was almost a whisper. "Let's get going."

* * * * *

Holly was deep into her own thoughts. Not that she had much of an option. Mason had been completely silent for the hour they had been on the road.

It was times like this, life-changing, critical moments, when she missed her father the most. He always seemed to find a positive twist to what others would consider the end of the world.

Only this time it really might be the end.

Science meant experimenting. It meant testing and trying to pinpoint the perfect path to success. She had learned there were often roadblocks along the way. Those who succeeded didn't wallow in the failures. Instead, they quickly reassessed and moved on to new tactics.

Yes, she thought, her father had taught her well.

She reached inside her mind, thinking about those lessons, remembering his great influence. She analyzed and discarded thoughts and feelings, pinning down what was truly important.

After a great deal of internal struggle, she accepted the truth of the matter. Her work was not going to be used the way she had hoped. It was time to deal with her new reality and use her work in a positive way.

She glanced at Mason. He was important to the future in some way. How she knew, she wasn't certain. She just did. There was something special about him. It was too abstract in her mind to completely understand.

He needed her.

She knew that too.

Being honest with herself, she needed him too. They were like two lost souls drawn together. They approached things differently but the goal was the same. They both wanted to save lives.

Holly knew Mason thought she disliked the fighter in him and she couldn't say it made her happy. Yet, she knew he was a good man. Her father would have respected him instantly. He was like that, her father. He read people like books. Holly had always considered herself to have the same ability.

She made a decision at that moment. Mason needed her strength and support to achieve whatever was ahead of him. She wanted to give it to him. Suddenly, she felt lighter, more like herself.

Sneaking another peek at Mason's profile, she asked, "How long will we be on the road?" His hair was pulled back with a leather tie, his jaw set in a firm line. He looked tense but it did nothing to take away from the pure male power he oozed. She wanted to make that tension goes away.

He didn't look at her. "It will be another twelve hours or so."

Holly glanced at the clock. It was almost noon and her stomach was starting to make noises. "Any chance we can eat soon?"

Still he didn't look at her, which made her grimace. "I want to go a few more miles first. How about I stop at the store and get you a snack?"

"I can live with that," Holly said, thankful for any form of nourishment. "You have to be hungry, too."

"I am," he said keeping his eyes on the road.

"Your metabolism is faster than most, isn't it?" Holly asked, hoping to learn anything she could about Mason.

He glanced at her direction but quickly turned back to the road. "Three times a normal man's. How did you know?"

Holly noted the reference to normal. She had already heard him make it several times. He wanted to be normal. Holly thought normal was overrated. She was a scientist. Creating a new definition of normal was what she did.

"A girl's dream come true," Holly said. "It would be great to be able to eat chocolate and not pay the price."

"You didn't answer the question. How did you know?"

"The rate you healed. It indicates a fast metabolism."

His tone was matter-of-fact, but she sensed it covered up darker feelings. "It got old fast. If I don't eat, I get weak."

"It comes with incredible perks though, at least from what I've seen so far." She tried for a cheerful tone.

"And negatives." He pulled into a gas station and stopped the truck. He pushed open his door and stepped out of the truck before she could ask any more questions.

Seconds later her door opened. "Come on," Mason said. "Anywhere I go, you go."

Swiveled around to sit on the edge of the seat, she studied him. He was every bit the warrior standing there, rippling with muscle, tall, broad and just plain sexy. But he was also a scarred, haunted man. His eyes reflected pain.

She wanted to see him healed. The need cried out from deep inside her. This man needed laughter. And he needed love. Her love.

And he needed acceptance.

From himself.

From others.

From her.

They had a special bond and she had no intention of walking away from what was between them. No matter how upset she was over his deceptions, she wanted this man.

Holly wanted to reach out and touch him but she didn't. "My protector?"

His eyes narrowed. "Yes."

Holly smiled and scooted off the seat to stand directly in front him. Her hand settled in the middle of his chest. "Who will protect *you* from *me*?"

He didn't move. "Why would I need protection from you, Holly?"

She flattened both hands on his chest. "That's exactly what I intend to find out."

Not giving him time to respond, she sidestepped him and began walking toward the store. She heard him mutter something resembling a curse just before the door slammed shut.

Holly smiled. He had met his match, whether he knew it or not.

Once she was in the store, she grabbed a package of Cheez Doodles and started to walk toward the drinks. Thinking about a candy bar, she took a step backwards and bumped into the hard wall of Mason's body.

The man moved as fast as a bullet train. She turned, peering up at him with mischief in her eyes. She grabbed an extra bag of Cheez Doodles instead of a candy bar. "My favorite," she said, indicating the bag.

Mason looked at the bag she already held. "I see that." There was a hint of a smile on the corners of his mouth. Holly liked it when Mason smiled. She got the feeling he didn't do enough of it. Silently she vowed he would start smiling a whole lot more.

Holly turned toward the store's refrigerator and selected a container of chocolate milk. Grabbing two bottles, she turned and watched Mason gathering several items himself. His choices included two hot dogs and an extra-large bag of Cheez Doodles.

Their eyes met across the store and Holly laughed. She covered the distance between them. "You like them, too."

To her pleasure, he smiled. "Yes, I like them, too." He looked at the milk she held. "Tell me you're not eating Cheez Doodles with chocolate milk."

"Everything goes with chocolate milk." She grinned.

Mason shook his head. "I'll pass on the chocolate milk. I think I'll go with orange juice."

Holly gave him a look of disbelief. "With Cheez Doodles? Now that *is* disgusting."

He grinned. "Everything tastes good with orange juice." Then he winked.

Holly let herself enjoy a secret smile as he paid the cashier. Mason was a whole lot more fun when he allowed himself to think he was normal.

Chapter Ten

They rode in silence as they ate, but not without eye contact. Several smiles were exchanged as the crunching of Cheez Doodles filled the truck. Holly was encouraged by his smiles.

The future was blurry at best. Being with Mason gave her an odd sense of calmness. Looking skyward, Holly silently thanked her father for instilling in her his outlooks on life. With that in mind, she reminded herself that she was simply entering a new path in life. Fear of the unknown was not her style.

Mason was part of her next step. She wanted to know about him for reasons having nothing to do with fear. He made her feel alive and fearless and new in ways she didn't quite understand.

Once they were done eating, Holly decided to probe and see what she could find out about him. "How long have you been a Black Knight?"

It took him so long for him to answer, Holly was beginning to think he wasn't going to. Finally, he said, "Five years."

"And before that?"

He kept his eyes focused on the road. "Delta Force."

She considered his answer. Everyone knew how covert Delta Force was considered. The Black Knights were the same, only they were considered myth rather than reality.

"Both tough jobs," she said and then added, "being the soldier no one claims." She studied his profile. "Why do you do it?"

"It's who I am," he said simply.

She knew there was more to it than that. "What about your family? Don't they worry?"

"I don't have any family," he said flatly.

Holly frowned. "You mentioned a brother."

"He's dead," Mason said so quickly, and with such conviction, Holly was taken aback.

"I'm sorry," she said quietly and then dared to push him farther. She couldn't seem to help herself. She needed to know about him. "No other siblings?"

"I had one. He was killed in the Iraq war."

"2003?"

Mason looked at her. "That's right."

"Were you there?"

He nodded. "Yes."

When he said no more Holly let out a frustrated breath. "This is like pulling teeth. Why are you so secretive?"

He stared at the road but she saw the way he tightened his grip on the steering wheel making his knuckles white. "In the eyes of many I don't exist. It's better kept that way."

"Too late," she said softly. "I know and I'm not going to forget."

Mason turned to her then, giving her his full attention, almost seeming to forget the road. "Holly —"

"You better watch where you're driving," she said pointing forward. Mason made a frustrated sound and turned back to the road. "Where are your parents?"

"Holly —"

"Please, Mason," she pleaded. "You know everything about me. I know nothing about you."

He gave her a sideways look. "All I know is what a file tells me. I don't know the important stuff."

Her brows dipped. "What do you consider important?"

His gaze moved between her and the road. "The things that make us who we are as individuals." His tone was serious. "What makes a person smile or cry or even laugh can't be captured in a government document. Those are the things that are ultimately important." Then he added, "Like washing down Cheez Doodles with chocolate milk."

She smiled for a moment but then moved forward. "I agree to some degree but our family history and relationships impact us as people as well." She needed to know more. "Where are your parents, Mason?"

He laughed then, but without humor. "You never give up, do you?"

"Nope," she replied, "so you might as well answer."

He sighed with resignation and she knew she had won a tiny war of her own. His grip on the steering wheel loosened and he dropped one hand to his lap. After long moments, he said, "Like yours, my parents are no longer around."

Holly considered what she had learned. Both of them were very alone in the world. Perhaps that drew them together. "How?" she asked in a half whisper.

"My father was called back during the Iraq war to help with a special intelligence mission. He was killed in friendly fire."

Holly gulped. "You lost your brother and your father to Iraq. I'm sorry, Mason." She slid closer to him, reaching for his hand because she couldn't help it. At first he held his hand limp in hers. "It must have been horrible."

Slowly he closed his hand over hers. "It was my mother who took it the hardest. She sunk into a depression and ..." His voice trailed off.

Holly felt his emotion like a wave of heaviness. She squeezed his hand. "And?"

"I left for a mission," he said. "I had to. While I was away, she killed herself."

Holly swallowed. Oh God, what he had been through would have destroyed a lesser person. She scooted the rest of the way to his side and rested her head on his arm. "I can't imagine what it was like."

Processing what she had learned, she realized she hadn't found out what had happened to his other brother. Now wasn't the time to ask any more questions. He had already shared far more than she thought he would.

This man, a warrior, so strong and fierce, yet so deeply wounded, touched her in so many ways. She wanted to comfort him. If only he would let her. She held her breath, hoping he wouldn't push her away. When he didn't, she let her eyes drift shut, feeling sleep reaching for her. At peace beside Mason, a man she hardly knew, yet on some level knew better than anyone else on earth, she slept.

* * * * *

Mason pulled his vehicle into a small diner just as the sun dipped beyond the horizon. Holly was curled up on the seat, sound asleep, looking sweet and angelic. When she had drifted off, he had been thankful for her silence. Somehow, the woman managed to get him to talk about things he simply preferred to forget.

Once he killed the engine, he sat looking down at her. Her knees were tucked up close to her body and one of her dainty little hands tucked beneath her chin. She took his breath away.

What was he going to do about her?

Her attitude baffled him. She wasn't angry and didn't appear freaked out over his differences. In fact, she seemed more eager than ever to get to know him.

She never did what he expected. She was a complex puzzle full of surprises. Most people, even some of the well-trained soldiers he knew, would be completely unnerved about being pulled from their lives, and thrown into some alien world.

But not Holly.

She seemed almost as if…as if…

Hell, he wasn't sure what was going on in that pretty little head of hers. His senses told him it wasn't trauma. No, his Holly Heart, his mate, was not doing anything a normal person would do under similar circumstances.

Like freaking out.

There was that damn word. *Normal.* Holly *was* normal, he reminded himself. He, on the other hand, *was not.* It was the ultimate separation between the two of them he could never bridge.

The urge to touch her was strong. Gently, he slid his hand down the softness of her hair. "Holly, Angel, wake up."

She stirred but didn't wake. He dipped his fingers into her hair and gently caressed her scalp. She made a soft noise, much like a purr. "Ohhhh," she murmured. "That feels wonderful."

Holly rolled to a sitting position, scooting closer to him as she moved. On purpose, he was certain. He fought the desire to pull her into his lap, to kiss her and make love to her until they were both lost.

He needed that escape and, more than anything, he feared he needed her. But he couldn't ask her to stay with him. It was too dangerous.

"Where are we?" She touched his arm, looking out the window.

A shiver of awareness raced through his body at her touch. His cock went rock-hard. He bit back desire. He couldn't believe the fire she evoked by simply touching him. Arion mates hunger for one another. Her eyes told of her own desire.

He had to work to keep his voice normal. "A small little town in the middle of nowhere," he said, willing his hands not to reach out to her. "Are you hungry?"

Slowly the corner of her mouth lifted. A hint of wicked intent laced her tone. "Starving."

The last remnants of the sunlight danced in her eyes, making them sparkle like fine diamonds. She was so damn beautiful and he wanted her like he had never wanted a woman. She was his mate, bound to him for all of eternity…unless he figured out how to undo what he had done.

They stared at one another and, with each passing moment, his will power weakened. He forced himself to close his eyes, breaking the spell wrapped around them. He had no option but to find a way to undo their mating before she knew about it.

Until then, he simply had to find the strength to keep himself in check.

He reached for the door handle, needing to put distance between them. His willpower, the ironclad control he was so well-known for among his fellow soldiers, seemed nonexistent where she was concerned.

Holly sat in the truck. He assumed she was waiting on him to come to her side. When he opened the door for her, she didn't move. "Holly?"

She turned her head to look at him. "What?"

Anger in her tone, he noted. "You're mad."

"You're observant," she retorted. "It must be those great warrior senses of yours, hard at work."

He held the door with one hand, dropping his head between his shoulders so she couldn't see his expression as he contemplated his response. This was like playing tug-of-war with his own mind and body.

Before he could answer, Holly slid down to the ground and faced him. Her hands went to her hips. "A warrior on the battlefield, a coward off."

His head popped up, eyes narrowed and dark. "What in the hell does that mean?"

She snorted. "Figure it out yourself." Grabbing her purse from the truck, she flung it over her shoulder and started walking toward the restaurant.

Mason let a low growl escape his throat as he shoved the door shut and quickly followed on her heels. Chasing after her was becoming a bad habit. His mind raced with options, emotions, anger...and yes, irritation. But it was short-lived as he analyzed her actions. *Damn*. She was trying to get an emotional response from him and he had taken the bait.

As he stepped into the diner, Mason found himself fighting a smile. The woman was impossible.

To ignore.

To resist.

He made a frustrated sound and silently added, *to win an argument with.*

Holly had slid into a booth and grabbed a menu before he was past the front door. Mason covered the distance between them, sitting across from her as he took in their surroundings, looking for escape routes and potential problems.

The first thing he noted was the emptiness of the place. They were the only customers. Good. The fewer people around, the less likelihood of trouble.

Several no-frills booths lined the walls with alternating red and yellow seats. Six regular tables covered in checkered cloths sat in the middle of the room. In the far back was a sign indicating a bathroom.

Turning to rest his back against the wall, he put one leg on the seat as he surveyed the scene behind him. The diner was connected to a bar by way of a huge cut-out door. He could see several pool tables and miscellaneous people milling around them. The sound of country music filtered through the air, as did the sound of pool balls clicking.

A waitress approached their table wearing a pink uniform and smacking gum like a teenager. Only she was more like thirty and had cleavage and big blond hair that screamed *look at me*. "Coffee for you folks?"

"Orange juice for me," Mason said and, indicating Holly with a nod, "Chocolate milk for the lady."

The woman smacked her gum. "Got it. I'm Janis. Be right back."

Holly sat down her menu and looked at Mason. "What if I didn't want chocolate milk?"

"But you did," he said with certainty.

"That's not the point," she countered tartly.

He brow lifted. "Why do you want to argue with me?"

She glowered at him. "Why do you want to avoid me?"

He smiled. "Want isn't the issue."

"What does that mean?" a challenge in both her voice and eyes.

"I've already told you, Holly. There are—"

Janis sat down their drinks. "What can I get you to eat?"

Mason sighed. "Holly?"

"Cheeseburger and fries," she said to Janis.

"Same for me," Mason said, "only make it two."

Janis eyed him. "Big appetite, huh?"

"Yes, ma'am." She tucked her pen behind her ear and grinned at him. She gave him a good several second inspection. "Looks like you handle it well. I like that in a man."

Mason didn't say anything. Janis turned and left swinging her hips a little too obviously as she did.

Mason refocused on Holly to find her frowning. "Janis was hitting on you."

"No, she was not," he said. "Besides, Janis is far from my type." Then he lowered his voice. "There isn't anyone who would take my attention from you."

Holly snorted and looked away. "Whatever."

"Holly," he said reaching across the table and covering her hand with his. She turned to look at him the second he touched her, questions in her eyes. He answered the only way he knew how. "There are things about me you don't know."

Her eyes narrowed dangerously. "Yes," she said in a clipped tone. "We've already established that."

His lips thinned. "Things you won't like. I am simply trying to protect you."

"Protect me?" she asked with disbelief in her eyes. "If this is how you protect me, then stop. One minute you want me, the next you push me away." Her voice quivered ever so slightly, giving him insight into her feelings. "Your form of protection is pretty hard to swallow."

She averted her gaze and he knew he had hurt her. "I'm sorry, Holly." He tried to relay how sincerely he meant the words in his tone.

She looked at him, surprise in her eyes. "Then don't do it anymore."

He laughed. He couldn't help it. Holly was so direct. "You never hold back, do you?"

"Not about things that matter to me."

Mason sobered quickly. She wasn't making things easy on him. "Tell me about yourself, Holly Heart. What matters to you?"

He was pleased to find her eager to talk. It was as if she let down some curtain and then him walk inside. She began talking without hesitation. About her parents, her research and even the dog she had as a child. Her voice wrapped around him like a soft caress. Watching her eyes twinkle and her expressions change kept him so spellbound he hardly remembered eating.

Mason paid the bill and was about to suggest they get on the road when her eyes lightened. "That's one of my favorite country songs. Come dance with me."

His eyes widened. "No," he said. "We have to go."

"Please, Mason. Just a quick dance. For a few minutes let's forget everything and dance."

"Holly—"

She cut him off with determined measure in her gaze. "I guess a tough guy like you doesn't dance? Or is it against some Black Knight code? If so, is there a manual I can read?"

He stared at her. She was going to be the death of him. Before he could talk himself out of it, he pushed to his feet and held out his hand.

Her brow inched up but she didn't move.

"Let's dance," he said, noticing the husky quality of his voice but not able to stop it.

His reward was her brilliant smile as she moved from the booth to her feet and placed her hand in his. "Thank you," she said sweetly.

As she stepped closer to him, Mason trailed his finger down her cheek. He felt her tremble in response and everything male in him roared with approval. "You make it very hard to say no, Holly Heart."

"Good," she whispered.

Tucking her arm under his elbow, he led her to the bar. Dim lighting filtered through the room while the jukebox switched to another slow, country song. Covertly, Mason surveyed the room.

There wasn't a dance floor so Mason simply pulled Holly into a dark corner and then into his arms. He was crazy for delaying their departure. Moving was critical to keep the Arions from tracking their position.

But here he was, dancing with Holly.

Together they melted into the shadows, her head on his shoulder. His hands slid up and down her back, along the perfect curve of her hip, and she answered him with a soft purring sound.

For the moments following, Mason pushed his concerns about the future aside. He was with Holly and nothing stood between them. Holding her was like coming home. He felt a peace he hadn't felt in years, if ever.

How long they clung to one another, swaying with the music, in perfect sync with every movement, he wasn't sure. He could have stayed lost in their little world forever.

Reality invaded with a crash from behind. He stiffened, scanned the room and identifyied the noise as nothing more than a broken glass. Still, he knew they had lingered too long.

"We have to go," he told Holly.

She nodded but her eyes were alluring, full of desire, and he found himself regretting the loss of their time together. Pushing to her tiptoes, she cupped his face with one of her hands. "Thank you for dancing with me."

He covered her hand with his before bringing it to his mouth. His lips brushed her knuckles. "Anytime, anything," he whispered.

They stood there, not dancing, not moving for long seconds. Forcing himself, he said, "We have to go."

"Um," Holly said. "I should go to the bathroom before we leave."

He nodded as his hand settled on the small of her back. He walked her through the bar toward the restrooms.

"When you're done, wait right here for me," Mason told her before they each turned to the appropriate door.

* * * * *

Mason stilled, but only for an instant of confirmation.

Holly.

He had heard her cry his name in his head. Her fear wrapped around him, making his breathing tight, as if he had a vice on his throat, strangling him. Pure terror like he had never known made his stomach twist in knots. Forcefully, he closed his eyes and let his senses take over.

Images came to him as clear as if he was seeing them firsthand. There were two men in the women's restroom, one standing in front of Holly, the other behind her, holding a knife to her throat.

He despised the Arions' use of humans to perform their bidding. Humans were rewarded for their participation. If effective in the assigned task, in return, the human would be turned into an Arion. The Arions won in this matter either way. They had their will acted upon without bringing attention to their race and they expanded their kind with only those who would do their bidding.

Mason closed the distance between the two bathrooms in a matter of seconds. Moving with the soundless grace of a well-trained Knight and the speed of a superhuman, he pushed open the women's door. He grabbed the man facing Holly and broke his neck. Before the man hit the ground, Mason had removed a shiny, round blade from his belt. Quiet and effective, it was often his weapon of choice.

In one quick motion, the blade was planted in the other man's forehead. The knife the attacker had been holding to Holly's throat fell to the ground, making a loud clattering noise.

He crumpled to the floor, whimpering with pain, but very much alive. Mason kneeled in front of him, removing the knife from his flesh. Using the man's shirt, Mason cleaned the blade.

Looking into his eyes, Mason's stare burned with pure fury. "When I clap, you will do to yourself what you intended for your victim." He held the man in his hypnotic gaze and then asked, "Do you understand?" The man nodded, his eyes glazed with the trance-like state Mason had placed him under.

Mason pushed to his feet and reached for Holly. She was trembling, her arms wrapped around her body. Framing her face with his hands he looked into her eyes, intentionally grabbing her with his power.

"I'm here," he said in a comforting voice as his thumbs wiped tears from her cheeks. "You're safe. I would never let anyone hurt you."

Her lips quivered. "I know."

"We have to go," he said, taking her hand.

She nodded, her eyes wide, her lips trembling as if she was icy-cold.

Mason pulled her behind him, guiding her into the hallway. He moved to release Holly's hand but she held it tight, insistently. Understanding her need, he tucked her hand under his elbow and then clapped, setting the man in the bathroom into action.

Taking Holly by the hand again, he pulled her behind him and toward the exit.

Chapter Eleven

Mason looked up at the sky with a grim expression on his face. Darkness had fallen with a thick cloud cover, eerie, like something out of a horror movie. The moon was a strange grayish color, ominous and half-covered. Thunder rumbled in the distance.

Inwardly he cursed their bad luck. Storms would only slow them down.

His senses told him there was no Arion presence in the direct area, but that didn't mean they weren't in danger. Humans were clearly at the Arions' bidding. And he had to put distance between them and the diner before the bodies of the two men in the bathroom were discovered.

Mason went straight to the driver's side of his truck, pulling Holly along with him, wanting to keep her near. He helped her slide into the truck. She stayed close to his side as he slid behind the wheel, holding his arm as if it was her lifeline.

He was glad to have her near so he could feel her alive and well. Damn, he had come too close to losing her. Once he shut the truck door, he wanted to hold her but there wasn't time. He needed to get them the hell away from the diner.

But he worried about her. She'd been through hell.

She was a strong woman but seeing someone killed was a tough thing. It was also hard to face the evil of a man intent on making a kill. She had faced two such men on this night.

Two too many.

He could feel her delicate little shivers. Minutes passed but her body still hadn't calmed. As soon as he felt it was safe, he pulled to the side of the road, fearful she was going into shock.

He turned to her, pulling her into his arms, stroking her back and hair.

"I'm so sorry, Angel. I'm here for you. I swear I won't let anything happen to you."

It was said true Arion mates had many abilities with their partners, including a calming effect. At this moment, Mason prayed it was true. Her heartbeat was too fast.

He kept touching her, stroking and caressing her with gentle reassurance. "Breathe for me, nice and slow, in and out."

She wasn't responding well. He leaned back, looking into her eyes. Mentally, he reached out to her, calming her. He held her gaze. "Let's try this again but keep looking at me. Let's breathe together, Angel. Okay?"

She just looked at him.

He reached for her mind, silently willing her to comply. "Breathe in," he said, sucking in a breath, feeling relieved when she did as well. Then he blew out a breath and she followed. They did this several times.

Gently, he caressed her cheeks with his thumbs. Her heart was beating a bit more normally now and he could see responsiveness in her gaze. "Better?"

She nodded but a choked sob escaped her lips and she tried to turn away from him. He didn't let her. He grabbed her and pulled her into his embrace, holding her as he whispered comforting words of love. At first she resisted, as if afraid to let go but, moments later, she clung to him, her face buried in his shirt.

She was more like him than he'd realized. A need to be in control drove her actions and reactions far more than he initially thought. He understood what that felt like.

The connections he felt to Holly were like nothing he had ever experienced or even imagined. She reached inside him and made him whole. Seeing the sharpened edge of a blade against her throat had been pure torture. He tightened his arms around her.

How could he ever walk away from her? Yet how could he not?

His mind raced a million miles an hour, taking twists and turns and settling on a major concern. What would Holly's reaction be to him killing those men?

Once she was over her initial shock, would she hate him for what he had done? Would she understand that he had been in soldier mode, protecting what was his?

He was a soldier, trained to kill when needed. And Holly was important to him both as a soldier and a man. If someone threatened her, he wouldn't hesitate to take his or her life.

Fighting evil sometimes meant kill or be killed.

He ran his hand down her hair, kissing her temple, her head and then her forehead. Tilting her chin up, he looked into her eyes, tears clinging to her lashes even though she had calmed.

She made an effort to smile. "I'm sorry I lost it like that."

His eyes went to her soft, full lips. "Don't be," he said lowering his head, brushing his mouth across hers and tasting the saltiness of her tears.

"You saved my life," she whispered against his mouth.

Silence filtered through the darkness, laced with their need for one another, their mouths and bodies touching, savoring the feel of just holding one another, of being alive and together.

Headlights flashed, shaking Mason back into reality. Reluctantly, he pulled back, feeling the ache of her absence immediately. Running his hands down her arms, he said, "We have to get on the road."

Holly nodded but, as he started to move toward the steering wheel, she grabbed his arm. His eyes went to hers. She hesitated, not saying whatever she was going to say. His brow inched up in question.

"Nothing," she whispered.

When she turned away, releasing his arm, he frowned, wondering what she had left unsaid. He pulled back onto the road as Holly snuggled up to his side and fell asleep.

He drove.

Thinking and thinking.

What had she *not* said to him?

* * * * *

Darkness enveloped the road while trees and brush almost seemed to close in around them. The gas tank sat on empty. Mason was thankful he knew the area well.

There was a self-serve gas station half a mile up the road. Holly still slept, no doubt exhausted by the trauma of the day. She didn't so much as twitch when he pulled into the station.

At one in the morning there wasn't a person in sight and Mason was thankful for pay-at-the-pump service. He had a special card, compliments of the government, traceable to someone who wasn't him but, then again, was. A little tactic needed in a world where electronic tracking was so easy.

The instant Mason stepped from the truck the wind changed. He would know the presence, any day, anywhere, so connected was he to the visitor.

David.

The two of them could always track each other. For Mason it took a great deal of effort. For David, it appeared almost effortless. Unless Mason was underground.

His eyes flew to the side of the building; dark shadows played against the wall. As he expected, David stepped forward. Mason moved toward him, closing the distance and meeting him halfway.

They stood facing one another, their eyes locking. Mason squared his shoulders, no fear in his stare, only contempt. Even now, looking at David, it was hard to believe he had turned so evil. Arions looked like normal humans. David *looked* like his brother. But he wasn't.

It was hard to swallow.

In appearance they had always resembled one another. There were small differences, such as height — Mason stood two inches above David's six feet. Where Mason was taller, David was broader.

Looking at David now, Mason wished he didn't resemble the man he had once loved. Their blood bond was so damn evident to anyone who saw them together. Even to him, as much contempt as he felt, their similarities were a reminder of what once was. The brother he had once known was dead. All that was left was this alien creature.

Who looked like his brother.

"What do you want, David?"

David's lips twitched with amusement. "Now, is that anyway to greet your brother?"

Mason's lips thinned. "My brother is dead."

David ran a hand in front of his body. "I am alive and quite well, Mason. Don't kid yourself. Denial won't change who or what I am."

Mason's mind shifted. He knew the instant Holly woke, a strange sensation because of its clarity. He could feel her confusion, almost hear her call his name. With an instinct and skill that was unfamiliar to him, he mentally reached out to her.

I am fine. Stay in the truck until I tell you otherwise. Don't argue this one, Angel. There is danger.

He thought the words but didn't think she actually heard them. But maybe felt them. Yes. He knew she understood. He relaxed marginally. There was too much risk to her with David present to let down his guard.

Shifting his attention back to his brother, he said, "Say what you will but the brother I once knew is no more." The brother he knew would never have been so evil. "We always differed in personality, but not in values."

Mason was disciplined and focused, where David had been wild and daring. Yet, Mason had always believed they had the same angle on life.

Obviously, he had been wrong.

David ignored Mason's words as if he hadn't spoken. "I come with one last offer, Mason. Join me. Together we will rule. One bloodline. A legacy of our own. Our children will rule after us, and then theirs." His eyes went to the truck, a silent message that he knew Holly was there. "I know you're attached to the woman. Bring her and I will assure her safety."

"Right," Mason said. "I met your human servants back at the diner. Nice way of ensuring her safety."

"You have my word," David said. "This is brother-to-brother. My word to you as blood."

Mason shook his head. "You never did understand the word no. Let me spell it out. I will not join you, not now, not ever."

David's black eyes seemed to darken to the depths of hell. "My patience wears thin, brother." He emphasized the word brother. "Your stubbornness will do nothing but seal your death," he looked toward the truck and then back to Mason, "and that of your woman by denying your spot by my side."

Mason laughed, taunting David with intent. "You always had a God complex, David. I knocked you on your ass many times when we were kids and I'll do it again, now. You know I can or you wouldn't care so much about having me on your side. I'm no fool, David. You'd best remember that."

The wind picked up speed, swirling the dust on the ground. David's eyes took on a predatory gleam. "I'm not so easily defeated, Mason. Test me now and people will die. Many people." He started to back away. One step, then two, before he stopped. "You have twenty-four hours. No more. If you don't come to me of your own free will, I'll consider us at war. Decide your fate."

Mason's response came quickly and with complete certainty. "You can give me an hour or a year, and my decision will be the same. I will never join you."

David's teeth clenched. "I sincerely hope you reconsider. Terminating you would come with regret but I will not hesitate to make it happen."

"There you have it. Our differences are evident. Terminating you wouldn't cause me one bit of regret. I sincerely hope you keep that in mind." Mason clutched his fists at his side.

"I'll be in contact," David said as he backed into the shadows and simply disappeared into the wind.

* * * * *

The minute Holly saw Mason approaching the truck she pushed the door open and ran toward him. He opened his arms to her, pulling her into the shelter of his body.

"I was scared to death when I woke up and you were gone," Holly said, clinging to his shirt with her hands as she looked up at him.

His expression was etched with worry and something else Holly couldn't quite identify. "I know. I felt your fear."

She rested her palm on his jaw. "What is it?"

"Nothing," he said, then averted his gaze, repeating the word as if he needed to convince himself it was true. "Nothing." He paused a heartbeat and then took her hand, pulling her with him as he walked toward the truck. "We need to get out of here and I need to put gas in the truck."

She tugged at his hand making him stop walking. He turned back to her, a question in his eyes and just a hint of irritation. "You spoke to me in my mind," she said quietly as if confirming she wasn't crazy.

"Yes," he said but, before she could read his expression, he turned away again pulling her with him toward the truck.

"Who was that man?" she asked from behind him.

"He was an Arion," Mason said evasively.

"How did he find us and what did he want?"

He dropped her hand and pulled out his wallet to fish out his credit card. "Arions can track anyone if they have their scent. They can get it from your home, your personal items, anything."

Holly frowned. "Can you do the same thing?"

He stuck the nozzle to the gas pump in the truck. "I have to have one-on-one contact with the person and my skills are far less effective."

"Maybe you just don't know how to use the skill. Perhaps it can be developed," she said thoughtfully. Then: "Who was he and what did he want?"

"I've already told you what they want."

Holly put her hands on her hips. "What are you not telling me, Mason?"

His eyes shut and then opened. His brother was evil. How did he tell Holly about a brother so evil...and so like him. Telling her would be like revealing his own darkness. Something he didn't want to accept, so how could he ask her to? "Holly, please. We need to get on the road. We'll talk later."

"Mason—"

"Holly, please," he said, interrupting her in a low, strained voice.

Holly sighed in resignation.

* * * * *

Sterling propped his feet on Holly's coffee table and stuck a Cheese Doodle in his mouth. He couldn't decide if Holly had four bags of the things because she liked them or didn't like them.

He'd spent the day trying to track down Roger to no avail. The man had simply disappeared. His connection to Holly might well have been a fatal one.

Pressing the buttons on the remote, he flipped the channels of the television, searching for a news update. There had been another abduction reported, a young woman from campus. He couldn't shake the feeling Arions were involved.

They had to be trying to breed but their approach was crazy. Arions could only impregnate their mate. To hope a random woman they abducted would be their mate... His thoughts trailed off. Unless...

He jumped to his feet, making tracks for the computer. As he waited for the computer to boot, he analyzed his thoughts. The Arions wanted Holly for her knowledge of genetics, to create and improve their race. Perhaps they were also trying other methods of breeding, like artificial insemination and cloning. The Arions were dogmatic in their quest for growth. Logically they wouldn't count on only one tactic.

The minute the computer was ready, Sterling began keying, eager to find some type of link to back up his conclusions. He started with a list of people, scientists and doctors, who might be able to help the Arions make such things happen.

Two hours later he found his link, a doctor in Canada who had been missing for several weeks. Marcus Phoenix had extensive experience with artificial insemination. Pulling a hand down the length of his long blond hair, Sterling let out a breath.

He needed to call Mason. Reaching for the phone, he went still. His senses sizzled with awareness of an Arion presence — one highly familiar.

Michael Roma, a former close friend. The strange thing was, he sensed no other presence with Michael. He was alone. Arions never traveled alone when seeking a battle.

Pushing to his feet, Sterling moved through the house until he was at the front door. When he pulled it open, Michael stood, back to him, his raven hair loose around his shoulders.

Slowly, he turned to face Sterling, black eyes locking with black eyes. "We need to talk," Michael said simply.

Sterling stood in silence, assessing Michael, wondering how a man he had once considered honorable and brave, had become his enemy. "I can't imagine what we have to talk about," Sterling said, getting angry as he thought of his friend's betrayal. "Perhaps it's a battle you seek rather than conversation."

Michael tilted his head back letting a deep roar of laughter escape his throat. "Always the renegade," he said, "looking for a fight. Well, old friend, you won't find one with me. I only wish to talk. How about inviting me inside?"

Sterling studied Michael intently. His Italian coloring gave him an edgy, dangerous look. But then, Michael was, if nothing else, a dangerous man.

When Sterling hesitated, Michael said, "I know where the man from the lab is, as well as several of the abducted women. I think we can save a lot of lives if we work together."

That got Sterling's full attention. Making a mistake with someone like Michael, especially an Arion version, could be deadly, yet... Slowly, he stepped back, offering a silent invitation. Michael followed Sterling into the living room and sat down on the couch. Sterling leaned against the wall, not willing to let down his guard.

Crossing his arms in front of his body, he studied Michael. "What's this about?"

No hesitation. "Mason, among other things."

"He won't join his brother," Sterling said fiercely.

"Good," Michael replied.

"Good?" Sterling asked in confusion. "Did you just say 'good'?"

"Mason may well be the only one who can ensure David's defeat."

Sterling let out a bark of humorless laughter. "Whatever your little game is, I'm not biting."

"No game," Michael said. "Arions are not destined to be evil. It's the soul of the human that determines the ultimate result. Otherwise Mason would already be no different than his brother."

Sterling blinked. "You mean if he had been transitioned into an Arion."

"He is an Arion."

"No," Sterling said. "Mason is not an Arion."

"He is and I believe he secretly knows it or at least suspects as much. Everyone knows he is the most skilled of the Black Knights. He simply doesn't accept his Arion abilities thus he cannot put them to use."

Sterling laughed but it was dry and sharp. "You're crazy if you think I'm buying this."

Michael gave Sterling a level stare. "You have the ability to sense the truth. Not only do you know he is different, you know me well enough to read the truth in me."

Sterling did know Mason was different. And he knew Michael spoke the truth. But, still, he worried this could be some Arion trick he didn't understand.

"Assuming what you say is the truth — Mason is Arion — what do you hope to gain by telling me?"

Michael leaned forward, elbows on his knees. "Mason can defeat David, and David knows it. He wants him on his side before it's too late."

"What's in this for you?"

"I'm on your side."

"But you weren't."

Michael's brows inched up. "Wasn't I?"

Sterling grimaced. "You want me to believe you were never on David's team."

"I did what I had to in order to stay alive," Michael said with a severity to his tone. "In the meantime I learned a hell of a lot."

Sterling knew he was telling the truth. This was a man of honor he had once trusted with his life. Letting out a breath Sterling walked to a chair across from Michael and sat down.

"You're certain Mason is Arion?"

"Absolutely," Michael said. "David made sure of it."

"How?" Sterling asked, mentally searching the past for clues. "We received the same injections. At the time we thought they were simply vaccinations." Sterling scrubbed his jaw. "Of course, you know that. You were there and a part of it all. I'm just trying to walk through all of this and make it come together."

"I understand," Michael said. "If you remember, I was among the men who volunteered to test the Arion enhancements. My little group thought we were the first. We weren't. David had volunteered to be the first test pilot, so to speak. He told no one, not even Mason."

"Apparently, he and Gina, who is now his Arion mate, plotted to spike Mason's injections long before any of us even knew about the Arion project."

"This is crazy," Sterling said.

Michael nodded and continued, "David intended to build a bloodline of ruling power. He was certain the Arion power would bring Mason to him of his own accord. When that didn't happen, he decided to come after him."

"Why not leave him alone?" Sterling asked.

"He has been enhanced to David's level and they are of the same bloodline. Mason might be the only person alive who could defeat David in a one-on-one battle. Look, there is much to be discussed. We need to get Mason involved and agreeable."

Sterling still had unanswered questions. "Why the hell did David ever think his brother would join him?"

"David still thinks he can bring Mason to his side. They're brothers and from what I understand they were once close. David believes he is doing the right thing, Sterling. He believes he can take over all of humanity and the end results will be a bigger, better place. He wants universal domination. If he succeeds here he won't stop. And like all power hunger monsters of the past, he sees no wrong in his ways. Why should his brother, the man who has always been by his side, not follow."

Sterling laughed, but not with humor. With bitter reality. "So your telling me he is insane."

A muscle in David's jaw jumped. "No. He's not insane. To me that makes him all the more dangerous."

"If this isn't insane, I don't know what is," Sterling countered.

"Evil," Michael said.

The word lingered in the air for long moments. "Right," Sterling said, a frown on his face. "Our best bet is to talk to Mason in person. He'll be more likely to accept this if he can see you face-to-face."

"So," Michael said standing up. "Let's go. There isn't a moment to spare. The Arions have some plans already in motion that we can't let them complete."

Chapter Twelve

The first thing Roger noticed when he woke was the splitting pain in his head. Then darkness. He was surrounded in blackness. He blinked. Was it his eyes or the room? Panic flared. He wasn't sure.

The restriction of his arms reminded him of the ropes around his wrists. Vaguely he remembered being tied up. Squeezing his eyes shut, trying to block out the complete blackness of the room, he suppressed a shiver of fear.

The strain of trying to see was unbearable. Absolutely unnerving.

Memories seeped into his brain, the strange men, the caves and the needles. God, the needles. His head thrashed from side to side as he thought of the pinpricks, of being held down. His mind conjured such vivid imagines, he could almost feel the needles break his skin and then sink into his tissue. A light perspiration dampened his brow.

What had they injected him with?

"Someone help me!" he yelled into the emptiness of the room.

His voice echoed as if in a cavern, answering him with his own words. He was so alone and scared.

* * * * *

Holly let out a sigh of relief when the truck stopped in the driveway of a small wooden cabin. She glanced at the clock. It was nearly three in the morning. She had offered to drive, worried he was tired, but he had refused.

A storm was rolling in, brought by brisk winds. Clouds covered the moon and stars and the night felt downright spooky. It was as if Mother Nature knew something they didn't. Thunder rumbled overhead seeming to get closer and closer with each roll.

"Please tell me this is where we're stopping," she said, sitting up straight as she tired to make out her surroundings.

Mason didn't answer. Instead, he drove to the back of the cabin and, to Holly's shock, straight into the middle of the woods. Jostled from side to side as the tires crunched on rough terrain, Holly held onto the seat with a desperate grip.

"What are you doing?" Holly demanded.

He put the gearshift in park, killing the ignition and lights. "Parking, of course." Then he actually had the nerve to chuckle. Holly couldn't see his expression through the shadows of the truck cab but he obviously thought something was funny.

She didn't.

Yes, she wanted the man to laugh more but his timing was crap, as far as she was concerned. With a more than a little irritation in her voice she said, "Why?"

As long as Mason's reasoning ended with them going into the cabin and getting some rest, she'd forgive his behavior.

"Switching vehicles."

He wasn't forgiven. "What?" she blurted. "Why? Can't we stay here a while?"

"I told you we have to get underground."

"Can't we rest until morning?" She hated the plea in her voice but, damn it, they'd been traveling for twelve hours and her backside was getting numb.

"Too dangerous," Mason replied as he pushed open his door. "Stay put. I'll be around to get you."

The minute he pulled her door open, she hit him with a question. "Whose cabin is this?"

He held out his hand to her but the shadows hid his expression. "Mine," he said flatly, offering no other information.

She slid off the seat to stand in front of him. "You live here?"

His hands settled on her waist. "You ask a million questions, woman."

"Because you're so secretive. Now answer my question. Do you live here?"

"No," he said. "I don't. I just want people to think I do." He turned without giving her time to respond, taking her hand in his and pulling her through the woods.

Holly followed nervously, well aware of the high grass or, rather, weeds. She didn't even want to know what might be crawling around by her feet. As soon as they were out of the woods and in an open clearing, Mason let go of her hand. Taking long strides forward, he left her standing there, staring after him.

"Hey," she yelped, starting off after him, her gaze darting anxiously toward the sky as thunder rumbled. A flash of lightning made her jump. Her eyes settled on his back moving rapidly away from her.

"Don't leave me here. It's dark."

She could just barely make out his actions as he stopped in front of a shed, grabbed the lock attached, quickly punched in a combination code and opened the door. He disappeared into the building just as Holly stepped up to the door.

How could he see? Holly peered into the blankness past the doorway. "Mason?"

A sudden burst of sound assaulted her ears, making Holly jump, her hand flying to her chest. "Jeez," she grumbled. "Mason!" This time she yelled his name.

Seconds later, he appeared, sitting astride a motorcycle, looking sexier than any man had the right to, and holding a helmet out to her.

"Put this on," he ordered.

Damn, the man was bossy. She grimaced. "As in, put it on and get on the motorcycle?" she yelled back over the engine.

His eyes twinkled with a hint of amusement. "Exactly."

Holly liked looking at Mason on the motorcycle. The idea of riding it with him didn't appeal. "Do I have to?"

He frowned and, despite the loudness of the motor, she thought he grunted. She made a face at him. "Fine."

Putting the helmet on, she expelled a deep breath. Holly flung one leg over the seat just as the first raindrop hit her nose.

Great! Would this night ever end!

Mason grabbed her hands, pulling them tight around his waist, silently telling her to hold on. It was also a hint of what was to come. She wasn't going to like the ride. The rev of the engine was her only warning before they took off through the grass. Holly gasped as her body rocked from the force of the movement. Though she was certain Mason couldn't have heard over the roar of the engine, she could have sworn she heard him laugh.

She had created a monster, laughing at all the wrong things. This was not funny. Not at all. Holly looked over his shoulder and quickly shut her eyes, appalled to see him heading straight toward the woods. Not to the road.

The bike jumped and jerked along with her body as rain began steadily pounding them. A thought hit her. Her things were in the truck. She didn't even have clothes to change into.

But Mason had her research tucked in a pouch he wore around his ankle. At least it was safe.

Something, at least, was going her way.

But not much.

* * * * *

Mason took each bump in the road with practiced precision. He had made this run over the mountain too many times to count. The rain, however, made the ride a bit risky, considering Holly was with him. She was clinging to him as if her life depended on it.

Smart woman.

Though he knew she had a firm grip, he was tense when the rain became a downpour, making visibility almost zero. It took all of his focus to keep them soundly planted on the ground.

Still, the risk of keeping her above ground far outweighed the risk of the ride.

It took an hour to get to their destination, a specific mountain which hid an underground cavern. Mason pulled to a stop and killed the motor. The rain had slowed to a light drizzle, giving them a slight reprieve from the onslaught of the prior downpour.

Pulling off his helmet, Mason felt Holly doing the same behind him before she slipped off the bike. "Where are we?" she asked with heaviness in her voice.

Mason climbed off the bike and turned to face her, only to find her hair plastered to the side of her face and what makeup she still had on smudged into dark circles under her eyes. Still, she looked adorable to him.

He handed her his helmet. "Take this so I can push the bike and I'll show you."

One side of the mountain was covered in trees, which hid a secret cavern door. It actually looked as if it was part of the mountain. It was a technology few knew existed, compliments of an Area 51 project years before. Mason pushed a button on the side of one of the trees, making the entrance open.

"Amazing," Holly said in awe. He looked at her, seeing the scientist at work even in the midst of her fatigue. Her mind didn't reject things she didn't understand. Instead, it seemed to absorb and analyze.

He motioned for her to follow. Rolling the bike through the door, he positioned it next to the three other motorcycles he kept near the doorway.

Holly placed the helmets on a rack holding several others. "I see you have quite the collection," she said noting the other bikes.

He shrugged. "I like to be prepared."

Holly shivered, hugging herself. "Too bad prepared doesn't include a hot bath."

He motioned toward the cavern. "I told you, ask and you shall receive."

"You better not be joking, because I really am not in the mood for your sudden run on humor."

He flicked her a curious glance. "Humor?"

She rolled her eyes. "Nothing. Just take me to the bathtub."

In silence, Mason led her into the cave, not stopping until they were deep into the center. He punched another hidden button, opening a panel in the floor. He nodded toward a ladder connected to the cavern wall. "Follow me down."

Once Mason was on the next level, he waited on Holly. As soon as she cleared the opening, he punched a button and closed the door. He felt safer knowing they were sealed beneath the surface. When she was close enough for him to reach her, he settled his hands on her waist to guide her to the floor.

"What is this place?" Holly asked, looking around at the small, bare cavern. "It's small." She swallowed. "Did I mention I'm claustrophobic?"

Mason grinned. "You are?"

Grimacing, she said, "Apparently, because I don't like this at all."

Mason chuckled. Never had a woman made him laugh so much. Again, he marveled at how amazing it was, what she did to him. She lifted his darkness, opening him up to feelings and responses he wouldn't have had before.

He smiled at her. "It gets better, I promise."

He turned to a panel of buttons and punched in a series of codes, making the wall slide open, displaying an elevator.

"Good grief," she muttered, following him onto the elevator. "What kind of maze is this?"

The corners of his lips hinted at a smile. "One very hard to break into."

She swallowed and nodded, her expression showing understanding. When the elevator doors opened, Mason grabbed her hand. "Come."

Right now all Mason wanted to do was wrap Holly up in his arms and make love to her. He'd spent the entire drive thinking about her. About them. Holly made him feel whole again. If he knew he wouldn't turn into some kind of monster, he would relish the bond between them.

Regardless of the long-term, at this moment he needed her. He wasn't sure he was strong enough to walk away from her. Not now, and possibly not ever.

Chapter Thirteen

Holly stepped out of the elevator and could hardly believe her eyes. She now stood in a fully furnished living room, complete with a plush brown sofa and matching chairs, a huge rock fireplace, well-placed pictures, end tables and even several lamps. She stood there, taking in the vision before her in stunned silence.

It was like stepping into some sort of story world.

They couldn't be in a cave, beneath the earth, and have such a normal setting. Could they?

It was nothing short of amazing. "How can all of this be down here?"

Mason's hands settled on her shoulders, as he stepped behind her. His hands moved up and down her chilled skin, warming her, comforting her, making her feel an odd calmness as she took in the strange surroundings. His lips brushed her ear, as tender as anything she had ever felt in her life. He spoke near her ear, his voice a strong force despite its hushed tone.

"It's a government safe house. In the past, places like this were set up and used for high-level officials during national threats. Now, all Black Knights live like this to protect them from the Arions. The walls are fortified concrete and steel."

"Amazing," she murmured. Her eyes moved to a glass door in the corner. Computers, wires and cables were telltale signs that it was a place of importance. "What's that room?"

"Surveillance area," he said. "I can see above the surface, including the cabin. Anywhere I have equipment set up."

"Amazing," she said again, because it seemed fitting. What other word described all that she had suddenly found herself faced with?

Mason made a sound of agreement. "Actually, a lot of this technology has been used for many years. There have just been improvements made as our know-how increased. Now, unlike in the past, it's almost impossible to find these caverns from the surface.

"Yes," Holly said. "The entrance was invisible."

He continued, moving so he faced her, his hands on her waist. "We have all the luxuries of a normal home. So..." he smiled, "how about that hot bath?"

Holly slid her hands over his. "A bath would be wonderful. Please."

Mason took one of her hands in his, drawing it to his mouth. He brushed his lips across her knuckles, gentle and tender, like a caress promising tantalizing possibilities.

Things she wanted and needed.

When he raised his mouth, his thumb found her palm, stroking lightly, sending waves of warmth up her arm.

"A bath it is, then," he said softly, still holding her gaze.

Oh, those eyes of his... Sometimes Holly felt as if she could get lost in those dark pools of temptation. They literally smoldered with an unspoken message. One her body echoed with a resounding "yes".

"This way." He stepped forward, holding her hand as he led her forward. Pulling her so she was side by side with him, he said, "Each room is connected tunnel-style. You have to walk through the living room, to the bedroom, to the kitchen."

Holly wasn't thinking about her surroundings any longer. She was watching Mason, so drawn to him she couldn't pull her eyes away. Wet clothes clung to his muscular frame, making a delicious vision too enthralling to ignore.

Just looking at him had her wanting.

Moments later, they stood in the bathroom, his hand still holding hers as he turned to face her. She was under a spell of sorts...his spell.

At least, it felt that way.

She hardly even remembered walking to the bathroom. Her eyes ran the length of his body. She could feel the heat he generated, even with inches between their bodies.

Desire washed over her like a tidal wave.

Their eyes locked and held. His were dark, sensual and, oh, so sexy. He knew what she was feeling. She saw it in those deep, dark eyes. The tension, not wholly sexual but definitively intense, laced the silence with possibilities.

She wanted to touch him with her hands, mouth and body. To feel his hardness against her softness. She loved how big and broad he was. His strength and power, both mental and physical, really did things to her.

This newfound sexual side of her personality was something unexpected and, thanks to Mason, quite fulfilling.

Forcing herself to look around the room, she was surprised to find a large garden tub against the far wall. Mason stepped toward her, his hands sliding to her waist and then running up and down her ribs. His touch sent a shiver racing down her spine and made her fall deeper into the warmth of passion.

Here she was, alone with the most amazing, sinfully sexy man she had ever known and it felt amazing. His hands kept moving, slowly, tantalizingly near the underside of her breasts. Her nipples tingled even as her thighs rushed with sensation.

He stepped even closer, bringing them thigh to thigh.

Yes, was all she could think as her hand went to the back of one of those strong legs of his, absorbing the feel of rippling muscle beneath the wet denim of his jeans.

She wanted this.

She wanted him.

The day had been nothing shy of severe in its impact on her future. Yet, all she had been faced with, the fear and confusion, the complete upheaval of her roots, didn't compare to the enormity of her need right now.

For Mason.

"You're so damn beautiful." His voice was husky and heavy, as if he too was lost in the moment. The raw need she felt in not just his words, but in his very presence, made her eyes fly to his face.

And she saw, in his eyes, answering emotions to her own; a mirror image of her own desire, her vast need for him, was there for her viewing.

He felt it too, what she felt, this feeling threatening to consume. He didn't try to hide it. It smoldered in his eyes like a raging fire threatening to consume her in its building flame.

The way he looked at her, as if he could loose his iron control over her, made her feel a surge of extra warmth. Never, ever, had anyone made her feel so female, both in and out of bed, as she did at that moment.

Because of Mason.

Maybe it was his protectiveness or perhaps his gentleness. Or maybe it was just the heat between them. The pure, hot desire that burned every moment they were together. She wasn't sure. But she liked whatever it was.

Thoughts raced through her mind as she felt the power of their connection, replaying all she knew of him and even of herself. Everything about Mason made her feel what she felt, not just one thing. It wasn't just physical. There was a bond, a reality beyond the physical.

She liked the way he wanted to take care of her, his strength and pride and pure maleness. It was crazy because she liked her independence. Still, Mason made her wonder how well she really knew herself. Maybe there were things she wanted all along and had ignored.

She touched his jaw, gently running her fingers back and forth. "I still can't believe what you did back there at the restaurant."

His reaction surprised her. His hands tensed at her waist as a tortured look flashed across his face. "They would have killed you, Holly. I had to act." His voice was etched with torment.

Holly realized he had mistaken her comment. She cupped his cheek with her hand. "Of course you did! You were amazing." She smiled as her voice softened. "My hero." Her fingers traced the round sensuality of his bottom lip. "You saved my life."

He swallowed so hard she saw his throat move. As if the feelings were her own, she felt emotion wash over him, painful and alive.

His voice was strained, tense. "Don't make me into some kind of hero. I'm not."

Pushing to her tiptoes, she brushed her lips across his. "You're *my* hero."

"Holly," he said, with a barely contained shakiness in his voice. "You have no idea what I am."

"Yes, I do," she insisted, meaning it. "You're a soldier." Her hand moved to his chest, over his heart. "You're also a good man." She smiled tenderly. "An amazingly sexy, good man, able to drive me to complete distraction when no one else ever has."

His expression didn't ease, remaining tense and worried. "You don't under —"

Holly kissed him, pressing her lips against his and swallowing his words before flicking her tongue between his teeth for the briefest of moments.

With a low growl that sounded almost strangled, Mason slid his arms around her back, molding her to his body. She melted into him, wrapping her arms around his neck, feeling as if her body was having a craving satisfied.

And perhaps it was.

She almost felt as if his touch, his nearness, was a need rather than a want. Though, lord only knew, she wanted.

His lips brushed hers, gently, back and forth, tracing them with his own but not actually kissing her. It was more like he was savoring the feel of her mouth against his, lips brushing lips.

It was highly sensual yet incredibly tender.

He whispered against her lips. Close. Intimate.

Tormented.

"Holly—"

She didn't want him to feel what he was feeling. What he was, he simply was. She accepted his differences from herself and others.

Even embraced them.

Her father had taught her that opening your mind to the new and unusual was what made you better and stronger.

If they came together to embrace their differences, she truly felt those very things could allow them to be so much more as a couple and as individuals. There was something unique between them. It felt like a union of sorts, linking their uniqueness and lending higher strengths in each. She felt it.

The word soul mate came to mind.

If you could truly have one, Mason was hers.

She knew him beyond the days they had been together. It could be an hour, a day or a year since the day she met him. It didn't matter.

This thing between them, whatever it was, extended beyond time. There was nothing scientific about her feelings for Mason but she had learned to trust her instincts.

She belonged here, with him. Her heart knew it. Apparently, her body did as well. He called to her on so many levels.

She pulled back from their embrace just enough to see his face clearly, pressing her hands against his chest, looking at him with her heart displayed in her eyes. She wanted him to see the truth, to know the reality of her feelings.

"I want you, Mason," she whispered urgently. "You and no one else. I know you're a fighter. I'm not going to suddenly decide I can't deal with who or what you are. I promise."

He stared at her, his eyes searching her features, probing and still haunted in some way. She had the oddest feeling, as if he reached beyond her mind, to her inner self, seeking.

He made a noise, something primitive and wanting, as his hand wrapped around her neck. He pulled her mouth to his, claiming it with an urgency she completely understood all too well.

She felt it too.

The instant his tongue touched hers, she moaned, feeling a rush of desire well inside. She clung to him, kissing him back with fervent need of her own.

He needed.

She needed.

The combination was potent, raw and almost breathtaking.

His hands slid down her waist to her bottom, cupping it, squeezing, and then pulling her tight against his body. She felt his arousal press against her, making her ache all the more. In her mind, she whispered *yes*. Knowing he wanted her felt good, right and exciting.

"See what you do to me," he said as he pressed his mouth to the sensitive spot behind her ear and then nipped at her lobe with his teeth.

"Thank goodness," she half-whispered. "I wouldn't want to feel like this by myself."

Mason laughed, soft and sexy, before pressing his lips to her neck. She loved feeling some of his tension slip away. Hearing him laugh felt good.

His words were serious though, his laughter gone quickly. "You make me feel all kinds of things I didn't think I still had in me."

Holly looked at him then, a hint of vulnerability in her eyes. "I do?" she asked, wanting to know he felt as overwhelmed by her as she did by him. She thought he did but hearing it, well, hearing it just felt better.

"Mmm," he said, scraping his teeth on her bottom lip. "And hotter than I have ever been for a woman."

Holly smiled at that. She wanted him hot. Her hands slipped under his shirt, palms pressing against the roped muscles of his abdomen. She loved the hardness of his body, so male.

"You make me bold and needy in ways I never felt before. Like now," she added. "I really want you to take this wet shirt off. I want to see you."

He didn't argue, tugging his shirt over his head with one hand and flinging it to the floor. Holly ran her hands down his shoulders, letting her eyes soak in his perfection.

"I love your body," she said as her eyes met his.

His returned gaze was frankly sexual. A slow, rather wicked smile slipped onto his lips. Whatever he planned to say or do, and judging from the look in his eyes he had something in mind, she didn't give him time.

She kissed his chest, small kisses, feathering them all over his warm flesh. Her tongue dipped here and there. Her teeth scraped. Her senses simmered with each and every moment. He smelled like spicy male in a way that made her nipples tingle and her body heat. She had never experienced anything like it. His smell absolutely turned her on.

And his taste.

There was a hint of saltiness but the flavor was pure addiction. The way everything about him could impact her on such an extreme level was like nothing Holly had ever experienced before.

Mason stood there, seemingly calm, but she knew better. His heartbeat pounded furiously in his throat, drawing her eyes and giving away the nature of his reaction to what was happening between them.

Which was what? She didn't know but she wanted it. Wanted him. Wanted what they were together.

He was a man of control and now, with her taking the lead, she sensed he was struggling to remain composed. On some deep level, she knew he battled with a desire to take control rather than give it to her.

And she took his willingness to fight his own internal battle for her as something special.

His breathing was another sign he wasn't unaffected. It caught in his throat as she scraped his nipple with her teeth. She smiled against his skin, flicking her tongue against the now hard nipple.

She liked being in control.

She wanted more.

She kissed downward, slowing lowering herself to her knees. His fingers touched her hair as she ran her hands down his jean-clad legs. Looking up at him she said, "We should really get you out of these wet clothes."

Her fingers went to the buttons on his jeans and made quick work of freeing them. Gaze dropping she found the trail of sexy, dark hair from his waistband to his navel. And then her tongue followed.

"Holly, come here." His voice was husky and laden with desire.

She looked up at him as her hands went to the buttons on his jeans. "No," she said defiantly. "I want to touch you."

He grabbed her hands. "You can. I want you to touch me but, right now, you need to get undressed before you catch cold."

She thought about his request for a long moment and came to a conclusion — it was his way of trying to take control again – consciously or not.

This time, control was hers.

She'd comply with his request, but on her terms and because she wanted to be skin to skin with him.

She leaned back on her heels and peeled off her T-shirt and, before he could respond, her bra.

With a low growl, he hauled her to her feet, covering her mouth with his own, his palms cupping her breasts, his fingers teasing her nipples.

So much for control.

She was putty in his warm hands, as they played across her waterlogged skin. Something about Mason's touch reached inside her, made her feel as if she was floating in a cloud of passion and emotion.

His tongue wildly delved into her mouth, primitive and demanding. She clung to his shoulders as he kissed her eyelids, her cheeks and her neck. Her head fell backwards as her desire began to control her body, making her feel as if she couldn't stand. As if he read her mind, his arm wrapped around her waist, holding her up, a strong force of power, control and comfort all in one.

Yet he didn't hesitate in his actions.

He continued his assault, tearing down her willpower, awakening each and every one of her senses, kissing and touching her like there was no tomorrow.

She murmured his name, wanting more — no, needing it. Her hands went to his pants again, fumbling in her efforts but needing to feel his skin against her own.

Her progress was halted as he scooped her up in his arms.

Chapter Fourteen

Kissing her as he walked, she hardly knew where she was until she felt her body being lowered. He gently placed her on the bed, a soft comforter absorbing her naked back while the hard perfection of his body slid down on top of her.

Spreading her legs without thought, she felt the sweet comfort of his body settling between her thighs, easing her ache in some ways while igniting it in others.

Resting his weight on his elbows, he stared down at her, his eyes dark and passion-filled. But there was more to his look than simple desire. Something stronger, more intense, played in his gaze, making her breath catch in her throat, and a strange flutter moved in her stomach.

Mason touched her cheek and whispered her name. His tenderness amazed Holly. For such a big man, he was so careful, so gentle with her. She actually felt as if she could feel his mind and body reaching for her own.

It was a rush, a powerful, yet strangely soothing, feeling.

The air was literally charged with some strange connection between them. Nothing else mattered. Not the past, not the future, not the government's super soldiers.

Nothing else mattered but them, now, together.

His index finger and thumb moved through a strand of her hair as he lowered his head, slowly moving his mouth toward her.

Ever so lightly, he brushed his lips across hers. Her eyes drifted shut as the impact of his touch, though light as a feather, raced through her body. A small sound escaped her lips at the contact, floating into his mouth, which lingered above hers, so near, yet not touching her own.

She swallowed, trying to catch her breath and gain her balance. This was a bit overwhelming, feeling so much, on so many levels.

Her eyes slowly opened, locking with his. So real was the connection she felt to him as she stared into his gaze, it was as if he was reaching inside her very soul and filling her with himself.

Suddenly, his hands were in her hair and his mouth closed down on hers, tasting her, once, twice, nipping her bottom lip. A slight flicker of his tongue touched her lip and then her teeth. Finally his tongue met hers in a slow, sultry brush that sent a wave of heat racing through her veins.

His tongue played along hers, sampling, teasing, pushing her into a deeper mode of passion. It was as if he was making love to her with his mouth, reaching out to her with his loneliness and asking her to accept him and want him.

Oh, and she did.

She replied with a tender caress of her fingers down his cheek, a soft purr into his mouth, a gentle prodding of her tongue. Acceptance was automatic. She loved Mason. Some might say it was crazy. She hardly knew him. But she knew he was the man she was destined to love.

She'd been waiting a lifetime.

For him.

For what they were together.

He took his time, kissing her as if he could do it for a lifetime, making her wet with the ache to have him inside her, so near and part of her. She clung to him, kissing him back, pressing her body into his.

He murmured her name, rolling them to their sides, face-to-face, placing small, hungry kisses on her even then. Her leg slid up over his hip as she snuggled close to his body, wrapping her arm around his back. His hand went to her cheek. His half-lidded eyes met hers, dark as night, alluring and mysterious.

There was scrutiny in his gaze, as if he wanted to confirm what he had felt in her touch and in her kisses. "There is something about you, Holly Heart."

A soft smile filled her face as her hand covered his. "I think there is something about us, Mason."

He kissed her then, his mouth hot and demanding as his tongue probed and played against her own. A fiery inferno of demand rushed through her insides. She clung to him, pressing close, feeling her nipples press into the hair on his chest as their skin melted together.

His hand slid up her back, molding her yet closer and closer. Her need was like his need, meshing together like one flame. "Too many clothes," she whispered against his lips.

"Yes," he murmured almost instantly, nipping at her lip and then running his tongue across it. "Let's get rid of them."

She nodded and made a sound of agreement. A quick, urgent kiss later, they both sat up and began removing first their shoes and then their pants.

When they were both completely naked, they turned to one another. For an instant, their eyes locked, their connection a scorching melting of their two gazes.

Holly wasn't sure who moved first but, side by side, they came back together, skin against skin, her thigh over his hip. Their mouths came within inches of each other's.

"Do you have any idea how much I want you?" he asked in a husky tone as their breathing mingled in and out, causing her nipples to tingle in the strangest way, as if he had touched her there.

"I want you, too," she replied in a barely audible voice. His erection pressed between her thighs. She needed him inside her. "Please. Now."

The tip of his erection slid against her wetness, teasing her, making her hips move to try and get to him. But he wouldn't let her. Instead, he took himself in his hand and slowly moved the tip up and down and all around her sensitive outer skin, making her moan and burn for what she didn't have.

Him inside her.

She couldn't take anymore. Her hand went to his, her lips against his. "Now, Mason. No more teasing."

Her hips arched and, before he could stop her, she pressed him inside, taking him, as they moaned together. Sliding down his length, her arms wrapped around him, hugging him tighter, to take him deeper.

"Mason," she whispered, not sure if it was in her head or out loud. Not caring. They kissed frantically, passionately, their bodies moving in a steady, growing pace.

His hand caressed her breasts.

Her hand stroked his back.

Their bodies pressed together.

And when the passion was so high she couldn't think, she could only cry out, she shattered. Her eyes squeezed shut as his body moved inside her, making each spasm seem more intense.

She knew when he joined her, over the edge, into the fire.

He shuddered and moaned and called her name.

Sated and exhausted, she clung to him, not wanting to let go.

* * * * *

Asleep, her long blonde hair spread like silky gold on the pillow, she snuggled deeper into the pillow and sighed. A smile on his lips, Mason gently pulled the blanket down to view the creamy white perfection of her naked body.

He ran his finger down her back and over the curve of her round, pert butt. She made a soft sound but didn't wake. Their lovemaking had been dynamic and lengthy. Each time he thought he was sated, he wanted her again. And again. Like now. He was hard just looking at her.

As much as he knew he should leave her alone, he wasn't sure he could. She was his mate. The need to see the confirmation was ripe. The proof that couldn't be disputed, the Arion star. Gently he moved his hand to her hair, brushing it aside to expose her neck.

He sucked in a breath. There, on the back of her neck, was the Arion star. His mark. Seeing the proof evoked powerful feelings of possessiveness, desire and other things he was afraid to examine too closely.

The need to be inside her, to take her, right then and there, was like a raging flame.

He moved between her legs, kissing the star as he pressed his body against hers. His mouth and hands were greedy, touching and tasting.

Slipping his hands beneath her he cupped her breast, tweaking her nipples with his fingers as he dipped his tongue into her ear.

Holly moaned, arching her soft curves against him. "Mason." It was but a whisper, but it was heavy with passion, making him hotter and wilder.

"Open for me, Angel. Let me in," he said hoarsely, nudging her thighs further apart and using his hands to pull her hips up for better access.

He slid his fingers between her legs. "Nice and wet," he said with satisfaction as he spread the silky proof of her arousal, caressing her sensitive flesh. Gently—but not too much—he pressed two fingers inside her, making her gasp and then sigh.

"I want inside you," he said, moving his throbbing dick to press against her swollen flesh, teasing them both as he wet the tip with her fluid.

"Now, Mason. Now," Holly demanded.

He didn't need more encouragement, sinking into her with a deep thrust that reached her core. He pushed until his hips framed her round bottom. Pulling her hips up further, he moved in yet deeper, surging in and out of her with slow, even motions.

Knowing Holly was his other half.

With each move, each touch and taste, his need grew well beyond the physical. Together they rode the wave of passion and, when he spilled himself inside her, he felt a rush of belonging.

And fulfillment.

He lay on top of her for long moments before rolling onto his side and pulling her tight, spoon style, against his body.

Holding her like he would never let her go.

Because it felt as if his life depended on it.

Chapter Fifteen

A loud noise startled both Mason and Holly from a deep sleep. Mason was out of the bed before Holly could even blink.

It sounded like a horn was going off. "What is it?" Holly asked, shaking her head lightly.

He was already pulling a pair of jeans from the closet. "Breach alarm. Get up and get dressed."

Holly's eyes went wide. "I thought it was safe here."

"It is," he said, jabbing one leg and then the other into his pants. Not bothering to button them, he headed toward a door Holly had thought was a closet and disappeared inside. Seconds later the alarm went off.

"Shit," he muttered, from inside the room.

"What?" she called, desperately kicking at the covers, getting her legs twisted and panicking, kicking harder and faster. Finally, she stood naked by the bed. She had no clothes to put on. Hers were wet and dirty. Indecision lasted a few seconds before she darted to the closet, yanking a shirt off the hanger. The black T-shirt she chose went to her knees and looked more like a dress.

Mason walked out of the other room with not one, but two guns in his hands. His expression was dark and intense, his body thrumming with battle readiness. He looked like some kind of ancient warrior, shirtless, shoeless and rippling with muscles.

"Stay here," he ordered in a clipped tone.

Her voice was urgent. "What's going on?"

Her answer was a glimpse of his broad shoulders as he disappeared from the bedroom into the living room.

* * * * *

Mason didn't know what in the hell was going on but he didn't like it. He held both guns to the elevator door as it opened. Though a gun wasn't about to kill an Arion, it would sure as hell slow one down.

The doors opened to show Sterling and Michael.

Sterling's hand went up, stop sign fashion, the instant the door opened. "Wow! Wait, man, Michael's with us!"

"He's Arion," Mason said harshly. "He's not with us unless…maybe you're like him now and he is with you?"

Michael stepped forward, fixing Mason in a hard stare while ignoring the guns. "He's not the one like me. You are and we both know it."

Mason laughed bitterly, fighting the wave of apprehension Michael's words evoked. "I am not like you." Without breaking eye contact with Michael, Mason spoke to Sterling. "What in the hell are you trying to prove bringing him here?"

"Michael can help us," Sterling said, stepping off the elevator. "He's not like the others, man, I swear. Put down the guns and hear him out."

"This is crazy, man. You're a fool," Mason spat back at Sterling.

"No," Sterling countered. "You are if you don't listen."

Something in Sterling's tone, combined with Michael's calm, watchful gaze, made Mason reconsider. Slowly, he lowered one gun. "Give me one reason to trust you," Mason said to Michael.

There was no hesitation in Michael's response. "You trust Sterling and he trusts me. If that is not enough, consider this. I'm alone. As you know, Arions never travel alone when going to battle."

Sterling added, "He's here to help. If I wasn't certain, I would never bring him here."

It was true, Mason trusted Sterling. He let the other gun drop to his side. "Talk," he spat at Michael.

"Why don't we sit down?" Sterling said, not waiting for an answer as he stepped past Mason toward the couch.

Mason and Michael stood face-to-face for long moments. "I can help you, Mason," Michael said in a low voice, meant only for his ears.

Mason stared at Michael. He said he was like him. Was he? With a curt nod of his chin, he motioned the Arion forward. He wasn't about to turn his back on him.

Michael walked past Mason, moving to sit on the couch where Sterling sat. Mason buttoned his pants and then inserted the guns in his waistband. Then he sat down in a chair directly across from Michael.

"Mason?"

Holly stood in the doorway to the bedroom, wearing only a shirt and looking worried. Surging to his feet, Mason started toward her.

"She is your mate," Michael said as if simply acknowledging a fact.

Everyone looked at Mason. "What?" Holly asked, confused. Mason shot Michael a go-to-hell look and covered the distance between him and Holly.

He had every intention of telling her about the Arion connection they shared. On his terms. Not like this. He turned her toward the bedroom, stepping inside with her and shutting the door behind him.

"Everything is fine, Angel," he reassured her, slipping his hands to her slim waist. "Please stay in here so I know you're safe."

Holly frowned. "I thought you said everything was fine."

He hesitated. "It is." He ran a hand through his hair. "I mean, it will be soon. The man with Sterling could be a threat. Give me time to sort it out, okay?"

Holly's eyes were wide with confusion and a hint of fear. "What did he mean... I'm your mate?"

He held his expression in check. Reaching out, he trailed his finger down her cheek. "Clearly we have a connection. It is easy for people who are perceptive to see what others might not." But there was more he didn't say and they both knew it.

Before she could respond he said, "Stay here. Please. Just until I make sure there is no danger."

Holly nodded. He could see from the look in her eyes it was killing her to bite back the questions she wanted answered.

Mason framed her face with his hands. "You make my T-shirt look damn sexy, woman." He kissed her forehead. "I'll be back in a few minutes to prove it."

He released her then and turned to the door. With his hand on the knob he looked at her over his shoulder. "Don't be running around like that in front of other men." Then he winked. His intention was to make her feel less apprehensive.

If only someone would do the same for him.

* * * * *

Mason stepped back into the living room, pulling the door shut behind him. Sterling was looking at him with an obvious question in his eyes.

Even though he knew the question, he said, "What?" It was easier than answering. He couldn't keep the irritation out of his voice.

"Does she know?" Sterling asked as Mason sat back down in the chair.

Elbows on his knees, Mason pressed two fingers to his eyes. "No. I planned to tell her." Then he opened his eyes, fixing Michael in his gaze. "In my own way."

"I responded out of surprise," Michael stated though he didn't apologize. "There is only one mate for an Arion. For you to find her is a blessing."

"I doubt she'll see it that way," Mason said with a grim tone. "Besides, I am still coming to terms with the whole thing myself. I don't see how it is possible that I have enough Arion in me to mate."

"Of course she will," Michael said, referencing Holly's response to their mating. His tone was reassuring. It was the last thing Mason expected from an Arion. "She loves you."

Mason found his guard easing with Michael. His senses told him Michael was indeed an ally. "We are offtrack. Cut to the chase. Why are you here?"

Michael went on as if Mason hadn't spoken, answering his previous question. "You are as Arion as I am, Mason. That's the answer to how you can mate."

He wanted to deny it. "I can't do the things you can do."

"Yes," Michael stated. "You can."

Sterling added, "Michael says you don't know how to harness the skills. He can teach you."

"Why would I want that?" Mason demanded.

A muscle in Michael's jaw jumped. "Because you are the only one who can defeat your brother. He tampered with your injections. He wanted a ruling bloodline. He thought being Arion would be enough. But it's not. Arions aren't evil. It's one's soul that is or isn't black."

Mason stood up, rubbing the back of his neck where tension had built. "This is not happening."

"We have to stop him, Mason. There are other Arions who are against him. I have a team of people ready to help. You alone can defeat David, blood to blood. You have to kill your brother."

"I thought your brother was dead."

Mason froze. Shit. Not now. He wasn't prepared to deal with Holly. He whirled to face her. She now wore his robe, sleeves rolled up, and it was still huge on her. "I told you to wait in the bedroom."

Her eyes flashed. "I don't take orders well." Then, "I thought your brother was dead."

"He is," he replied flatly and then brusquely added, "To me."

Mason averted his gaze, not able to stomach the look he knew he would see in her eyes. He hadn't been completely honest with her. How could he tell her his brother was Arion? Hell, that he was Arion. It killed him to think of her rejection.

A long, pregnant silence filled the room. Finally, Holly said, "Sterling, is there any word on Roger?"

Sterling's eyes went to Mason's and held. He took his time answering, searching Mason's expression before speaking. "Michael here," he said, motioning with his head, "knows about Roger and the abducted woman from the news."

Holly's eyes narrowed marginally on Michael. "Is he...is he dead?"

Michael gave Holly a direct look. He never minced words. "The last I heard he was alive, yes, but that doesn't mean he is now."

Holly tilted her head to the side as she continued looking at Michael. "Your eyes, they're black, like Mason's and Sterling's. Are you a Black Knight as well?"

Mason and Michael locked gazes. One of Michael's brows inched up in silent challenge. "I was," Michael responded to Holly but continued looking at Mason.

Her voice held a hint of trepidation. "And now?"

Mason swallowed as he forced his gaze to Holly's, praying he was able to hide the anguish in his eyes. "Holly, I've asked you to wait for me in the bedroom."

Her chin tilted up defiantly. "I'm not a child to be sent to her room."

Michael stood. "You two need to talk. I'll wait." His simple statement held a deeper meaning, which Mason quickly understood. He had to deal with Holly before he could focus on the other issues.

Sterling stood as well. "We'll wait in the security booth."

"No," Mason said in a sharp, but low, voice. "We'll talk now. Holly *will* wait in the bedroom." His eyes locked with Holly's. She glared at him, fists clenched at her sides, and then, with a disgusted snort, turned and disappeared into the bedroom.

The door slammed behind her.

A pregnant silence followed.

"Well?" Mason said to the two men. "Speak up. Obviously, there is still much to discuss."

Sterling fixed Mason in his gaze. "She's a strong woman. She'll understand."

"And you need her right now," Michael added. "Together you will be stronger."

Mason wasn't so sure Holly would understand. The only thing he was certain of at the moment was his need to figure out what in the hell Michael was all about. He couldn't deal with Holly until he knew the whole big picture of matters and what risk it might subject her to.

Quietly, Mason said, "Make me understand how I can possibly be Arion."

Mason sat on the couch with Sterling by his side, silently absorbing the details Michael relayed about the Arions and his own connection to them.

Michael's gaze settled on Mason's features as he concluded his story. "You are the key to fighting your brother. There are plenty ready to follow you. Now, you must decide if you are willing to rise to the challenge."

Mason's gaze sharpened for a fraction of a second. "Our government is what needs to be followed, not me."

Michael gave him a hard look. "The corruption is deep, Mason. Our country has Arions deep in its core."

Mason stared at him in surprise, a horrible feeling of dread filling his heart. Things were much worse than he had expected. "Since when?"

"Power feeds deceit," Michael said with grimness to his tone. "Almost from the beginning of the Arions' escape, there has been corruption at the top of government ranks. We need a leader who offers hope." Michael paused. "*You* are that hope."

Mason ran his hand across the back of his neck where tension was quickly building. "I would think my family ties to David would be a negative."

"Quite the opposite," Michael assured him. "If you, as his brother, will stand and fight, so will others."

"Mason," Sterling said quietly. "You can do this. I know you can."

Mason leaned forward, resting his elbows on his knees as he let his head drop between his shoulders. It was so much to digest and think about. He needed time to think.

When it was evident Mason wasn't going to speak, Michael said, "There are several critical issues we need to address as quickly as possible."

Sterling added, "The Arions are responsible for having abducted the women the news has been talking about."

Mason's head raised. "They're trying to breed?"

Michael nodded. "Most definitely. Cloning will follow. They are searching for a team of people who can make it happen."

"What?" Mason said, blinking. "Breeding isn't fast enough for them?"

"That's part of it but it's even more complex than timelines. Recently, it was discovered that Arions can only breed once they mate," Michael explained. "This gives them few options, since mating is so rare. Without a female with the perfect chemistry, an Arion simply cannot reproduce. They must find their mates to breed."

"Clearly humans can mate with Arions. Mason is an example of this," Sterling added.

"They're crazy if they think to abduct women and find Arion mates for them. It'll turn into some kind of sex camp."

Michael sighed heavily. "No doubt they will become a party to some not very nice things. They will be kept in hopes of a later match, while being used in artificial insemination experiments."

Mason scrubbed his jaw. "Jesus, this is crazy."

Sterling nodded. "We have to rescue them."

"Yes," Mason agreed, "but we can't afford to send them back to their homes. We can't have them spreading their stories. What in the hell are we going to do with them?"

"They won't talk," Michael said. "Arions have the power to wipe out memories." In a lower voice, he added, "There is much for you to learn."

"Apparently," he said tersely.

"We need you to lead this fight, Mason." Michael spoke with conviction, his eyes probing Mason's.

Mason ran his hand through his hair, pushing to his feet and walking toward the fireplace. He gave the two men his back as he responded. "This is a lot to digest. I need time to think."

"There's little time for consideration. We must act," Michael insisted, urgency to his tone.

Mason turned, sharpness to his movement. "I'm aware of this." He needed time to deal with Holly, amongst other things. "Once I become familiar with my skills, how are you so certain I won't follow my brother?"

No hesitation. "You won't. You're a good man, Mason. David isn't. I hate saying that to you because I know it causes you great pain. Your brother draws evil to him. Holly is pure and good. She would know David for the darkness he represents. The fact that you were able to mate with her speaks worlds about who you are."

Holly filled his mind with concern in so many ways. "They had humans try to assassinate her."

"When?" Sterling asked, shifting on the couch to see Mason more clearly.

"On the trip here."

Michael nodded. "They want her one way or the other, either on their team or dead. They believe she can help them continue to make enhancements. There are others they could use for this effort but they believe she is special."

"I was hoping she might be able to study the Arion weaknesses so they could be more easily defeated," Sterling suggested.

"That could be a good and bad thing," Michael added. "Mason and I are Arion, as are many men willing to stand with us. Anything we can use on the Arions can be used on us as well."

"Yes, but there are many, like myself, that need an advantage," Sterling argued.

Mason's lips thinned. "Holly will never help you with combat-related issues."

"Give her a chance by sharing all the facts. She's a smart woman. Surely she will see the need to defeat the Arions."

Mason sighed. "I need some air," he said, shaking his head. "I left Holly's bag at the cabin. I'm going to go get it. When I get back, we can make plans."

"Will you lead us to victory, Mason?" Michael asked.

Mason knew the answer but he needed time to accept it himself. "Ask me when I return."

Sterling and Michael sat watching his retreat. "We must act." Michael's tone was terse.

"He'll come through," Sterling assured him. "The connecting cavern is mine," he said, pushing to his feet. "Perhaps we should clear out and give Mason and Holly some space."

* * * * *

Mason forced himself to take a deep breath as he walked into the bedroom. Holly sat on the end of the bed glaring at him, anger alive in her eyes.

"Don't you ever treat me like that again," she said through clenched teeth.

"You gave me no option," he said moving to a drawer and pulling out socks before retrieving his boots. "I told you to give me a chance to ensure your safety and you came out there anyway."

"But it wasn't about my safety, was it, Mason?" Her voice was raw with bitter challenge. "It was about keeping secrets."

He didn't look at her, couldn't. He walked to the side of the bed, sitting down, giving her his back. "I can't do this right now."

He felt her weight lift from the bed as she stomped around to face him, hands on her hips. "You can and you will! You've turned my life upside down and have the nerve to tell me not now?!" She glowered. "That's a load of crap and apparently so is everything you tell me."

Holly's eyes were accusing and it twisted his insides into knots. "I didn't lie to you, Holly. I spoke the truth as I see it."

Her tone was crisp. "But you knew you left out important details."

What could he say? "Yes," he said tightly. "I guess I did."

"You said your brother was dead." Anger etched her features as she stared at him.

"He's Arion, Holly. How was I supposed to tell you something like that? Besides," he bit out tightly. "He is dead to me."

"You should have been honest," she said in a voice that trembled. "What did you mean when you said Michael is like you?"

Mason tried to find the words to tell her he, like Michael, was Arion but they just wouldn't form. Abruptly, Holly turned on her heel and marched into the bathroom.

Two hands dashed through his hair in an act of utter frustration. His mind raced with options. Resolutely, he stepped forward. He had to make this right.

Holly was standing with her back to him, her shoulders slightly hunched over, arms wrapped tightly around her. When his hands settled on her shoulders she didn't move away. He saw that as a positive but, when she spoke, some of his confidence faltered. "I kidded myself into thinking we had something special. Maybe it's just extreme circumstances and a whole lot of adrenaline."

He squeezed his eyes shut. "God, no, Holly." He slid his hands around her stomach, pulling her against his body, needing to feel her close. "We do have something special."

She turned then, facing him but allowing his hands to remain on her waist. Through their physical connections he felt their soul-deep link. As upset as she was, she didn't move away from him and he knew she felt the link between them despite her anger.

Her voice and her eyes held so much pain it made him ache with guilt. "Then why won't you trust me?"

He averted his gaze momentarily. "It's not about trust. It's...complicated."

"I see." Bitterness etched her tone. She stepped out of his reach, breaking their physical connection. He felt the emptiness instantly. "Too complicated for me, I guess."

He was grasping for the right approach. "Holly," he said in the midst of a breath that was both a plea and a worried sigh.

Before he could find the words to finish his sentence, she said, "If this is all we can be together, two people who can't trust and share together, I don't want any part of it." She tipped her chin up. "I won't do this thing with you and me. Not like this."

He pressed his fingers to his temples. He couldn't tell her now. He needed time to think. "I'm going out for a while," he said before turning away from her and leaving the bathroom. Gathering his clothes, he left the room without another word or look at Holly.

He was having a hard enough time not condemning himself for what he had become. He wouldn't survive seeing the horror of his confession in her eyes. Not now.

Chapter Sixteen

Pushing his motorcycle to stable ground, Mason didn't bother with a helmet. Straddling the bike, he kicked the engine into gear. The rain had cleared, leaving sunshine in its place. He had spent a lot of time underground over the last few years. The feel of the sunshine warming his shoulders felt good. It represented space and freedom, things he didn't feel he would ever completely have again.

Nor would Holly.

How was she going to feel about living underground once she figured out how long-term it would be?

The news Michael had brought with him was hard to digest. Holly was his real concern. She was an amazing woman, a scientist with dreams of making a difference. The last thing she had wanted was to create super soldiers. Instead, she had become linked to one. No, he thought bitterly.

Worse.

An Arion.

He took the rocks and bumps on the tough terrain with reckless force, pushing himself and the bike to the edge, pressing for a release. Knowing he wouldn't find it but trying anyway.

Burning in his mind was the inevitable. He would have to tell Holly the whole story.

Today.

* * * * *

Holly was furious. She paced the bedroom floor with angry steps. It was easier to be mad than to deal with the pain lurking just below her surface, threatening to fog her brain or, worse, make her break down.

She had to get out of here.

She couldn't be trapped like this.

She wouldn't be ordered around like a child.

Thinks, think, think. She paced some more. She stopped. Think!

She paced.

Maybe if she left the state... She stopped walking again, finger on her chin as she thought.

Her parents had left her a small condo in San Francisco. Leaving the state would hide her from the Arions. Wouldn't it? Her teeth found her bottom lip as she tried to decide. She threw her hands up and dropped them again. What option did she really have?

She couldn't stay here knowing Mason wouldn't be honest with her. How could she trust her life to him when she didn't even know what was truth and what was fiction?

She couldn't.

The worst part was...it was quite possible she loved him. Sure, she had only just met him but he made her feel things no other could. But it didn't matter. She couldn't live like this.

Leaving was her only option.

Gathering her still-damp clothes, Holly dressed quickly. Then she moved to the bedroom door, pulling it open slowly as she peeked through the opening. No one in sight.

Tentatively, she stepped into the room, ignoring the growling of her stomach. It had been hours since she'd eaten. Now, heading toward the elevator, she thought of the trip back to the cabin. She'd have to walk. Riding a motorcycle wasn't an option. Breaking her neck simply wasn't appealing.

Mentally she tried to calculate how long it would take her to get to the cabin. It had taken them about an hour on the motorcycle but it had been raining. Two hours at least to walk, she guessed.

Stepping onto the elevator, she blew out a breath. What were the chances Mason would have left the keys in the truck? Maybe there was a set in the cabin. She hoped.

Stepping out of the cave, Holly squinted into the sunlight, covering her brow with her hand. Even her purse was in the truck. If her cell phone wasn't dead she could call a cab. She hoped. Looking at her surroundings, she frowned. Well, once she was back in civilized territory. Even then, could one get a cab out this far in the mountains?

At a different time, under different circumstances, she would have enjoyed the spectacular view of mountain peaks on the horizon and the billowing trees crowning the cave. One of the things she loved about Nevada was being surrounded by such beauty.

But now wasn't the time to take in scenery.

She started walking to the west, hoping and praying she was right about the direction of the cabin.

* * * * *

Mason reached for the truck door when he sensed something was wrong. Holly. She wasn't in the cave. Letting his eyes shut, he reached inside his mind. After a long moment, he cursed as he took off in a jog toward his motorcycle. The stubborn woman was walking in the middle of the mountains. Didn't she know how much danger she was in?

At that very moment he wished he had full use of his Arion skills. David and his kind traveled with the wind, at speeds unheard of by humans. He had to get to Holly before someone else did.

Uneasiness crept over him. Something was not right. She was in danger. He didn't think it was an Arion. But what? Five minutes passed, then ten. Where in the hell was she?

Then he heard her scream, but in his head. Holly was terrified. He felt her in his mind, calling his name. For him to feel her so clearly, she had to be close.

The minute he turned the next corner, he saw her. She stood stiff and still. Sound rolled through the air, not perceivable by human ears, but Mason was Arion. For once in his life, he was glad. There was no mistaking the rattlesnake's dangerous warning.

He jumped off the bike, making the tires skid off into the dirt as it landed on its side. Blessed with Arion grace and speed, Mason was behind Holly in seconds, his footsteps almost soundless.

In his mind, he was thankful he had been above ground. He would never have sensed her danger from the cave. A small whimper escaped Holly's lips but Mason didn't have time to comfort her. Reaching for his belt, he grabbed the round knife of the Black Knights.

It swished through the air with a hiss before plummeting into the snake's neck, chopping off its head. Turning to Holly, he reached for her and she fell into his arms, her body trembling.

"Oh, God," Holly whispered into his shirt.

Mason held her tight. Twice now he had found her in trouble, fearing he would lose her. No way could he let that happen. He loved her. The words came to his mind with certainty but he kept them to himself. "It's okay, Angel. I'm here."

She clutched his shirt, looking up at him, tears streaming down her cheeks. "I thought... If you hadn't... How did you—"

He ran his hand down her hair in a soothing motion. "I seem to have a sixth sense where you're involved."

Her lips trembled. "I just knew it was going to bite me." She let her head drop to his chest.

"But it didn't," he told her, kissing her head.

A muscle in his jaw locked. Seconds later and he would have been too late. He'd witnessed the aftereffects of a few snakebites. Not pretty. She shouldn't have been outside of the cave in the first place.

"Why aren't you in the cave?"

She looked up at him again; her eyes were red, her cheeks streaked. At least she had stopped crying. "I," she paused as if she struggled to find the words or didn't want to speak them, "I...thank you for being here for me."

Not an answer. As much as he wanted to demand a response, he needed to get her back underground. There would be time for explanations later. Gently he ran his thumbs under her eyes, wiping away the dampness.

His hands settled on her neck as he leaned forward and kissed her forehead. "Let's get back to the cave."

Her hands went to his wrists, unshed tears pooling in her eyes. "I can't go back there," she whispered.

He fought the urge to demand yet again. They were out in the open, exposed. "I need to know you're safe, Holly." The words, spoken in a low voice, held steel determination. "The cave is the best way to do so."

"I'll leave the state," she said desperately. "No one will find me."

He felt a pang of anger as reality washed through his mind like a dash of salt in an open wound. She wanted to leave him. And pain. He bit back both emotions. "Yes," he replied firmly, "they will. I can't let you leave."

Holly made a jerky movement, dropping her hands to his waist and trying to shove away from him. He held her with ease. "This isn't fair," she cried.

Mason pulled her close, enfolding her in his arms, giving her comfort he knew she needed. She stilled, not fighting, burying her face in his shirt. Softly, he said, "I know it's not fair but I can't change the cards that have been dealt."

She didn't look up at him. "Please just let me go," she murmured.

For now? Forever? He wasn't clear on her meaning but it didn't matter. His answer was the same. "I can't, Holly." His voice was raw with hard-spoken honesty. "I couldn't bear it if anything happened to you. You mean too much to me."

She wouldn't look at him. "I wish I could believe that," she said softly.

He leaned back, taking her chin between his fingers to force her gaze to his. Her words were like a slap in the face and he needed to see her expression to know if she had meant them. Certainly he had given her reason to doubt him. Still, it wasn't easy to accept.

Searching her eyes, he saw turmoil of his own making. He let out a deep breath and released her chin. He was torn over Holly. He wanted to protect her from the Arions, from him, from anything and anyone who might harm her. On the other hand, he couldn't bear the thought of her not being with him.

He didn't know what to say to her. "We have to get back."

"No," she said, tipping her chin up defiantly.

He was losing patience. Her safety was his first motivation. "This is not up for discussion."

She struggled uselessly against his grip as though she thought she might actually get away this time. He saw it as the desperate act it was, holding her tightly until she got it out of her system.

"You can't just order me around," she said through clenched teeth.

His resolve was ironclad. "Better me than the Arions."

She looked like she might argue but instead said, "I need my bag and purse."

His eyes narrowed suspiciously. "Once I have you safely underground, I'll pick them up."

"I don't want to go back. Let me go!"

"No," he said simply because he wasn't in the mood to play word games.

"Yes!" she ground out angrily, her fists balled at her sides.

A muscle in his jaw jumped. "No, Holly," he said in a soft voice that defied the tension in his body.

Her shoulders slumped with defeat. "I hate this."

"I know."

She stared at him.

"We have to go," he said, releasing her arms and then reaching for her again as he sensed she might bolt. He fixed her in a hard stare. "Running will get you nowhere. Don't doubt my resolve, Holly. If I have to forcefully take you back, I will."

"Ohhh!" she glared at him. "You're a damn monster!"

Mason stiffened. "And you'd best remember that in the future."

He turned on his heels, walking briskly to the motorcycle, fighting his raging emotions. The truth was out. He was a monster. And now he knew how she really felt about him.

He straddled the bike, kick-starting the engine with a roar that didn't half match the one raging in his mind. He maneuvered the bike, stopping in front of Holly. "Get on."

Holly stood, hugging herself, struggling to catch her breath. Mason looked dangerously fierce sitting on the motorcycle. His sandy brown hair blew around his shoulders, his solid body humming with edginess. He looked every bit a formidable warrior.

He wouldn't look at her.

She had hurt him. He seemed so untouchable, yet she felt his disruptive emotions as if they poured into her through her very cells.

He wasn't a monster. Not at all. He was a protector. Far different. Her protector. But not just hers and she knew it. He had made it his life's work to serve others. Oh, how she wished she could call back her words.

Never in her life had she lashed out at someone. Mason confused her. She wanted to be with him, was willing to give up her past, even her future. All she wanted in return was honesty. And love, she added silently.

He revved the engine, turned stone-cold black eyes on her. "Now, Holly."

His tone cut through her like a knife, hard and uncaring. He was hurt, she reminded herself. She slipped her leg over the seat but didn't wrap her arms around him. Somehow, she doubted he wanted her to touch him.

She sensed his frustration as he rotated around, fixing her in a heavy-lidded look. He grabbed one of her hands, turned, grabbed the other and wrapped them around his waist. Holly let her head fall onto his shoulder. She couldn't help it. He felt safe and, even mad at her, comforting and perfect.

God, she loved him. How could she leave him? It didn't take away the sting of his dishonesty. On the other hand, the mistakes he had made with her didn't diminish her love for him.

She had simply been hurt and desperate when she ran from the cave. And stupid.

When they arrived at the cave, Mason started pushing the bike toward the entrance. "I can let myself back in so you can go back to the cabin."

"Not a chance," he said without looking at her.

Holly rolled her eyes but didn't argue. It was useless. They walked through the cave without saying a word to each other. Once they were on the elevator, the silence seemed unbearable, thick and intrusive. "Mason?"

Slowly he turned his attention to her, fixing her in an unreadable stare and letting his brow inch up. The elevator doors opened.

Holly threw her hands up. "Nothing." She stepped off the elevator to find Sterling and Michael in the living room. Sterling, who was pacing, stopped and stared at them. "Where the hell have you two been?"

"To hell and back," Mason grumbled holding the elevator door with his hand. "Don't let her out of your sight. I'm going to the cabin."

Holly shut her eyes, blocking out the emotions that roared inside. Hoping her emotional state wasn't obvious to Michael and Sterling. After several seconds, she opened them, new determination taking over.

Her hands went to her hips as her eyes darted from Sterling to Michael. "I am sick and tired of being left in the dark. What isn't he telling me?"

There was an uncomfortable silence. Michael, looking far from rattled by her demand, said, "What *has* he told you?"

Her lips pursed. "Only that his brother is Arion. Actually, the Arion leader or something of the sort."

"Nothing else?" Michael asked in a cautious tone.

"No, nothing," she said shortly. "I can't go on like this. I need to know what I'm dealing with." She made a face and firmed her jaw. "I have a right to know."

Sterling walked to the couch and sat down, patting the cushion beside him. "Why don't you sit down, Holly."

She sighed. It would be easy to decline. Well, maybe not easy, but tempting. Being bossed around and controlled by these men was getting old. Still, she wanted to know what was going on. When she didn't move immediately Sterling's brow inched up.

The action set Holly off again. "Don't look at me like that. I'll sit if I like." She moved forward. "It just so happens, I like." She spoke the words with more bravado than she felt.

Michael laughed. "You should be quite helpful in achieving our cause. Most would be intimidated. But not you."

Holly sat down, giving Michael a shrewd look in the process. "What cause are we talking about exactly?"

"This is between you and Mason," he responded with a slight twitch of his lips, as if he understood her attempt to draw out information and was amused by it.

She wanted to scream in frustration. "Have I no rights? I have been swept from my home and my life, with little to no explanations. Surely, I deserve to know why."

"You know why," Sterling insisted with a hint of irritation in his tone. "You've seen firsthand the danger you're in."

Holly was speechless for a moment as she replayed the recent events. Her lashes fluttered downward to her hands resting in her lap. Mason had been gravely injured protecting her.

Feeling Michael watching her, she looked up and met his gaze. His scrutiny was intense and a bit unnerving, as if he was looking into her soul.

She flicked a quick look at Sterling. "Yes, I do know the danger I'm in. That's not my point, as I believe you are well aware."

"Holly," Michael said, drawing her attention. "Mason *needs* you. We *need* you. There are big stakes at risk here and you impact them in ways you don't yet understand."

A sudden premonition of danger sent a chill down her spine. She swallowed. "Meaning?"

"Again," he said in a neutral voice, "there are things you and Mason need to discuss. Mason has much to face. Without your support he will not be as strong."

Her first instinct was to question him but she knew he would simply evade answering. Besides, she wanted to be by Mason's side, to help him any way she could. It hurt he wouldn't trust her enough to tell her everything that was going on.

She let out a long sigh and then her thoughts became words as if by their own design. She didn't mean to verbalize her feelings. "If he would only trust me enough to let me help." The words were spoken softly, almost to herself.

"He will," Michael reassured her. "Just give him your patience. He is struggling to accept some things about himself and fears how you will respond when you learn all there is to know. Sometimes it's necessary to come to terms with things in one's own mind before you can speak it out loud."

The words wrapped around her like a blanket and then seeped into her mind, penetrating her hurt and evoking understanding. She looked at Michael, seeing his words as the voice of experience. Knowing he was right.

Perhaps Mason simply needed to know she didn't think he was the monster she had called him.

Perhaps she needed to encourage rather than demand to get her answers.

* * * * *

Mason stepped into the cabin, cursing the need for nourishment as he flipped on the lights. Hearing Holly call him a monster still had his gut in knots yet his body demanded food.

Just another reminder he wasn't normal. Not even close. He kept food at the cabin for just such occasions. Once he had made himself a couple of sandwiches, Mason moved to the sofa and dropped down onto the cushions.

He ate as his mind chased answers. The implications of being Arion wore heavily on him. Even having Michael around was weird as hell. He was a damn Arion.

And so are you, he reminded himself.

It was hard to accept he might somehow hold the key to conquering the Arions. If, indeed, he was the solution, the person who could bring down David, he had no choice but to take on the role of leader. The question was, would Holly stand by his side?

He wanted her to, but of her own free will. He wanted her to accept their pairing without influence. He sighed heavily. No way could he tell her about their mating and have her feel she could choose.

He just hoped she chose him, monster that he was, because he'd already made his choice. He had to have Holly Heart, one way or the other. If the world was depending on him, he needed the comfort and strength she brought him. She was the only salvation he, and maybe the world, had.

* * * * *

Holly stood in the kitchen, surprised at how well-stocked it was. A cook she wasn't but she could manage to whip up some form of food.

The results of her efforts were two huge stacks of sandwiches and a massive pan of soup, the canned kind — ten cans, to be precise — because that was all she knew how to make.

The amount of food she had witnessed Mason and Sterling put down told her to plan for big appetites, making what she considered an enormous amount of food. She had to feed three of them. She had eaten the first sandwich she made, starving and impatient for food.

Once her work was done, she went in search of Michael and Sterling. They were behind the glass doors of the surveillance room, absorbed in conversation. She didn't knock. What was the point? Even though neither man had looked her direction, she knew they were aware of her. There was a subtle change in their postures, she was beginning to recognize.

These men didn't get surprised easily, at least, not from the likes of her. And she was quickly figuring out these men and their special skills could be irritating. It was hard to have an advantage with people who were superhuman. Correction, she thought, a bit uneasily, super soldiers.

Pulling the door open, she stood half in-half out of the room. "I made some food. Anyone interested?"

Surprise flashed in Michael's dark eyes and, for just an instant, she thought she saw a hint of admiration. He smiled, showing perfect white teeth. He reminded her of a handsome vampire from some horror movie, striking and alluring, but, oh, so dangerous.

"Thank you," he said. "I, for one, would love some food."

"Me too," Sterling said, smiling. He, too, was attractive, light to Michael's darkness, and softer in ways she didn't quite understand. But still deadly, she had no doubt.

"It's ready when you are," Holly said before slipping out of the doorway and moving back toward the kitchen.

Holly sat the sandwiches on the table, which was a mere few feet from the stove. Michael and Sterling came into the room, making the small kitchen shrink with their large frames taking up what felt like half the space available.

Finding a seat and sitting down, each man grabbed a sandwich and finished it off before Holly could even get them a bowl of soup.

"Man, you guys can eat," she mumbled as she sat a bowl in front of one and then the other. "What do you two want to drink?"

Both men answered at once, "Orange juice."

Holly smirked as she pulled open the refrigerator. She had already noted the top shelf full of orange juice. As she pulled two glasses from the cabinet, she asked, "What is it with you guys and orange juice?"

Sterling reached for his fourth sandwich. "We have a chronic vitamin C deficiency."

Holly sat a glass in front of him. "Huh," she murmured thoughtfully. Sitting the other glass in front of Michael, her mind racing with possibilities, she added, "I'll have to look into that."

"You could try," Michael said, "but some very qualified doctors have made attempts to figure it out and failed."

Holly turned to him and arched a brow. The one thing in life she was quite arrogant about was her skill as both doctor and researcher. "Not qualified enough, apparently."

A rich laugh escaped Michael's mouth. "Confidence isn't an issue for you, is it?"

Holly pursed her lips. She preferred Sterling's rather quiet demeanor to the outspoken likes of Michael. "Nor for you," she said, flipping her hair over her shoulder and turning to replace the jug of juice in the refrigerator. The action gave the men her back, telling them she was done with their remarks.

She replaced the jug and was about to turn when Sterling laughed and said, "He was irritatingly arrogant, even as a human."

Holly stilled. The room went silent. All three of them knew Sterling had spoken when he shouldn't have, inviting her to draw assumptions. So Michael wasn't human anymore?

Mason's words came back to her. *Now he's like me.* What did that mean?

Holly was about to turn and ask what Sterling had meant when she became aware of Mason. She felt him before she saw him, which was unique and unnerving but not unpleasant. She actually felt her skin tingle where his eyes touched. Slowly, she turned toward the doorway.

Mason stood there taking up the entire entrance with his large body, one hand over his head as he leaned on the frame. Momentarily she found herself distracted from her question, consumed by Mason's presence.

His hair still hung over his shoulders, giving him an untamed, masculine appeal Holly found mesmerizing. His presence was potent in its attack on her senses. But then, it always was.

He wore an expression of aloofness that made her heart sink. His eyes rested on her face, intense and unreadable. Had they been alone she would have gone to him. She longed to wrap her arms around him and make the distance, both physical and mental, disappear, to tell him he wasn't a monster.

Instead, she motioned to the table. "I made some food," she said quietly. "Are you hungry?"

Slowly, he stood up straight, giving her a quick nod. "I am," he said, looking away from her toward the table.

"I'll get you something to drink," she murmured in a low voice as he walked to the table and sat down.

When Holly sat a glass of orange juice in front of Mason, Michael said, "Holly wants to tackle our vitamin C deficiency."

Mason eyes went to Holly's face, clearly probing for something, but he didn't speak. Holly fixed him in her determined gaze, trying to send him a silent message. But words seemed needed, so she said, "There are a lot of things I can do to help," she paused with intent, "if you let me."

Comprehension flashed in his eyes as he held her stare for long moments. When he finally spoke, his voice was soft but firm. "I never doubted that for a minute."

She believed him. He was being protective of her for reasons she didn't completely understand, keeping things from her based on some agenda he felt shielded her from something, but he didn't lack faith in her abilities. The point she had hoped to make, and she thought she had, was that she needed the full opportunity to help.

She needed to be included.

"I need a lab to work in," she said sitting down in the only empty chair, which was directly across from Mason.

"Didn't I mention, I plan to take you to the main government lab? This was just a resting point. You'll love the facilities there. Everything is state of the art."

Holly's stomach flip-flopped. Was he leaving her there, without him?

"You can't take her there," Michael said in a hard voice. "The Arions have people inside."

Mason and Sterling cursed under their breaths.

Expelling a breath, Mason said, "We have a small cavern directly below here that could be used as a lab. The problem is, we need equipment."

"I could get my things from the University lab," Holly suggested.

Mason gave her a disbelieving look. "Doesn't the equipment belong to the school?"

"Some of it," Holly said, "but my father contributed greatly to that lab. If you take me back, I can get the basics. Of course, depending on what I need to achieve, I may need other things and some assistance."

"You can't go back there," Mason said in an uncompromising tone.

Holly studied him a moment. The hard lines of his expression warned her how on edge he truly was. She didn't feel like arguing with him. "I could make a list."

Approval and surprised flashed in Mason's eyes.

"I'll go to the lab," Sterling offered.

"There are other things we need to discuss and act on as well," Michael said, meeting Mason's eyes with a silent message clearly passing between the two.

Mason gave him a quick nod and a short, clipped response. "I am well aware of that." Clearly dismissing the idea of having a discussion at that very moment, Mason picked up a sandwich and started to eat.

Holly could tell the undercurrent of tension suddenly filling the room was due to her presence. Pushing her chair back, she stood up. "I'm going to shower and change."

"Wait," Mason said reaching for her hand to stay her. "I'll go with you."

The inference that he would actually be showering with her didn't slip past anyone in the room. Not that it embarrassed Holly. It didn't. She was more concerned that he hadn't eaten.

"Don't you need to eat?" she asked. He looked at her with narrowed eyes and she realized he thought she was avoiding him. In a low voice, she reassured him. "I'll wait on you."

His expression softened. "I ate at the cabin." He pushed to his feet and locked gazes with Michael. "I know," he said. "We need to talk. And we will. Soon."

Michael grunted. "There is little time to waste."

Mason's lips thinned. "I'm no fool."

"If you were, I wouldn't be here."

The two men stared at one another. It was Mason who gave him a curt nod, breaking the contact and then reaching for Holly's hand, guiding her to her feet. Mason hadn't looked away from Michael in defeat, but rather dismissal.

The act spoke volumes to Holly about just how much power Mason yielded. She exchanged a look with Sterling. Michael was dangerous. Both knew Mason could be far more so if and when he chose to be.

But not a monster. A trusted friend to Sterling. And a hero. Her hero. But what was he to Michael?

Chapter Seventeen

Roger blinked into the darkness, feeling as if he was going to lose his mind. Tears burned his eyes. How long had he been tied to this bed? He couldn't remember. Vague images of sharp, blinding light, followed by shadows and voices, male and female, flashed through his mind.

Time ticked in long minutes. He counted...one, two...one-hundred. Was there any hope of a new tomorrow? Would he die soon? Maybe it would be better if he did. He couldn't stand the blackness. It swallowed him like a consuming hatred, unforgiving in its torture and its pure longevity. It wouldn't go away. If only he could.

As if his mind had conjured it, a flash of light made him cry out. It sent shooting pains into his pupils. Why? Why did it hurt?

Then a voice.

A woman.

He couldn't make himself open his eyes.

The light, it hurt.

"Roger," a soft, feminine voice purred, offering comfort and perhaps salvation. He knew it. How, he wasn't sure. But he knew. A soft caress moved down his cheek.

"Yes," he whimpered," please, help me."

"I can make you strong, Roger," the voice whispered. "Untouchable and more powerful than you ever imagined." A warm breath moved over his ear. Seductive. Promising comfort and relief and so much more. "I can make you feel like you have never felt before."

"Who are you?" he asked in a trembling voice, needing to know.

"Open your eyes and look at me." A kiss brushed his ear. "Open, Roger."

"I... Yes," he whispered, blinking, blinking, trying to open his eyes. "I can't."

"Open," she said, again caressing his cheek with her finger. "You can do it. Open your eyes."

Slowly his eyes accepted the light. He blinked. Bringing the woman into focus took only a moment once his lids lifted. Long blonde locks fell down her creamy, bare shoulders. She wore a white camisole and looked as pure as an angel. "Holly?" he asked confused, desperate, hopeful.

Could Holly have come to save him?

She smiled. It was a sultry, inviting smile. "No," she said, "I'm Carrie." She sat down on the bed and leaned forward, her smell, so similar to Holly's, a sweet jasmine scent, rushed through his senses.

Leaning forward, she pressed her soft curves against his needy body, slipping her delicate hand along his jaw, pressing her breasts against his chest. Her mouth came close to his, her breath mingling with his. "I can be your very own Holly," she promised and then brushed her lips across his. "I can be anything you want me to be, Roger."

His heart pounded in his chest. She was so like Holly and she wanted him. Holly had rejected him. Carrie wanted him. She smiled against his mouth. "And I can make you powerful, like Mason, only better."

She was saving him, offering him more. He would never feel less than other men like Mason. Could it be true? "What do I have to do?"

Carrie smiled her approval, her midnight blue eyes twinkling with pleasure as she pulled back enough to look into his eyes. "I will be your guide. Just do as I say."

* * * * *

Gina stood at the monitor and started laughing, an evil, sultry sound. Her eyes met David's. "So, my dear husband, Carrie was a good find, was she not?"

His expression was hard. "Better if she had mated with one of the men."

Gina waved a dismissive hand. "Regardless, she's serving us well."

His brows inched up. "This Roger is a weak man. She didn't have to work too hard to persuade him."

Gina shrugged. "Don't underestimate her. We wore him down and searched his mind for the exact things to use against him. Besides, all that matters is the result. We get him on the inside of the Black Knights' planning sessions and we will be set. Nothing will stop us."

Chapter Eighteen

Stepping into the bedroom with Holly's hand in his, Mason pulled the bedroom door shut.

"How will they get to the other rooms without coming through here?" Holly asked with apprehension lacing her tone.

He looked down at her, a predatory gleam in his eyes having nothing to do with her question and everything to do with how he was feeling. Holly brought out possessiveness in him. It coursed through his veins like hot lava materializing in different forms. At present it was coming out in a combination of desire laced with a massive dose of emotion.

"There's an elevator. They can take it and come back around."

Her brows dipped. "One of those secret panel things, I guess?"

He didn't answer. She didn't expect him to.

He could tell the edginess of his mood was making her wary. He couldn't help it. The desire to claim her, to make her know she was his, was stronger than his need for air. When she had first tried to run from him, he had been hurt. Now he just wanted to make her his, period, the end.

His forever.

But he had also decided he wouldn't tell her she was his mate. The forever had to come from her heart and her body. That's where he planned to start, with her body. Here, now and later.

He pulled her close, his arms slipping around her waist. "Why are you acting so nervous?"

Her small, delicate hands, which he loved so much, settled on his chest. Green eyes met his black ones. "I'm not nervous." She wet her lips with the pinkness of her tongue, tempting him without realizing it. "I just don't understand your sudden mood change. You were mad and now…"

He quirked a brow. "Now?"

"Now you're…you're…something, I don't know what." She paused, obviously trying to understand what she saw in him. "Aggressive."

"Hungry," he said, lowering his head until his breath caressed her lips. Then their lips touched, a barely-there brush, his senses absorbing their softness with intense pleasure. "For you."

Unable to wait any longer, his mouth slanted over hers. Impatiently, his tongue slid between her teeth, exploring and stroking. A low moan purred in his throat. God, she tasted good. Holding Holly made him forget everything else. And right now, he just wanted to be with her, to get lost in all she offered and all they could be together.

"No," she said, pulling back slightly, breaking their kiss, but barely, as if it took will power. Her lips still touched his as she whispered, "We need to—"

He cut her off with his mouth. Contradicting the "no" she had given him, her tongue met his with equal need. Her body seemed to melt into his harder one.

"So sweet," he murmured as their breath mingled together. His lips lingered above hers as he soaked in her nearness like a healing mist. It didn't make sense, he knew that, but it felt as if her pureness could save his tainted soul. With Arion blood he would surely need salvation.

Maybe Holly could give it to him.

Once he had thought he could keep a distance from her, to protect her.

Now he wondered if her nearness wasn't the exact thing that would give him the strength to be all he needed to be. For her. For humanity.

His lips met hers again, his tongue slowly stroking hers. He slid his hands down her tiny waist, across the sexy curve of her hips, and then he cupped the roundness of her bottom. He pulled her against his body, tightly, possessively. She trembled and it wasn't fear. He could smell her passion, delicious and inviting.

God, he needed her.

But then Holly surprised him, abruptly pushing on his unmoving chest. "No, Mason. We have to talk." Her voice was soft but urgent. Her chest rose and fell in rapid motion.

He kissed her neck over and over. "Later, Holly. I really need you right now."

Holly made a soft sound in her throat. Surrender. "I need you, too, Mason," she whispered and then moaned as one of his hands cupped her breast. "But I don't want there to be any walls between us," she managed in a trembling voice.

He froze for several seconds and then let out a short bark of bitter laugher. He raised his head from her neck and looked down at her, letting her see what he was feeling.

Something about her words rekindled her earlier pain. "You don't think the fact that you think I'm a monster might be a wall between us?" he asked in voice filled with both passion and pain.

"I never should have said such a thing." She touched his cheek. "I am so, so sorry, Mason. I didn't mean it. I was angry and hurt and...wrong."

His eyelids slipped downward as he fought the powerful mix of emotions and desire raging inside, threatening to take control. He needed to make love to her. It was as if he was going to explode without the release of touching her. And he wanted to believe she didn't think he was a monster, if only for now.

His need wasn't rational and, while it was on the most elemental level a man needed a woman, it also went far beyond, to deeper reasons. Facing what was before him, who he was, what he was, he needed to feel his connection to Holly, to know he wasn't alone. He didn't understand exactly what was happening to him but it burned with fiery need in his veins.

What in the hell was he turning into that he couldn't even control his physical needs?

She wanted to talk and he just wanted to find a way inside her. "Perhaps I am a monster, Holly," he said in a low voice.

"No," she whispered.

He looked up at her. "What if I said I can barely contain the urge to throw you on the bed, tear your clothes off of you and bury myself inside you? Because at this moment, that's how I feel and, believe me, it's driven by far more monster than human." His voice was deep and low, his body shaking ever so slightly with his barely contained need.

Holly pressed her body to his, wrapping her arms around his neck. "Then do it."

Her blue eyes, so pure and angelic, like the heavens above, met his. In them, he found a much-needed invitation to take her, to possess her. Silently she told him she understood his need was far more than physical.

He dropped his forehead to hers, his chest rising and falling with heaviness, reaching for restraint. This need, clearly a part of his Arion makeup, consumed and controlled. He didn't like it. But he couldn't stop what burned inside him.

Holly tugged at his T-shirt, slipping her small hands to rest on his bare stomach. "Stop fighting it. We'll talk later."

He lifted his forehead from hers searching her expression with barely contained lust. If she moved her hands, he might snap. "Holly—"

"I want you, Mason," she whispered as her hands skimmed his ribs, caressing him with their warmth.

He snapped. A low growl disappeared into her mouth as he claimed her lips, delving his tongue between her teeth, tasting her as if he was a starving man. And he was. For Holly. His mate.

He unleashed what he felt, the powerful intensity of his feelings for her in the kiss, possessiveness, hunger, the absolute need for her. And love. Damn, he loved her. She whimpered into his mouth as her hands slid to his back and her soft curves melted into his hardness. It was like a calling had been answered in his mind and body, even beyond.

Yes.

He picked her up, hands cupping her backside, her legs wrapping around his waist. He went down on the bed, on top of her, while her legs moved to his thighs, wrapping around him as if she didn't want him to get away.

He couldn't stop kissing her. Tasting her felt addictive, as if he needed it, needed her, to breathe. His tongue challenged her, wanting everything she would give him, and she didn't disappoint. She kissed him back with so much passion it felt as if she had become a part of his very being, as if a powerful force had consumed them, pulling them into their own world.

His need was her need.

Her need was his need.

She tugged on his shirt, trying to pull it over his head. "Take your clothes off," he whispered near her ear.

She nodded but didn't move. Her legs had him tightly pulled to her body. Clearly she didn't want to let him up. He tugged his shirt over his head and tossed it to the floor.

Immediately, her hands explored his shoulders, her mouth pressing against his chest. When her tongue flattened on one of his flat nipples, he felt it like a line of fire in his blood.

"You have to let me up if you want me to undress," he said, nipping at her bottom lip.

"Kiss me first," she whispered.

And so he did but something changed as he did. He felt his raging need soften, turning to passion, simmering with a feeling to be savored. Seemingly in tune with him, she eased into his new mood along with him. His tongue caressed hers, slow and easy, their lips pressing together with delicious friction.

When he pulled back to look at her, he brushed strands of blonde hair from her eyes. "I love kissing you but we both definitely have on too many clothes."

With obvious reluctance, Holly slipped her legs from around his body. Mason found himself smiling as a wave of tenderness swept over him. How had he gone from such dark intensity, to such different feelings? But he knew the answer. Holly had some power over him. Something about her brought out his better side.

Sliding off the bed, he quickly started to undress. He watched Holly do the same, enjoying every glimpse of ivory skin she offered.

He moved to the mattress, eager to get his hands on her naked body. She met him at the footboard, bared to her beautiful skin, climbing onto the end of the bed on her knees. Her mouth and hands went to his chest, touching and kissing and driving him wild. His hands settled in her hair. She never ceased to amaze him. There wasn't a shy bone in her body when it came to making love.

His hands moved to cup the round fullness of her breasts, not too big, but not too small. They fit in his hands perfectly, as if she were made for him. It felt like she was. How could he deny the need for her he felt? How could he ever walk away from her?

His fingers found her nipples, rolling them and pinching them with gentle care. Her head tilted back, exposing her beautiful white throat. He bent down to touch it with his lips and then his tongue, feathering kisses across the exposed area.

He slid his fingers into her hair, palms on her cheeks. "Holly," he whispered because he didn't know how to put the immense feelings of need he had into words. She was so beautiful, so amazing, so Holly.

"Make love to me, Mason," she responded, her eyes fixed on his, her voice laced with passion.

He let his hands slowly slide down her face, to her neck. "Whatever you want, Holly."

"I want," she whispered, her eyes shutting as his hands slid down her shoulders.

His voice was a low murmur. "I want."

Her nipples, drawn tight with arousal, drew his eyes. He was well beyond hard as it was. He ached to feel her body wrapped tightly around him.

But he also wanted to feel the rush of pleasing her. Knowing she had never really been pleased, but let herself be by him, really felt powerful and good.

Intimate.

Unique.

Right.

He trailed his index fingers around the hardened peaks, watching her face, enjoying the look of pleasure he saw in her expression. Bending at the knees, he ran his tongue around one nipple making her hands go to his head and her breathing quicken.

Exactly what he wanted.

To please her.

Silently he guided her backwards, spreading her legs so he could settle between them, even as he flattened her against the mattress. "I need you, Holly."

She wrapped her arms around his neck. "I need you, too. It's crazy how much."

They kissed then, both craving one another, both funneling those feelings of need into the kiss. With each stroke of their tongues, urgency grew between them and their bodies pressed closer together.

Long moments later, he broke their kiss. Looking down at her, he willed her to hold his gaze, wanting to see her eyes as he slid inside her body. She sucked in a breath as he entered her but didn't close her eyes. Once he was deep in her core, he stayed there, feeling the completeness of the moment.

Lost in what they were together, he knew she felt it too. It was in her expression and her very being. This feeling of oneness was profound, overwhelming and completely right on some elemental level.

Staring into each other's eyes only served to enhance their connection, somehow seeming to kick up their passion level one more octave.

In turn his body became all the more demanding.

Making him want to move and feel her more fully.

And when he did, so did she, as if she too needed what he did. Still looking deep into her eyes, he moved in and out of her, stroke by stroke, feeling the essence of their passion seep through to his nerve endings.

"I want you on top," he told her but didn't give her time to respond. Rolling over, he pulled her on top of him.

She sat there, naked and perfect, blonde hair streaming down her shoulders. "Damn, you're beautiful," he said hoarsely.

"Prove it," she said, starting to move and urging him to do so as well.

She used his chest to prop herself up, gliding along his length with perfection in each stroke, his hands anchoring her as they held her waist.

Moments later, they were in a frenzied whirlwind of passion, bodies moving and sliding, as moans of pleasure slipped through their mouths. And just when he thought he couldn't last, she cried out his name and arched her back and he felt the ripples of her release.

His body responded with conviction, delving deeper with one last stroke, before sending a shockwave of release through his body.

Just as Holly had sent a shockwave of emotion straight to his heart.

* * * * *

Holly collapsed on top of him, her face buried in his neck. Long moments later, she leaned up and looked into his face, her hands sliding to the sides of his face. "You're not a monster."

In a quick movement, Mason flipped her on her back, positioning himself over her, weight on his elbows. "Not when I'm with you."

"Not ever," Holly told him in a voice filled with belief and determination.

His eyes shut a long moment. "You don't understand, Holly."

"Then make me," she said firmly.

His eyes opened, fixing her in his tormented gaze. "I have no right to expose you to the things in my world yet I find myself wanting to hold on to you, to keep you by my side."

Holly cupped his cheek. "I want to be by your side, Mason."

"You were leaving today," he accused in a low tone, his eyes searching hers.

"Because you weren't honest with me," she said with frustration etched in her tone, "not because I didn't want to be with you."

"I didn't lie to you, Holly," he said with conviction. "When I said my brother was dead, I meant it. The man I knew is no longer."

"But you omitted important details."

Abruptly, he rolled off of her, moving to the side of the bed. He sat on the edge of the mattress, back to Holly, hunched over so his elbows rested on his knees. He didn't say a word. He didn't know what to say.

* * * * *

Holly stared at the rigid line of Mason's back for a long moment before she struggled to the side of the bed. She made a quick trip to the bathroom to clean up before returning to the bedroom.

They needed to talk.

She found Mason sitting exactly as she had left him.

She sighed. He needed her but felt guilty about it. Whatever he wasn't telling her was killing him. Obviously, his brother was an issue. Having a brother who was Arion was clearly eating him alive.

Holly moved, stopping in front of Mason and then dropping down to her knees. His hair hung in his face, hiding his expression from her viewing. With her hands, she reached up and pushed it back, willing him to look at her with her actions.

He kept his eyes on the floor. "Mason, please talk to me."

He lifted his gaze giving her a view of his stormy expression. "I've been sitting here trying to figure out what exactly I should be saying," he admitted roughly.

The tension in his body radiated through his eyes. "Just tell me," she said gently and then added a plea, "Believe in me."

A sharp wave of emotion flashed in his eyes. "Believing in you isn't the issue. How would you have responded if you had known up-front about my brother? Would you have been so quick to accept my protection?"

"You aren't your brother. The bond I feel with you, whatever it is, I don't understand it, but it makes me more confident than I could be in any other person. I believe in you." She took his hand. "Now, you have to believe in me."

He took both her hands in his. For several seconds he seemed to battle some internal war. Finally, he said, "You won't like what I have to say."

She squeezed his hands. "Believe in me, Mason."

He let out a long breath and then started talking. "Michael says there are Arions who want to fight David. They want to overthrow him out of power. He somehow has it in his head that I can lead these men in the battle. He thinks I am the only one with the power to defeat David."

She didn't understand. "That's good, isn't it? That men want to fight the evil David represents?"

"It means war, a battle to death."

She swallowed. With his brother. A battle to death. "I understand. I don't want you to die."

He laughed. "I don't kill easily. You've already seen that firsthand. Besides, David wants me to join him, to become a part of some ruling blood line. He won't let anyone kill me until he's certain he can't turn me."

She was still processing, trying to put everything together. "He wants you to become Arion."

He stiffened. "Holly," he said in a very low, tense voice. "I am Arion."

She blinked. He hated Arions. "I'm confused."

"It's true. I didn't know until Michael told me," he said but shook his head almost immediately. "That's not really true. Deep down, I think I knew. I was aware I had skills other Black Knights didn't. I just didn't want to face the facts."

"I see," she said but she wasn't certain she did. Mason had told her so many evil things about Arions it was hard to adjust her thinking to include Mason as one of them.

"Do you?" he asked. "The monster you called me truly does live inside me. Whenever I feel its poison trying to take me over, somehow you bring it under control. But what if one day I can't rein it in?"

Holly fixed her gaze on him. "Perhaps the monster is in your mind, Mason. If you are Arion—"

"I am," he said firmly. "It was hard enough for me to accept my brother as Arion. Accepting myself as one has been hell. But there is no doubt. I am Arion."

She continued as if he hadn't spoken. "Then Arions as a race are not evil."

"I'm not so certain," he replied tersely.

"If your human brother committed a crime would that mean you were evil and so was all of humanity?" She paused to let the words sink in, not expecting an answer. "People are evil, entire races are not."

"There's no way to be certain."

"I'm willing to chance it. If you're to fight the Arions, I plan to be by your side when you do." She bit her bottom lip. "That is, if you want me by your side."

"It's war, Holly."

She frowned at him. "I understand what it is. I might not like war but I know when it's unavoidable. One of the whole reasons I was against super soldiers was because I was afraid it would cause someone to do just what they did, get power hungry. And I was right. I knew someone would think a Super Soldier program could lead to world domination."

He stared at her. "I think I'm falling in love with you, Holly."

Her expression softened. "Good," she whispered, "because I'm pretty darn certain I'm already there where you're concerned."

He pulled her to him, wrapping his arms around her waist as he bent his head, lowering his mouth just above hers. Slowly, gently, he claimed her mouth, tenderly stroking her tongue with his.

His mouth lingered above hers, his breath mingling with hers as one. "Be sure, Holly. Once I decide to hold onto you, I don't know if I can ever let go."

"I'm sure," she whispered against his lips. "I want this. I want us."

Chapter Nineteen

Mason found Michael and Sterling sitting at a table in the surveillance room absorbed deep in conversation. Having freshly showered and changed, he felt like a new man. His hair was neatly pulled back, as was his attitude.

He and Holly had taken a shower together. He couldn't remember ever taking a shower with a woman. Not that it would have been the same as it was with Holly anyway. Somehow, he had managed to find the ability laugh and truly relax, if only for a short while, and despite the evils facing him. Laughter had turned into making love again.

Holly was amazing.

She gave him hope.

Guilt raged in his mind. Should he have told her about their mating? He wasn't ready to tell her. Yet, in all fairness, he knew she had a right to know. Their connection would have ramifications for her. He would never want another woman. If she knew, knowing Holly as he did, she would feel obligated to stay with him. He needed her to choose to be with him on her own, because it felt right to her.

If she saw the harsher sides of him, his battle face, and wanted no part of him, he wanted her to be free.

He had to know she wanted him, good, bad and ugly — all that he was or could be.

Mason entered the surveillance room and both men stopped talking, each staring at him. The wordless question was in both men's eyes. Would he agree to lead a team against David?

Mason answered. "I'll do it. Let's talk about how to get started."

Neither man moved or spoke immediately, as if they were afraid he would change his mind.

"And Holly?" Sterling asked.

Mason sat down at the table, in the empty chair between Michael and Sterling. "She offers her assistance."

"She knows now?" Michael asked.

"About everything but the mating." Mason's lips thinned as he let his eyes slide between the two men. "And I advise you both to keep your mouths shut."

Michael's brow furrowed. "Why didn't you tell her?"

Mason gave him a hard look. "I have my reasons." His tone said he wasn't willing to elaborate.

He changed the subject, further proving his position on the matter. Mason didn't want to talk about him and Holly. It was a private matter between the two of them. "What's the first step in defeating David? Where do we start?"

Michael gave Mason a look, but didn't press for more information about Holly. "I have new intel. Roger is being moved."

Mason's brow inched up. Sterling responded to the silent inquiry by unrolling the map he had in front of him and pointing to a circled section. "He's here now. He's being moved to Area 51."

Mason looked at Michael. "Area 51 has reopened?"

Michael offered a quick nod of confirmation. "Yes, run by David. My sources say the abducted women are already being held there."

"Why didn't they take Roger there to start with, I wonder?" Sterling asked.

Michael's response came with certainty. "Something's changed. They intend to keep him if they are taking him to Area 51."

Sterling's eyes narrowed. "So he has become useful. Why, I wonder? Is Roger able to carry out Holly's work?"

"Good question," Michael said. "None of my people know. It's not his ability in a lab. He doesn't have Holly's skill. He's a follower, not a mastermind. I'm the only one close enough to David to find out what's really going on."

"When are you due back?" Mason asked.

Michael's voice held a certain raw tension. "Tomorrow."

"What aren't you saying?" Mason asked.

Michael hesitated. "There is much for you to learn. You represent the leadership of many. If anything were to happen to you...well, the results could be devastating."

Mason let out a bark of disbelieving laughter. "I'm not planning on killing myself or anything like that."

Michael ignored his remark. "The point is, if we are to save these women, or Roger for that matter, I need to go back to Area 51. I would prefer to train with you first. A day will come when you will face David and it's critical you be prepared."

He continued, "And we have men to think about. Black Knights and Arions who want to join the Knights. We need to figure out where to set up a main facility and when and how to notify both our teams. It's critical we pull everyone together into one force under your leadership."

All three of the men looked up as Holly walked into the room. Her blond hair bounced in a shiny halo around her heart shaped face. Her bright smile was as much a part of her outfit as her sleek black slacks and matching knit shirt.

"Any progress in here?" Holly asked as she walked behind Mason and slid her hand onto his shoulder.

Mason ignored the interest in the watching eyes. Instead, he looked up at Holly. "We were talking about where Roger and the abducted women are being held."

"He's alive?" she asked urgently. "Are we certain?"

"As I said before, he was the last I heard," Michael said, "but that could change at any moment."

Holly swallowed visibly. "Can we help him?"

"We will," Mason told her and then looked at Michael. "The way I see it, we are better grabbing Roger during his transport."

"Agreed," Michael said, as Sterling chimed in his murmur of approval. "We can get the women after I size things up from the inside. I should have the details of Roger's movement in the next few hours."

"I've been thinking," Holly said, drawing three sets of eyes. "This vitamin C deficiency you guys have could be a key to fighting the Arions." Holly paused and squeezed Mason's shoulder. "The bad ones, that is."

"How so?" Mason asked quietly.

"What if I could come up with some sort of vitamin C zapper, like a virus that eats up the vitamin C in your body?"

"Can you do that?" Sterling asked, a bit surprised.

"I won't promise. Many consider me overly ambitious," Holly said with a degree of tension in her voice.

"Are you?" Michael asked.

"No." She said simply with no hesitation.

Michael studied her a moment. "That could be helpful but we need a battlefield tool to take them down, on the spot, during battle."

Holly gave Michael an irritated look. "I'm aware of that. I was thinking some sort of tranquilizer-type bullet."

The room was silent a moment. Mason reached up and took Holly's hand from his shoulder, holding it in his own. "What do you need to make this happen?"

"The basic lab you have said you could set up here is fine for now," she said. "And a sample of each of your blood, of course."

Michael pushed to his feet. "You can have my blood. Just make this happen."

Holly met Michael's gaze. "I'll do my best."

"And that is better than most will ever achieve," Mason said quietly as he stood. His eyes met hers, a message of pride there for her to see.

Holly was forever surprising him, and always for the good. He wished the surprises he still had in store for her didn't exist. He hated having secrets between them.

* * * * *

Mason watched as Holly extracted several tubes of blood from Sterling and Michael. She had been pleasantly surprised to find he already had a small lab in place that simply needed enhancements and expansion.

When it was his turn to give blood, he sat down and extended his arm. Holly went to work, wrapping his arm with a tight band.

"Tell me about your powers," she quietly encouraged him.

"I have much to learn about them myself," he said with a shrug.

Holly inserted the needle into his vein. "But you know some things," she insisted. "Everything I can learn about Arions and Black Knights will help me with my research. I want to chart the traits of humans, Black Knights and Arions so I can compare."

He nodded. "I understand. I think Michael will be the best one to help you. He knows things I should but don't. Secrets about what I can or can't do physically and mentally."

She closed up the last tube and popped the band off his arm. Holding cotton on the extraction site, she bent his elbow to hold it in place. "Can you read my mind, Mason?"

He reached for her, pulling her to stand between his legs. "If I could?"

Her answer came quickly. "Can you?"

"No." He hesitated. "Yes. Sometimes I feel what you feel. I know you're upset, or angry, or sad. I don't hear your actual thoughts but I feel your feelings. It's like a tunnel from my mind to yours."

She frowned. "Sometimes I think I can feel what you feel."

"Maybe you can," he whispered, knowing how close she was to suspecting their bond was deeper than normal man and woman.

She slid her hand to cup his cheek. "You can't control my thoughts, can you?"

Again he hesitated. "I can control people with my eyes. It's a hypnotic trance-like state. It's purely Arion. It's one of the things I knew was different about me. Black Knights have very limited abilities in mind control."

"So you could do that to me?"

He met her eyes, willing her to see the truth he offered in them. "I would never do that to you. You have my word."

She smiled. "Then I believe you."

"Even after everything we've been through together?"

"You have never broken your word to me. Until you do, I will believe you are good for it."

Mason ran his hands up her thighs and squeezed her bottom. "I don't deserve you," he whispered.

Before she could respond, Michael came barreling into the room. "Okay, I just got word. Tonight is the night they move Roger."

* * * * *

Holly stood in the weapons vault, which was on the same floor as the lab, watching Mason strap on weapons. She looked around the room and sighed. Weapons of all sorts—guns, knives, explosives, anything and everything—surrounded her.

Mason slipped a gun in his shoulder holster. "Stop worrying. Everything will be fine."

Holly hugged herself, willing her voice to be strong. "Don't you dare go and get yourself killed."

His hand stilled on the belt he was about to adjust. Instead, he reached for her, and pulled her into a hug. Kissing her head as she wrapped her arms around him, he said, "I fight, Angel. And I'm good at it. I don't die easily."

Holly leaned back and looked at him. "I know what you are, Mason. I just want you to come back to me."

His expression softened with understanding. She saw what she felt in his eyes. They needed each other. In a soft promising of a voice, he said, "I will. I promise."

Then he kissed her. And she clung to him, praying he really would. She had lost her parents. Now that she had someone else to love, she didn't want to lose him too.

Holly walked him to the elevator and kissed him there too. Mason looked at Sterling, who was staying behind to guard her. "Keep her safe, man."

Sterling's lips twitched and then he winked at Holly. "As long as she doesn't run off again, we'll be fine."

But she couldn't smile. "I think Sterling should go with you guys. You need all the help you can get."

"Sterling's not Arion. We are. They also want him dead, and me alive," Mason told her for the third time. "Michael has my back."

Michael met her gaze, his tone serious. "I would die to protect him, Holly. He is the future." Holly nodded and Michael continued, "And so are you. He needs you by his side. Stay here and stay safe."

Sterling touched her shoulder. She felt a growing friendship with him. Perhaps through his bond with Mason. She wasn't sure. It simply was.

She hugged Mason, pushing to her tiptoes and whispering in his ear. "I love you."

"And I you, Angel."

* * * * *

Holly was determined to be of use in defeating the Arions. Her best asset was her scientific mind. Sterling and Holly sat in the only chairs in the lab, two metal back seats, as she drilled him with questions. She was taking notes as quickly as her hand would write.

"Claws?" she asked and gulped, looking up from her pad of paper. "Arions have claws?"

Sterling laughed. She shot him a look. He held his hands up. "Sorry, your expression is so priceless. Mason doesn't have claws."

She was still frowning. "They come out during battle when anger kicks in. I've seen Mason in battle. No claws."

"That's what ripped his side up, isn't it?"

"Yes," Sterling said. "He was trying to save me."

She had thought Sterling to be a very hard man when she first met him. Now, she knew it hid a much more complicated Sterling, an honorable, good man. A much softer man than she had imagined.

Holly reached forward and touched his hand. "As you would for him."

"Yes."

Holly's thoughts went back to her work. "If all Arions don't have claws, I assume there are other traits not universal to the race?"

"Yes. It seems some have more power and ability than others. They might have the same skill, but with an extra ability to harness the power they hold in a more advanced way."

Holly thought a moment. "That sounds like a mind control issue. We need an expert in that area. I'm not it. What about other physical traits that are not shared?"

Sterling hesitated.

"Just tell me," Holly told him with irritation in her voice.

He nodded but his discomfort was obvious. "Some Arions, when they reach a certain level of fury, have fangs."

"Fangs?"

"Yes, almost wolf-like. We have no real idea what the aliens were like. The bodies disappeared years back. It was very secretive. By that time, though, the DNA extractions, and even some cloning, had been done and stored."

Holly pressed two fingers to her now-throbbing temple. For a brief instant she felt panic. She was in love with a man who was basically part alien. Who could have fangs and claws. Love. She loved him. Fangs or claws, he would only kill for the better of good. She knew that in her heart.

"Of course, there is also a rumor that David has contact with the true alien race used for this whole experiment."

She snapped out of her own thoughts quickly. "You're kidding."

He shrugged. "It's a rumor. But somehow, some Arions have learned to harness their powers on a greater level, which seems to indicate someone, somewhere taught them. Then, there are the mating habits of Arions. I don't see how we would have figured that out without help."

Uneasiness made her stomach flip-flop. "Mating habits?"

Sterling eyed her closely as if he wanted to gauge her reaction. "Yes. Arion men can have sex with any female but they have only a few potential matches to mate with."

"Mate?" Holly asked with distaste in her tone. "That sounds very caveman-like."

"It's actually a profound and unique bond, one that is lifelong once the mating ritual is performed. The mating process is not at all beastly or caveman-like. It's far more complete than human ways. Once you mate, you never want another. Mates have the power to bring each other happiness beyond what human relationships bring."

She tilted her head to study him. "Meaning?"

"There are mental and physical bonds the two share. Ultimate trust exists. I have seen the blessing it can be but I have also seen the pain it can deliver."

She swallowed. "Pain?"

"Losing a mate is like losing part of one's self. Some never recover the loss. And mates can be used against each other. The male is very possessive and protective. His mate's safety will come above all else. Her pain will be his pain."

"I see," Holly murmured.

Could she be Mason's mate? She felt a strange bond with him. She had from the moment she met him. They had only known each other a short time but she knew she loved him. And she knew him inside, his mind, his heart and his soul. There was no question to her, he was a good man. Could she say that so easily about another?

Sterling pulled her from her reverie as he continued, "Here is the thing that makes me wonder if these aliens, whatever they are actually called — Arions is David's name for his race — might be involved in this. See, Arions can only produce children with their mate. Since a mating can only take place if the two people have a certain connection, a mate can be difficult to find, thus making reproducing difficult."

Holly's stomach flip-flopped again. Mason was Arion. If he ever wanted children, she couldn't give them to him. Not that she was his mate, but the bottom line was, she couldn't have children. And she couldn't stand the thought of another woman with him.

"So you think the Aliens want to use humans to expand their race?"

"Yes, maybe. It's something to be considered."

"It would indicate we have a much bigger problem to deal with than simply David trying to dominate," Holly said with concern.

"Yes, I'm afraid so. But the fact that mating is being so focused on is enough to be of concern, with or without the true aliens involved."

"So David is taking women to try and mate them with his men?" she asked.

Sterling nodded. "Exactly."

Holly thought about the implications of David's actions. The things she needed to accomplish felt overwhelming. She looked skyward and said a little prayer. She couldn't fail. "I need to compare your physical makeup to Mason's and Michael's. And to a normal human's, preferably male, but I can use mine to start. The common genes need to be identified. I need...I need a lot of things."

She sighed. Then she looked at Sterling. "This is going to take me time and resources. In the mean time, I need to help us all stay alive. Teach me how to shoot a gun."

His eyes widened. "What?"

"You heard me." She stood up and sat down her pad and pencil in her chair. "Teach me. I need to be ready to fight."

"Mason said you don't like guns and fighting."

"I don't like senseless death, mine included." She motioned for him to stand. "Teach me."

"I'm not sure how Mason will feel about this," Sterling said with concern.

"Mason doesn't control me," she said, narrowing her eyes at him. Her look dared him to argue. "This is my life and I choose to take responsibility for it."

Sterling pushed to his feet. "You're a pain in the ass, Holly Heart."

Holly laughed. There was a hint of admiration in his tone. "You ain't seen nothing yet."

"That's what I'm afraid of," he muttered as he moved toward the door.

Chapter Twenty

A mile from Area 51, shadowed in the darkness, as still as if part of the forest, Mason and Michael hid.

Two Arions were transporting Roger. One of which was Tad. Mason was looking forward to another confrontation with him. Unfortunately, tonight wasn't the night for payback. But that day would come. Tad needed to be eliminated.

The other was a man named Paul McIntyre. He had once been a good man. Or so Mason had thought. Obviously, he hadn't been as good a judge of character as he had once surmised.

Still, they were taking no risks. Not with an innocent human involved. He and Michael each held guns. They would take the two Arions down with bullets and get the hell out. If they took them off guard, they would get a few well-placed bullet holes before the Arions shielded themselves from the bullets. They had the mental ability to deflect what they knew existed. It's why he didn't bother using weapons at Holly's place when he had been confronted. While on the attack, the Arions are always ready for anything.

Weapons were best used when an element of surprise was in place. Like tonight.

The motorcycles he and Michael had used for travel were hidden a mile away. They had finished the remainder of the trip by becoming the wind. With Michael's assistance, Mason had managed to get a hold of that part of his power, at least to some degree. To become the wind was an Arion trait he had never utilized.

The experience had been exhilarating, not to mention effective. Wind travel was a silent, rapid method of movement.

The trip to Area 51, once they ditched the bikes, had been only minutes. Of course, they had taken most of it on motorcycle to accommodate bringing Roger back with them. Still, the cave was fairly close. Something that had given him little concern in the past since he had thought the 51 facility closed. Now, it was too close for comfort. He agreed with Michael — taking it over as their headquarters was a critical maneuver.

The Arions were traveling by jeep. Mason knew this thanks to Michael's insiders. The road was deserted at this time of night so when the first sign of headlights flashed, Mason knew it was them.

Michael was on the other side of the road. He trusted him to do his part. They would converge on the jeep, catch the Arions off guard, hopefully wounding them enough to slow them down, and pull Roger out.

Mason counted to ten from the first instant the jeep came into sight, just as he and Michael had planned. Then, he moved with the speed of wind and the lightness of air.

He and Michael reached the jeep at the same time. Tad was driving, which put him on Michael's side. Even in the midst of battle, Mason felt a sting of regret for missing that matchup.

Mason took McIntyre, who sat in the passenger's seat, nailing him with three bullets to the chest. He heard Michael's shots, felt the jeep jerk to a stop.

Michael had control.

McIntyre held his bloody chest, gasping for mental control of the pain, which he would get in mere seconds. Checking for Tad, needing to know with certainty he was down, Mason found him slouched across the steering wheel.

Michael had hit him in the temple with several bullets. Tad might not survive. Likely, wouldn't. Even Arions, if hit in the right spot, died like everyone else. The head, the temple to be precise, was one of those spots.

Michael didn't screw around. A good thing, since Tad was damn powerful. Of course, Michael knew that going into this mission and probably chose his mark accordingly when the opportunity presented itself.

Mason reached for Roger, who was in the backseat, whimpering despite the tape over his mouth. The man was a complete loser. No fight whatsoever. Why Holly cared about him, he would never understand.

Drawing a knife from his belt, Mason reached to cut the ropes around Roger's hands. Roger dropped against the seat as if he thought Mason was going to cut him.

"What's the holdup?" Michael said fiercely. "McIntyre is moving."

"Give me your damn hands, if you want to live," Mason spat at Roger through clenched teeth. And then, because he knew the man had probably been terrorized, but mostly because an image of Holly ran through his mind, he added a bit more softly, "I'm not the enemy."

He still didn't move. Mason lost patience. He grabbed him, lifting him out of the jeep as if he was a paperweight. He was a fairly small guy and did little to test Mason's Arion strength.

Michael shot McIntyre again. This time in the temple. One shot, two shots. "Let's go!" he yelled at Mason.

McIntyre wouldn't be following.

But there could be other Arions nearby. They were close to Area 51. Again, Mason thought, too damn close for comfort.

Tossing Roger over his shoulder, Mason had speed on his mind. He could carry Roger and still escape faster than any human could follow. Especially since he was so damn scared he wasn't doing anything but shake.

Taking off in the direction they had come, Mason was silently aware of Michael bringing up their rear, guarding them. Guarding him. Michael was acting like his damn bodyguard.

He didn't like it. He didn't need protection. He gave it.

Once they arrived at the location where they had left the bikes stashed, Mason sat Roger down on his feet. Fixing him in a hard stare, he said, "I'm going to cut you loose." His tone was low but laced with hardness. "Then I'll take the tape off but keep your mouth shut. We could have been followed. In case you haven't figured it out, Arions have exceptional hearing."

Roger nodded his comprehension but his eyes were wide with fear. Mason yanked his knife from his belt and cut the rope from Roger's hands. He reached for the tape but hesitated, again thinking of Holly's wishes. "This will hurt. No way around it. Faster is better." He didn't give him time to respond. He yanked. Roger yelled.

Mason growled. "Shut up!" he whispered through clenched teeth, his eyes flashing dangerously.

Roger shut up but tears rolled down his cheeks.

Michael appeared with a scowl on his face, took one look at Roger crying and rolled his eyes. A few seconds later, Michael appeared with Mason's bike. Mason climbed on the familiar machine, feeling comfortable straddling a means to escape. "Get on before I leave you."

Roger didn't move. Mason revved the engine. Roger moved. He hardly had his leg over the seat before Mason took off. Michael appeared on his bike, bringing up the rear like a watchdog.

Mason let the wind's energy wrap around him, feeling long-suppressed power inside him begin to come to life, knowing things were changing and so was he.

Wondering at the implications.

* * * * *

Holly still couldn't believe the caves housed so many rooms. She pushed the safety glasses to the top of her head and stared at the target she had just shot a very big, very loud gun at. She had missed the mark horribly. She frowned. "I'm not very good at this, am I?"

Sterling laughed. "It's your first time. You're doing fine."

She tilted her head and studied him. He was a good teacher, both patient and understanding. The more she was around him, the more she understood what Mason saw in him. "What color were your eyes before your transition?"

He looked surprised. "Blue."

Holly grinned. "Blond-haired, blue-eyed stud, huh?"

He laughed. "I don't know about that."

She laughed this time. "Oh yeah, I get the feeling you were quite the ladies' man. Probably still are."

He stiffened. "No."

She had started to put the goggles back on but instead pushed them back on top of her head. There was something in his tone. "Why not?"

He shrugged and picked up a gun, not bothering with goggles, firing at the target until he emptied the weapon. He was on his mark every shot. She looked at the target and then at him. "Want to talk about it?"

"No." He sat down the gun.

Holly did the same. Her arms hurt from holding it up so long. "Why not?"

No response. After a minute, she made a frustrated sound "Are you always so stubborn?"

His tone was clipped. "Yes." Abruptly, he laughed but humor had little to do with it. "I hope Mason knows what he got himself into."

Holly stiffened. That hurt. She didn't even know how to respond.

He looked at her, his expression showing he sensed her change of mood. "Hey, now," he said with a different tone. "I was joking." Then in a softer voice, he added, "Mason is lucky to have you."

Holly sank down in a chair. "Talk to me, Sterling."

He sighed and seemed to contemplate what he should say. "Mason and I have always felt it unfair to involve ourselves with human women."

Holly thought of how Mason had fought their attraction. "I think that's very honorable but it makes for a long, lonely life."

"We take the hand life deals us and do the best we can with it," Sterling said with a shrug that didn't fool her into thinking he was as nonchalant as he wanted her to believe.

But she agreed and respected his feelings about making the most out of things. She just didn't want him to be alone forever. "If you knew more about what you are, would that help you feel more comfortable about relationships?"

He took a long time to answer. "Maybe, I don't know."

"Maybe is better than no," she said, meaning it, feeling for Sterling and others like him. They were victims of power hungry people. They deserved a solution. "I commit to do my very best to give you as much normalcy to your life as I can. You have my word." Her voice held heartfelt conviction.

Sterling smiled though there was sadness in his eyes, contradicting the lift of his lips, making them seem even blacker, even haunted. His voice, deep and a bit raspy, echoed in her ears, filled with just the slightest hint of defeat. "I believe you, Holly Heart. I believe you."

At least he believed she would give it her all. It was better than not believing in anything.

* * * * *

Holly paced the floor in front of the fireplace as Sterling sat on the couch watching. Worrying her bottom lip with her teeth, she turned desperate eyes on him. "Shouldn't they be here by now?"

He didn't hesitate. "No."

Holly glared. "Don't you have any other word in your vocabulary?"

He didn't say anything but he suddenly seemed more alert. Holly noticed. "What?" she asked urgently and, before he had time to respond, she added, "What?!"

"They're back," he said, pushing to his feet and walking toward the elevator.

Holly followed on his heels. The elevator opened and Roger stood there, looking meek and scared and incredibly small, between the much larger bodies of Mason and Michael.

A quick look at Mason reassured her he suffered nothing more than irritation. Holly held her arms out to Roger. "You're alive, thank God."

Roger stepped forward, wrapping his arms around her and dropping his head to her shoulder. His posture was that of a child.

Holly met Mason's eyes over his shoulder. She could actually see a muscle jump in his jaw. Her eyes narrowed with realization. He despised Roger holding her. His feelings were so intense she could feel them as if they crawled across her very own skin.

His dark eyes met hers and she saw a warning in them. One she would have ignored except she got the distinct impression Roger would pay for her actions, not her. She released Roger's arm and stepped back from him. Assessing him, Holly thought he looked thin and pale. The distinct shaking of his hands only added to the impression of fragility he made.

Holly asked him, "Are you hungry?"

He nodded. "Yes."

"Let's get you some food and then I'll give you a checkup."

She linked her arm through his and pulled him forward, ignoring the scowl on Mason's face and the disapproval on Michael's. But then she changed her mind. She was angered by Mason's behavior but the things he was now facing were tremendous.

Holly stopped walking. She turned to Sterling. "Could you take Roger to the kitchen and make sure he eats?"

Sterling gave her a quick nod. Roger hesitated, as if he didn't want to leave Holly's side. "I'll be there in a minute," Holly told him with a reassuring smile.

Michael took the hint. He followed the others. Or maybe she took his hint. He had truly given her the evil eye. Coming from Michael, it wasn't to be taken lightly.

Mason stood utterly still, his expression etched with anger and something else she couldn't quite identify. He looked big, untouchable and incredibly masculine.

Her warrior. Holly took several steps until she stood directly in front of him. Without hesitation, she wrapped her arms around his waist, pressing her thighs to his and hugging him tightly. He kept his hands by his sides.

"Please don't look like that," she implored. "He's just my friend. Nothing more. A friend who has been through hell."

His tone was stiff and cold. "A friend who wants you as a man wants a woman."

"As I am sure many women want you. And I can't stand the thought of anyone else touching you," she said honestly. Before he could respond, Holly laid her head on his chest, listening to his heart beat, loving having him so near.

His hands settled in her hair, as his body seemed to relax. "I'm not used to feeling this way about someone," he admitted quietly.

Holly looked up at him. "I'm not either. Half the time I don't know what to do with all the feelings you provoke in me, Mason. The intensity is overwhelming." Then trying to lighten the mood, she teased, "My first reaction to your anger over me and Roger was to hit you." She laughed as his brows inched up. "I didn't figure that would go over well. You had Sterling and Michael to protect you."

He smiled down at her, laughing lightly. "Do you know something?"

"What?" she asked, smiling back at him. She liked it when he smiled.

His hand stroked her hair. "I'd forgotten how to laugh until you came along. Now, I go from angry to laughing in mere seconds." His hands cupped her face. "You do that for me."

"I do?" she asked, a bit stunned by his words. No one had ever made her feel so special. Like she personally impacted their life. Oh, she knew her scientific abilities had helped others. But Mason made her feel like she, the woman and person, made a difference for him.

He nodded, a tender expression on his face. Holly looked at him, stunned by his transition. He no longer looked the warrior. He looked like a man in love.

His voice, a soft caress, wrapped around her heart. "Yes, you do," he said. "I also want you to know, that as Roger whimpered and cried, I contained my irritation. For you, not for him."

Holly inched her hands up around his neck. "I was so worried about you."

He caressed her cheek with his thumb. "Let's go take care of Roger and get him settled. I want to be alone with you."

She nodded, smiling at him and making sure he saw the love she had for him in her eyes. He needed to know.

Holly slipped her hand into Mason's as they started walking toward the kitchen. Abruptly Mason stopped in his tracks, pulling Holly around to face him. He fixed her in an eye level stare. "I don't want you to talk to Roger about any of our plans. Not your ideas, not our strategies to defeat the Arions, none of it."

Her brows dipped. "You can trust Roger."

He hated how damn protective and blind she was about Roger. "Arions have ways of dragging information out of people. He's weak, Holly. Even if he didn't intend to give away information they could make him. He might not even know he did it."

"Well, they could do the same with me," she said, obviously defensive.

"No," he said. "They couldn't. You're different."

"How can I be different?"

He stepped closer and mentally assessed how to tell her what she wanted to know without revealing what he wasn't ready to tell. His hands settled on her shoulders. "You know I've touched your mind, Holly. I know who and what you are. You are nothing like Roger. Some people are more susceptible to hypnosis, intimidation and power, the three favorite tools of the Arions."

She looked like she might argue. He almost laughed. No one argued with him when he gave orders. But Holly was Holly and she would always fight for her opinion. She wasn't a soldier trained to take orders. And he liked her that way.

Most of the time. "Please trust me on this, Angel."

Her expression softened instantly. "I do trust you."

She said the words so easily. Not telling her about their mating was a betrayal she didn't deserve, a form of breaking her trust in him. He could only hope she would see things through his eyes and understand.

He tucked a strand of her hair behind her ear. "Thank you."

When they walked into the kitchen, Michael and Sterling sat on either side of Roger as he ate what appeared to be soup. They were each asking him questions. Mason released Holly's hand, letting her go to Roger. He didn't like it, but what could he do?

He motioned toward the door as he looked at first Michael and then Sterling. Knowing they would follow, he turned and left the room.

Chapter Twenty-One

Standing in the surveillance room with Michael and Sterling, Mason said, "Something isn't right."

"Agreed," Michael and Sterling said in unison.

"It almost felt too easy, taking Roger back," Mason said thoughtfully, his mind racing through option after option.

"I don't know about easy," Michael said. "We left two dead Arions behind. I doubt that was in their plans." He frowned. "But I agree. Something doesn't feel right."

"Roger seems like he's hiding something to me," Sterling input.

"But what?" Michael asked. "I can't get a good sense of what. Usually I can."

Sterling continued, "He seems nervous. Yet when I ask him questions he has a perfect answer for everything."

"He seemed afraid of us when we took him," Mason added.

Michael dismissed that idea. "That doesn't mean anything. He was scared, period. I think the man walks through life jumping at his own shadow."

Mason shrugged. "Maybe it's simply that he wants Holly and I have her."

Sterling let out a bark of laughter. "If he would have seen the look on your face when he hugged Holly, he'd be terrified for certain."

Mason fixed Sterling in a hard, go-to-helllook. "I told Holly not to tell him anything. Not even her ideas to fight the Arions. At least, not until I figure out what's bothering me."

"Good idea." Michael pulled out a chair and sat down at the table. "Let's talk about taking over 51."

Mason sat down. "Yes, let's. I'm tired of being on the defense. It's time to take an offensive position."

* * * * *

It was a long time later when Mason finally left the surveillance room, a plan in place to take over Area 51. His mind was on Holly, pressing him to locate her, wanting to hold her.

He found her in the lab.

Roger sat in a chair as Holly took his vital signs. Mason leaned on the doorframe, eyes watchful.

Holly looked up at him, answering the question he never asked. "He's dehydrated and needs rest. Where will he sleep?"

"Sterling has an extra room next door."

"Won't Michael be using it?"

His tone was flat. "Michael won't be staying."

Her eyes met his over Roger's head. She understood. Don't ask in front of Roger.

She gave a barely perceptible nod and refocused on Roger. "Let me take a tube of blood and you can get some rest."

Roger stiffened and started to stand up. "No. I don't feel up to giving blood."

Holly frowned at him, pushing him back down into his chair with a firm hand on his shoulder. "You have to, Roger. What if something's wrong?"

"Tomorrow," he insisted. "I need rest."

"Not tomorrow, now," Mason said in low voice he intentionally allowed to hold a hint of threat.

Holly and Roger both looked at Mason. Silence filled the air, heavy and tense. After several long seconds, Mason spoke. "Take his blood, Holly."

She nodded. Roger swallowed visibly.

Mason watched Roger the entire time Holly was withdrawing his blood. He was hiding something. No doubt about it. Mason didn't take his eyes off Roger but he spoke to Holly. "Have you tested any of the blood samples yet?"

"No, I was planning on doing it tomorrow. I spent most of the time you were gone today filling out questionnaires with Sterling." She smiled as she disposed of the used needle. "And learning to shoot a gun."

Mason's brow inched up.

"You hate guns!" Roger exclaimed.

Holly gave him a look. "I hate being helpless much more."

"Angel," Mason said with a completely serious tone, one holding pride and tenderness, not surprise or anger. "One thing you will never be is helpless." Then he turned his gaze on Roger. "Come with me. I'll take you to Sterling."

Roger scowled a bit but stood up. Mason's eyes locked with Holly's. "Meet you upstairs." And then, certain Roger wasn't looking, he winked. Holly rewarded him with an angelic smile.

Damn, he loved her smiles. He loved her.

He was looking forward to some alone time with her. The battle plan they had drafted was going to take a lot out of him. He needed Holly. She helped him stay focused on what was important. She helped him remember he wasn't the bad guy.

Unfortunately, right now, he had to deal with Roger. And the man was most definitely trouble.

* * * * *

Mason didn't say a word to Roger until he was inside Sterling's living room. The instant Mason stepped off the elevator, Sterling's eyes settled on his face.

"Problem?" Sterling asked.

Mason looked at Roger, fixing him in a hard stare. "Perhaps we should ask our visitor that question."

Roger fidgeted. "I don't know what you're talking about."

Mason crossed his arms in front of his body, his legs spread wide. "Oh, you know. Why didn't you want Holly to take your blood?"

He averted his gaze. A sign he was lying. And he was. Mason could practically smell his dishonesty. His senses were getting stronger. "I told you. I'm tired."

Mason walked toward Roger.

Roger took several nervous steps backwards bumping into the wall.

Trapped.

Mason didn't touch him. He didn't have to. His anger was like an electric current in the room. His power was charged, thick with its presence, and far more alive than it had ever been in the past.

Mason's voice was low. Calm. Too calm. Threatening. "If you put Holly in danger, I'll kill you. No hesitation."

"I...I swear. I would never hurt Holly." Roger was trembling. He looked like he might cry.

Mason gave the man a pity look. "You're pathetic."

Exchanging a look with Sterling, Mason knew he understood the risk Roger represented. Mason moved with impatience toward the elevator, edgy from his power, now racing through his veins like some sort of liquid heat. Michael had been right. Accepting his Arion genetics allowed him to bring his skills to life.

Controlling them was now his concern. His mind was powerful, as was his body. In anger, it could be deadly. Control was critical.

Mason found Holly facing the kitchen counter, one foot propped on top of the other, writing on a notepad. He watched her for several seconds, just soaking in her presence. It was said the female in an Arion mating had the power to keep the male calm and focused. Now he believed it. She wrapped around him like a second skin, holding him together and making him complete.

Just being near her made him relax.

Holly looked up, as if she sensed his presence, and smiled at him. "Everything okay?"

He walked toward her as she sat her pad and pencil on the counter and turned to face him. He rested his back against the counter and pulled her with him, her thighs resting against his.

Settling his hands around her waist, he said, "They are now."

Holly's hands settled on his chest. "I was worried about you tonight. It's going to be hard for me to get used to you always being in danger."

"We, Holly," he said. "*We* are both always in danger."

Her connection to him, as his mate, actually could offer her some extra protection but she would always be in danger, with or without him. David had made her a target. That was a fact that wouldn't change.

"I know," Holly said in a barely audible voice. Then, in a normal voice, "You know I'm not blind. I see the writing on the wall. That's why I asked Sterling to teach me to shoot a gun."

He tucked a strand of her hair behind her ear. "I think that's a good thing. I'd like you to learn every possible way to defend yourself. I know you don't like violence but protecting yourself is critical. There are skills you can learn, things I can teach you if you allow me to."

Holly nodded. "Arions don't seem to die easily. How can I defend myself against something like that?"

"A gun will kill an Arion. It just has to be at the right spot, which means catching them off guard. Their mental ability allows them to deflect a bullet if they know it's coming."

Holly gave him an odd look. "You're talking about Arions like you aren't one."

He sighed. "I know. Arion is the name David gave his people. As in, Hitler's better race. He wants the same thing. To rule the world with his new race. I will always be a Black

Knight, Arion blood or not, and so will our people. Anyone who joins us becomes a Knight, with or without alien enhancements."

"Our people?"

He traced the line of her jaw with his thumb. If he was to be the leader, as his mate, the Knights would be their people. But she didn't know that. "I consider you part of this. I hope you do as well."

Her voice was soft, her green eyes, bright and compelling as they locked with his. "Of course, I do. You know I do."

He leaned down and brushed his lips across hers. The touch made his body surge with awareness, only it wasn't merely physical; it was much more intense and utterly consuming. He felt her tremble slightly and knew she felt it as well.

Whatever it was.

She searched his face. "I don't understand what you make me feel." Her voice was a barely-there whisper.

"This is new to me, too," he told her in complete honesty. "When I am with you, Holly, I feel stronger, more able to face what's before me. For that, I can't thank you enough."

Her eyelashes fluttered, settling against her ivory skin like half moons and, for a minute he thought she was blocking him out.

But then she looked up at him, raw emotions in her eyes. "I've only loved two people in my life, my mother and my father, and they both died on me."

He slipped his hand to the side of her face. "I don't die easily, angel. I'm far more worried about you than me."

Her expression was completely serious. "I don't die easily, either. I want to learn to fight. Teach me what you can teach me."

Mason smiled. He couldn't help it. "You never stop amazing me, Holly Heart. You hate fighting but now you're determined to learn to fight."

She frowned. "I hate death and, as I told Sterling, mine in particular." She paused. "And yours. I don't want you to die."

A mate could join minds with his partner. He was only beginning to understand how it worked. But he was certain it was a benefit he would be thankful for. As he became stronger, and so did their mental bond, he could lend her some of his power. It would be far more effective, however, if she knew about their mating. He couldn't wait too long to tell her.

He had to make everything that might impact her safety available to her as quickly as possible. "As I said, there are many things I can teach you. Just using a gun will not be overly effective. Not for you. It might buy you seconds but that won't be enough."

Holly nodded. "Thank you for rescuing Roger."

He didn't say anything. What could he say? At this point he wished like hell he had left the man with the Arions.

She responded when he didn't. "You don't trust Roger."

His expression was grim. "I'm afraid I don't, Holly. I think they got to him."

Her voice held a hint of hurt. "I don't want to believe that."

"I know you don't."

"He didn't want to give me his blood. Why?"

"I suspect they promised him Arion power and gave him the first injections toward gaining his transformation, to win his loyalty. It is a common manipulation tool for David."

"But they held him as if captive." She frowned. "Didn't they?"

"They did but that isn't uncommon either. He hadn't been with them long enough to prove he could be trusted." He thought a minute. "Then again, it could have been a setup. We might have been meant to rescue him."

"But you weren't injured."

"No," Mason said thoughtfully. "But…"

"What?"

"Something's not right. I hope like hell Michael isn't walking into a trap."

"Where exactly is he?"

"He went back to the Arion base to coordinate a take over of 51."

"Which means what?"

"He will gather several key people, bring them to fight by my side, from the outside in. He will lead a group from the inside out."

She swallowed. "When?"

"Soon," he said, wanting to change the subject. "Enough talk for tonight. Right now, I just want you to come to bed with me."

Holly leaned into him, pressing her forehead against his chest. He ran his hand down her hair and her back, understanding her silent need for comfort.

Finally, she looked up at him. "I just want to pretend all of this doesn't really exist." She stared at him and then added, "For just tonight."

A soft smile turned up the corners of his mouth. "I can think of many ways to take your mind off things. Come to bed and let me show you."

Mason took her hand and started moving toward the door. He was all for getting lost in Holly and forgetting everything else. If only morning wouldn't hold the grim truth. Life was changing forever. They could never go back. And the only good part about the new version of life, at least to Mason, was Holly.

A few minutes later, Mason pulled Holly onto the bed and into his arms. He simply held her for long moments, loving how perfectly she fit in his arms.

Moving to his side, he raised up on one elbow, looking down at her. She rested on her back, her eyes wide as they searched his face. Her delicate little fingers traced his bottom lip.

"You're beautiful," she said softly.

Taking her hand in his, he brought her fingers to his lips and then smiled at her. "Isn't that my line?"

"I like it when you smile. You should do it more often."

His expression became serious as he moved one hand to rest on her stomach. "I spent a lot of time hating what I am. You make me think it's not all bad. It brought me to you."

"And you to me," she said, turning to her side to face him and sliding her elbow under her.

"I traveled with the wind today. I simply became a part of it. It was amazing," he told her. The need to share his experience with her was unique, almost necessary.

She blinked. "Like, as in, part of the air?"

He nodded. "Something like that, yes."

She pressed her hand to his chest. "That makes you safer, right? It's easier to escape an attack like that?"

He heard the worry in her voice. "I'm not going to die on you, Holly."

She looked at him, wide-eyed, her lips parted as if in invitation. He leaned forward, bringing their mouths close and then brushing his lips over hers.

Her arm wrapped around his neck. She looked into his eyes, not hiding the depth of her emotions. "I am really not used to worrying about someone so much. It tears me up thinking about you getting hurt."

"Ah, Angel, I feel the same." He whispered his response as he lowered his mouth, kissing her as the last word left his lips. As he pulled her closer, savoring how well she fit him, his head swam with the perfection of their bond.

She was his woman and his mate. He would die for her.

Chapter Twenty-Two

Mason's eyes opened as his arms tightened around Holly, instinctively ensuring her safety. She snuggled closer, cuddling up to him like a sweet little kitten. He wanted to enjoy the moment but he couldn't.

Something had woken him. Another sign his senses were getting stronger. To wake him from his sleep when nothing obvious was happening indicated as much. Gently, he started to set Holly away from him but she wouldn't budge.

"Mason?"

"Yeah, Angel, I just need to go check out the security cameras."

She sat straight up. "What? Why?"

He sighed and reached over and turned on the light. "It's just a feeling. Go back to sleep."

She sat up in the bed, naked to the waist, frowning. "No way. Toss me your shirt."

Despite the circumstances, he almost grinned. He had a gorgeous blond, his Holly, naked and sated from his loving, in his bed.

It was hard to ignore.

He reached for his shirt, scooped it up and handed it to her. While she pulled it over her head, he stuffed his feet into his jeans, not bothering to button them, and padded across the carpet to the camera room.

As he expected, Holly followed. Mason sat down in front of the monitors. There were six, all showing different angles of the caverns. Nothing obviously seemed wrong. Holly sat down in a chair next to him as he signed on to the computer.

After a few keystrokes, he started maneuvering the angle of the cameras. A camera outside the lab brought Sterling into focus. He was clearly on alert.

"What's he doing?" Holly asked.

Mason clicked to the surrounding areas. And there was Roger, just as he expected, opening the lab refrigerator. "Stealing his own blood."

Holly gasped. "I can't believe it."

Mason leaned back in his chair. "It's amazing what the promise of power does to people."

Holly just sat there a minute. "I thought I knew him."

Mason slid his hand to her leg. "As I thought I knew many of my men, not to mention my very own brother."

Holly slipped her hand over Mason's. "I know and I'm sorry. What do we do about Roger?"

Mason ran a hand through his long, loose hair. "See what he knows. Find out if Michael walked into a trap." He sighed. "Get dressed. You might be of assistance. Roger has a soft spot for you."

* * * * *

Mason and Holly entered the lab to find Roger sitting in a chair, looking like he was going to be sick. Sterling was propped up against the wall, arms and legs crossed. "Took you long enough," he said dryly.

Mason fixed his eyes on Sterling. "I assume you set him up?"

"Oh, yeah." Sterling grinned. "I told him I thought you had overreacted and I didn't want to tick off Holly by locking him in the room. I gave him the freedom to show us his true colors."

"Why, Roger?" Holly asked softly.

He looked at his hands where they rested in his lap. Finally, he looked at her. "I knew they injected me with something and I didn't want you to think badly of me."

"What did they inject you with?"

He averted his gaze. "I... I don't know."

"You do know," Mason said tersely. Holly looked at Mason. "He knows, Holly."

"Maybe he doesn't."

"Trust me on this, Holly," he said softly, his eyes fixed on hers. "I know."

Her expression said she was trying to understand, to make up her mind. It was several seconds before she turned back to Roger. Her voice said she believed Mason. "Why, Roger? Why would you do this?"

His face crumpled, knowing she didn't believe him, knowing he was busted. "It was join them or die."

Holly didn't move to comfort Roger as Mason thought she would. Instead, she looked at him. "Mason?"

He stepped to her side, laying his hand on her back and speaking close to her ear. "No, Angel, he's lying."

Holly nodded and spoke only to him, in a very soft voice. "I really don't want to talk to him right now."

Mason understood. Facing betrayal from someone you cared about was hard to swallow. "You want to go upstairs and wait for me?"

She nodded again. He kissed the top of her head.

When Holly had stepped onto the elevator and Mason knew she was no longer able to hear, he turned to Roger. "Was this all a setup?"

Roger looked at the ground. "I don't know."

Mason crossed the room and effortlessly lifted Roger, his shirt balled in his fists. The chair toppled to the ground and Roger's toes dangled in the air.

"I could make you talk but I think this method is much more enjoyable."

Roger was breathing hard, his face etched with fear. "Please, I didn't know what to do. They had me tied up. I was scared. I really did think they would kill me."

Holly's appalled voice rang through the air. "Mason!"

Mason grunted under his breath. Damn, what was Holly doing back?

"Mason!" Her hands touched his shoulder.

He looked down at her and then back at Roger, meeting the whimpering man's eyes and willing him to answer. "Was it a setup?"

"Yes!" he yelled. "But you weren't supposed to kill their men!"

"Who got killed?" Holly demanded.

Sterling touched Holly's arm. "Holly." It was a plea for her to back off. "Mason needs to know what Michael is facing."

"Put him down, Mason!" Holly demanded.

Slowly, Mason lowered Roger but only because Holly asked him to. "Who gave Michael up?" Mason said as Holly grabbed the chair and sat it upright, allowing Roger to sit down.

Roger looked at Holly, a plea in his eyes. "I don't know."

Mason stared at him, irritation and distaste trying his patience. Sterling must have expected as much because he said, "Roger, I highly recommend you tell us everything you know."

"Tell us, Roger," Holly said through clenched teeth.

He swallowed. "They wanted me to find out where Holly was being held."

"And you would have told them?" she asked incredulously.

Roger moved to the edge of his chair. Mason's hand flattened on his chest. "I had no choice!"

"You always have a choice," Holly said in a shaky voice. "I considered you a friend."

Mason pulled his hand back from Roger's chest. Without looking at Sterling, he spoke to him. "Get him out of my face before I do something I'll regret."

Sterling looked at Roger. "Would you prefer to walk or shall I find another method of transport?"

"I'll walk." He stood up and took a step toward Sterling, and then turned back to look at Holly, "I really am sorry, Holly. I never meant for this to happen."

Holly turned away from him, arms crossed in front of her body. She could hardly believe Roger had betrayed her. It hurt, yes, but it made it made her angry more than anything else. Angry at the betrayal and angry at the Arions for their intent to destroy all that was good.

It made her more dedicated to battle against the Arions than ever. She needed to test all the blood, to start her research.

Now.

She knew when Roger was gone and she was glad. Crossing to a supply cabinet, she yanked out a handful of supplies before turning back toward Mason. He stood near the doorway watching her. She held up a needle and syringe as she sat down in a chair. "I need a sample of my blood to compare to the others. Have you ever taken blood? I don't like sticking myself."

Mason crossed the room and knelt down in front of her, his hands on her knees. "I'm sorry, Holly."

She let out a bitter bark of laughter. "You didn't make Roger betray me. Why are you sorry?"

"Because you have to go through this. Because I lost my temper."

"Are you kidding?" she said with a very unlady-like snort , quite out of character for her. "I wanted to hit him. Yes, sure, I was upset at first, when I saw you being aggressive, but you knew what I didn't." Then she added, "Can you take my blood?"

He took the supplies from her hands and put them on a small table that sat next to her chair. "It's the middle of the night, Angel. Come back to bed with me. Start fresh in the morning."

Her eyes shut and she swallowed. "I really need to get started if I'm going to find answers."

"Tomorrow," he said, as she opened her eyes and looked at him. "Please." He let the word linger in the air. "Come to bed with me. We have a huge battle ahead of us. Let's take tonight to rest. Give yourself a little time to digest all of this."

"What are you going to do about Michael?"

"I'm to meet up with him tomorrow night. The problem is, he's bringing men to join us. One could be the traitor."

"You won't be able to trust any of them," Holly said, laying her hand on top of one of his.

His expression was grim. "I'm aware of that."

"So what are you going to do?"

"The only thing I can do," he said, "make the best of the worst. I'll meet up with them and deal with it as the moment indicates necessary."

Not a good answer. "That's not much of a plan."

He smiled but it held no happiness. "You call it how you see it, don't you, Angel?"

Her lips began to tremble. "I really hate this, Mason."

He took both of her hands in his. "Me, too. Me, too." He stood and helped her do the same. "But I would hate it a whole lot more if I didn't have you. It's your conviction to do what's right that has helped me see why we have to stand up and fight." He kissed her forehead and then added, "And why losing simply isn't an option."

Holly wrapped her arms around his waist, pressing her ear against his chest. Listening to his heartbeat always calmed her for some reason.

"Let's go to bed," she murmured.

* * * * *

The next day, Holly spent hour after hour in the lab, determined to find a way to contribute to the challenges ahead. The problem was, research took time. It was almost evening when an idea occurred. She raced to the elevator, eager to find out what Mason and Sterling had to say about it.

She found them sitting at the kitchen table, eating sandwiches as they reviewed some map. Without even waiting for Sterling to finish his sentence, she raced across the kitchen and leaned her palms on the table.

A bit breathlessly, she announced, "I've got an idea!"

Both men looked at her. Mason's lips hinted at a smile. Damn, he looked good, she thought. She shoved aside the thought, refocusing on her idea. A glance at Sterling told her he was irritated by her interruption.

Holly didn't care. "Sedate them."

"Sedate who?" Sterling asked.

"The Arions." Holly pulled a chair out and sat down, excitement in her face. "Don't you see, if you can't kill them, sedate them. Like a wild animal. Even if it doesn't knock them out, it should deaden some of their mind powers."

"Huh," Mason said thoughtfully. "Interesting concept."

"It'll work," Holly insisted. "I know it will."

"We could test it out," Mason said, running a hand across his jaw.

Holly was encouraged by Mason's response. "A tranquilizer gun would be no different than shooting a regular weapon."

Sterling shook his head. "They could still deflect the bullets. It won't work any better than a gun."

"It will," Holly insisted. "From what I understand, a bullet won't kill them, at least not easily, and they can block the pain. Once you get the tranquilizer in them, they won't be able to block the pain of the next bullet. They'll at least go down. I hope." She frowned. "I think. Really, I'm almost positive. I don't have the ability with my limited resources to test the theory. You'll have to do hands-on testing." She looked between both men and then said, "I say it's worth a try."

"I agree," Mason said, without hesitation. "I'll see what I can get my hands on but it'll have to wait until tomorrow. I can't risk being delayed before meeting Michael."

"Why don't Sterling and I go pick up the supplies?"

Mason's disapproval was instant. "No way. I want you here, underground and safe."

Holly's eyes flared with irritation and a hint of anger. "I can't live like some kind of caged animal, Mason."

A muscle in Mason's jaw jumped. "Until I get things a little more controlled and at least know who the enemy is, you're going to have to live within some boundaries."

"You mean caged, like an animal?" She pushed to her feet, shoving the chair back with her legs. "Maybe you should just use the tranquilizer gun on me. Then you certainly could keep me locked up, couldn't you?"

Mason's eyes followed her movement but his face was a mask—no expression, no anger. Just nothing. "It is as it is, Holly."

Holly was livid, her hands clenched in tight balls by her side. "I don't need a babysitter. At least send Sterling without me."

Very quietly, but with a definite tenseness to his tone, Mason said, "I'm not leaving you here alone."

"It's worse than alone. We have Roger to think about," Sterling added.

Holly's head turned to Sterling. Her tone was icy. "He's locked up. It's not like he's going anywhere." She turned back to Mason. "Have you decided what to do with him?"

Mason pushed his chair back from the table as he stood. "I don't have time to deal with him. Right now, he's staying under lock and key."

"He's not an animal either. You can't leave him locked up forever." Her hands went to her hips. "As for leaving me here alone, or rather, alone with Roger, this place is a fortress. No one is getting in who doesn't know how. Sterling can get the tranquilizer and be back in no time. We can't afford to go without something that could make a difference."

Mason and Sterling looked at each other. Holly glared at both of them. "Well?"

"I have a friend who can get what we need," Sterling offered a bit tentatively as if he wasn't sure Mason would appreciate his input. "If I leave right away, I can be back not long after you leave. I think I should try and get what we need, Mason."

Mason took several steps, stopping a mere inch in front of Holly, ignoring Sterling. They were so close, she could sway and they would touch. He looked down at her, his eyes dark and brooding. "Woman, you're going to be a pain in my ass for the rest of my life, aren't you?"

Holly blinked.

The rest of his life? They had never talked about forever but it was there, in the back of her mind, wanting to be talked about. But then there was the baby thing. She couldn't have them. She told herself that didn't matter but she would always wonder if it did to him.

"No," Holly said quietly, the wind suddenly knocked from her sail. "No, I'm not."

She started to turn but his hand snaked out to stop her. "What's that supposed to mean?"

"Whatever you want it to mean," she said, staring at his chest. His very nice chest with a nice cotton shirt pulled snug across rippling muscles. Damn, why did she always want him so badly?

"Holly—"

She looked up at him, not letting him finish his sentence, not wanting him to. "I don't want to talk to you right now, Mason." Then she did something she never did. She rambled. "And I definitely don't want you to touch me." She shook her arm where his hand rested but he didn't move it. "When you touch me, I forget everything we should be talking about, that I don't want to talk about right now."

Sterling cleared his throat. Mason frowned. "And yes," Holly added before they could speak, "I know that makes no sense to you but it makes perfect sense to me. Just let me go back to the lab."

A long pregnant silence filled the air.

His hand dropped. "As you wish, Holly," Mason said, taking a step backwards.

There was something about the way he said her name that kept her from moving. Her eyes went to his face but he turned, as if intentionally guarding his expression.

Sometimes, no, most of the time, she could feel what he was feeling. Now, she couldn't. It was almost as if he had shielded his emotions from her. And perhaps he had. He had powers he was only now learning to use. Thinking he had shut her out that completely felt like a sharp prick in her heart.

She turned on her heels, moving toward the door as quickly as possible. Yes, she had wanted some space but not like this.

Would she ever understand her feelings for Mason?

* * * * *

Sterling took one look at Mason's face and said, "You both took each other wrong. You're both under a lot of stress. Go after her."

Mason stood rigid, unmoving. "I won't force myself on her. Mate or not, if she doesn't want to be a part of my life, so be it."

Sterling had known Mason a long time. He was a trusted friend who was unique in his abilities, both mentally and physically. David's turn for the worse had messed with his head though. Sterling knew Mason needed Holly if he was to lead them all to a better tomorrow.

Leaning forward, arms on the table, Sterling said, "I don't believe that for a minute. She loves you. It's clear to see. Don't let what you're facing skew your judgment."

Mason looked at the clock on the wall. "I have to leave soon."

He wasn't letting him off that easy. Sterling's voice was firm. "All the more reason to clear things up before you go."

Mason sighed. "I do need to show her how to monitor the perimeters while we're both away."

Sterling pushed to his feet. "I'll be here. She'll be fine. Unless you've reconsidered and want me to go? I'm worried this could be a trap."

"I need to know someone is here for Holly. And you won't be here when you go for the tranquilizer. I want her to understand what to do if something goes wrong."

Sterling didn't like idea of leaving Holly alone any more than Mason did but he really wasn't keen on Mason going to meet Michael alone. Not after what they knew about Roger.

He also wasn't convinced the tranquilizer thing would work. Still, it was worth a try and leaving Holly alone in the cave was safer than taking her above ground. They did need every advantage they could get.

Sterling let out a frustrated breath. He had few options. "I'm going to leave now so I can get back as quickly as possible. The less time she is alone, the better we will both feel. You know, it might be good for you to tap into some of those special powers you possess. "

"I feel better going with what I know. There is too much on the line for me to get carried away with things I don't even fully understand." Mason's voice was thick with worry as he reverted back to the prior subject. "You really think she'll be fine here alone?"

"It will be an hour at the most."

Mason was silent a long moment before he gave Sterling a quick incline of his head.

Chapter Twenty-Three

Holly looked into the microscope without really seeing what was before her. She was thinking of Mason, of their fight and their future or, rather, lack of one.

She could see the writing on the wall. If the Arions weren't completely shut down, and soon, there would be a major change in humanity. Mason could easily be the leader of what would be a group of people fighting for freedom and goodness. He would need children to rise up and follow in his footsteps as leaders.

She couldn't give him what he needed.

The emptiness quickly building inside was suddenly replaced with an awareness that washed through her mind, a warmth that only one presence gave her.

Mason.

She turned toward the doorway moments before he walked into the room. How did she know he was there? This weird sense of understanding him and knowing him was starting to rattle her a bit.

They looked at each other, eyes locking, yet neither spoke. Holly took in his appearance with open regard. His hair was pulled back with a tie and he had changed into all black. He had a knife and a gun holstered to his belt and she was certain there were other weapons she couldn't see. He looked big, dangerous and ready to act. She could literally feel the edginess he felt as if it was a hum on her own skin.

Holly knew the weapons were necessary but they made her worry. He was going into danger. She didn't want him to get hurt. "You look like a walking arsenal."

"Just trying to be prepared," he said flatly.

"When are you leaving?"

He stared at her, not responding immediately. "Soon," he finally said. "I need to show you some things in the equipment room."

"Does that mean Sterling is going for the tranquilizers?"

"It does."

She knew how hard it was for him to give in. Even now, she sensed his hesitation to leave her alone, his fear for her. It was hard to stay angry when she felt his concern, so real and alive, as if it were her own. "Thank you."

He didn't acknowledge her words but she saw the surprise flash in his eyes before he wiped it away. With a nod of his head, he motioned her forward.

Holly followed him to the small equipment room. It had a countertop, two rolling chairs, which faced the large monitors, and equipment sitting on metal shelving. Mason sat down in one the chairs and pulled the other out for Holly.

He showed her how to log in to the system, what to watch for and what alarms could go off and why. She took in all the information, hoping—no, praying—she wouldn't need to put it to use. She had seen what an Arion had done to Mason. She knew they were dangerous.

The last thing he showed her was how to send him a distress message on a silent beeper he carried. "The system has special wiring that will reach above ground even beneath all this rock. If you call my cell phone it will be detected so, whatever you do, don't use it. This device will be safe."

"Is that why you can't call Michael and warn him?"

"Exactly. The signal would be picked up and tracked. It's too big a risk."

Mason swiveled his chair to face Holly's. "There's something else." He seemed to hesitate. "If you should have trouble and you can't get to the computer, there is another way to contact me."

Holly turned her chair halfway toward him, a question in her eyes, but instead of explaining how she could contact him, he asked, "Is being around me the rest of your life such a horrible thought?" His voice was soft, even gentle. Still, Holly sensed his apprehension. Her heart sped up, adrenaline pumping through her veins in some unknown form of anticipation.

She swallowed, feeling as if her throat was suddenly far too dry. "Not for me but it sounds like it would be for you," she said, with edginess to her tone. And because she didn't want to talk about the baby thing, she said, "After all, you said I would be a pain in your ass and that's a direct quote."

His eyes narrowed. "I don't want someone who whimpers and whines, Holly. Your convictions make you more, not less, in my eyes."

She made a sound. "You have a funny way of showing it."

"You knew I wasn't serious. Why did you respond to it out of the context we both know it was meant?"

"I…I don't know, Mason." She looked down, not wanting him to see what was in her eyes.

He grabbed the arms of her chair and turned her to face him, his arms locking her into a captive position. Her eyes went to his instinctively.

"I love you, Holly." His voice was a soft caress touching her heart. It began tearing down her walls. "I want us to spend the rest of our lives together. If you don't want that, if what I am scares you, then tell me so. Don't search for an out. I won't force you to stay with me." He hesitated. "I will force you to let me protect you. I won't let you get hurt."

His eyes met hers, searching her expression in some soul-deep way, almost as if he could read her mind if he tried hard enough. His eyes held something raw and needy and his voice was urgent, but low. Her shields seemed useless with Mason. And she really didn't want them to exist anyway.

With Mason, she felt the need to share her thoughts and feelings, good and bad. It was a fear of holding him back, of keeping him from having children, forcing her to shield herself at all.

"What aren't you telling me, Holly?"

She averted her gaze, staring at her lap. In a very soft voice, she asked, "What makes you think I'm not telling you something?"

He gently took her chin between two fingers and made her meet his gaze. "I can sense your feelings, just as you can mine. You know I know when you're upset. I feel your distress and I also know you really want to tell me what's bothering you."

With obvious trepidation in her voice, she said, "I'm not able to be everything you deserve to have in a woman."

"Meaning what?"

She shut her eyes since he still held her chin. "Haven't you wondered what I am doing for birth control? It's not like I have a pharmacy nearby."

In an instant, she was in his lap, legs over the arms of the chair. His arms were strong and comforting and she clung to him, soaking in the power of their connections, wanting it to last forever.

He slid his hand to her cheek and made her look up at him. "Are you telling me you think you're pregnant? If you are, please don't think I'll be upset. It's not the best of circumstances but how could I be upset about having a child with the woman I love? We will just have to pray my genetic changes won't be a problem."

Her stomach twisted in knots. "I'm not pregnant."

He studied her as he gently brushed hair behind her ear. "Talk to me, Holly. I don't understand what you're telling me."

She sighed and then started to explain. "I was talking to Sterling and asking him if he dated and —"

Mason stiffened. "Why would you do that?"

Holly gave him a look. "That's not the relevant issue here. He told me how Arions mate. He also said they only have a limited opportunity to have children."

"That's true," Mason said. "It must be with their true mate or conception won't take place."

"You will need a child to carry on your role should this turn into what it seems it will. I think it will become a war of leaders, with you as one leader and David as the other, good against evil."

"It's too soon to make those type assessments," Mason said frowning.

She didn't look at him as she spoke. "I can't have children so, even if I was your mate, I can't fulfill your need. You need to find a mate who can."

Mason ran his finger down her cheek. "Angel, look at me."

She shook her head no.

"Yes," he insisted as he used his finger to tilt her chin up. "I want you. If that means we don't have children, then we don't. Frankly, I would be afraid of what would happen to a child, considering all my genetic tampering."

She wasn't accepting that answer. It would be greedy and wrong of her. She wanted, even needed, Mason, but there was more than her needs to be considered. "Find your mate, Mason, so the future can be bright with your heritage."

He stared down at her, his heart in his eyes. "I have found my mate, Holly Heart." Then he lowered his voice, "You."

"No," she whispered. "I won't do whatever has to be done to make it so. I know there is some sort of ritual or something. Sterling said so. You need to find someone else compatible who can give you a child."

Finality in his voice, he held her gaze. "It's too late. What is done is done. I chose you."

"I won't do that to you," Holly whispered, trying not to cry.

Mason leaned down, brushing his lips over hers. "There is much we need to discuss, Angel, but not now. I have to go. Just know this," he said with a husky quality to his voice, "I choose you. There is no other I can mate with. I should have talked to you about this before now." His fingers laced into her hair. "I wanted you to choose to be with me despite what I am, not to force the ritual on you."

Then he kissed her, slanting his mouth over hers and dipping his tongue into her mouth. Holly sighed into his mouth. He tasted of love and desire and made her feel cherished. When he pulled his head back, they stared into each other's eyes.

His hand slid along her body, his desire to touch her, to please her, taking over. It hadn't been his intent. There was no time. But he raged with a sudden need to please her. To hear her call his name in pleasure. His hand moved to her thigh and inched between her legs, stroking her. She whimpered into his mouth and it only served to drive his need to a roar.

His head lifted, his eyes locking with hers. Long seconds were spent staring at one another before he lifted her. Somehow his desire to simply bring her pleasure had turned into a burning flame that he no longer controlled.

He was leaving her tonight… Who knew what would happen. He had to go knowing she was his. At least, for the moment. He pulled her pants down even as he turned her to lean over the chair. "What if someone comes," she whispered.

He didn't even consider her words. "I need you, Holly." He released his throbbing cock and then molded his body to hers. Animal need was controlling him. He slid inside her, hearing her gasp, a mix of shock and pleasure.

He felt like tilting his head back and yelling with a possessive claim. His hips pressed into her round, perfect ass, even as his hands held her hips. Each stroke was like a rocket of sensation. He sunk deeper, and harder, and she pressed against him with equal impatience.

She was making loud sounds of pleasure and he felt the animal in him answer with the rage of pure need. Harder, faster, more...closer. He wrapped his body around hers, filling his palms with her breasts, and his body shook with release.

Holly cried out his name...and then she spasmed around him. And slowly, he calmed, the beast inside now fulfilled, as was the man.

He helped her get dressed, kissing her cheek, her lips and her hair. Finally, he cupped her cheeks. "There is something important I need you to remember," Mason told her. "If you should get into trouble and can't get to the computer, reach out to me with your mind."

"What do you mean?"

His eyes met hers. "Our bond is strong, Holly. You already know we share much more than other couples."

"Why is that? It's true, I know. Are we... I mean, is it because I am compatible as your mate?"

"Of course you are. We both knew we belonged together the moment we met. As I said, there is much to discuss, Angel. The ability to communicate in our minds is not something I could do with anyone else, nor could you. If you get into trouble, focus your energy on reaching out to me and you will."

* * * * *

Holly sat in the lab, analyzing the Arion blood against a few formulas she had put together. Her resources were so limited, it was frustrating. There were ideas bouncing around in her head, good ideas to deplete the vitamin C in the Arions bodies, but she simply didn't have the resources to test them.

When Mason left, she had buried herself in her work, trying not to think about the danger he was in. It was unnerving, thinking about him against those creatures. He wasn't like them. They were evil and that changed the whole way they approached battle.

And what if Michael had been betrayed and now Mason was walking into a trap?

Holly looked up, staring into space, willing herself to stop worrying, to be calm. But she wasn't calm. The gun she had sitting on the table next to her was proof of that.

A loud sound made her jump, her hand flying to her chest.

She knew that sound.

It was the alarm.

Holly grabbed the gun, pushing her chair back so quickly, she stumbled forward and had to catch herself on the table. She looked down at the gun and gulped. She didn't need to be bouncing around with a weapon she hardly knew how to fire.

She needed to get to the equipment room. She whirled and took off in a jog toward it, holding the gun so it pointed at the ground, aware of its cold steel presence in her hand, silently giving her some semblance of comfort.

In that moment, she decided she was going to learn to master using a gun and any other weapon she could. Not just use them, master them. It wasn't in her nature to sit back and became a victim. She wouldn't do it.

The minute she stepped into the equipment room, she centered in on the problem. Mason had left a camera set up to monitor Roger. She could see smoke surrounding him as he pounded on the door.

Fire.

Holly sat down the gun, the threat of intruders gone, and started toward the elevator. A strange feeling, black and ominous, made her turn back and grab the gun. The extra time only made her more frantic. She had to get to Roger before he burned to death.

She punched the elevator button over and over. "Come on," she yelled at it. "Come on!"

It felt like a million years before it actually opened though it was only seconds. Holly ran inside the car and punched the close button the instant it was in view. There was no way to get to Sterling's cavern without going to the main level and then taking another elevator.

By the time Holly stepped off the second elevator into Sterling's living room, smoke had funneled under Roger's door and was forming a cloud inside the cavern. Holly started coughing, her throat and lungs burning almost instantly.

"Hold on, Roger," Holly screamed in a raspy voice as she moved toward the room Roger was being held in. "I'm coming."

Unlocking the door with shaky hands, she shoved it open and jumped backwards in case flames might surge outward. Roger fell forward, onto the ground, coughing and choking.

He was covered in black soot and his lungs were filled with far too much smoke, but clearly he was okay.

A fire extinguisher hung by the elevator door, as it did on all floors. She couldn't get a grip on it without getting rid of the gun. In a matter of seconds, she battled a desire to hold onto the weapon and the need to put out the fire. She shoved the gun in her pants but it didn't fit and she was afraid she would end up shooting herself.

With no time to analyze the intelligence of her decision, she sat the gun down at her feet. In the next instant, she yanked the extinguisher off the wall and moved toward the flames. Pulling the release, she began shooting a white wash of spray everywhere she saw fire. Holly wanted to scream out with joy as the flames turned into smoke, inch by inch, disappearing and taking away the threat.

When the fire was finally out, she dropped the extinguisher to the ground, exhausted and breathless. She wiped perspiration from her forehead with the back of her hand and then pressed her palm against it. Her skin felt too hot to be normal and her eyes burned as if she had acid in them.

The flames had been like a living thing, scorching with intent. God, they could have died.

She smiled, but just barely. It took too much energy. It always felt good to prevail. It would feel better later when she got cleaned up.

"Holly."

Something about the way Roger said her name made dread snake through her veins. Slowly, she turned and brought him into focus. He stood facing her, the damn gun in his hand.

She looked at it and then raised her eyes to his. "Now I know why I didn't want to put the gun down." A bitter laugh escaped her lips. "In the midst of saving your life, I forgot I was dealing with a traitor."

His eyes flashed with anger and something she couldn't quite identify. "It didn't have to be this way. I loved you but you chose Mason."

Jealousy. That was the other something in his eyes. "You set that fire, didn't you?"

"Where are the others?" he asked, ignoring her question.

Holly's eyes narrowed. "You're a fool, Roger. Mason will kill you for this."

He back stepped toward the elevator. "Get in the elevator, Holly."

Holly shook her head. "I don't think so, Roger."

"If you think for an instant I won't shoot you in the arm or the leg, and even kill you, you're wrong," he said. "I'm through with you, just like you are with me. They prefer you alive but they'll be fine if you are dead. You choose."

Holly stared at him, hardly believing this was the Roger she had considered a friend. Gone was the soft, nice man she had known. Had his whimpering the night before been an act? It must have been, because this was not the same person. Holly believed he would kill her. She saw it in his eyes.

She had never been afraid of dying but she wasn't overly fond of the idea. And Mason needed her. Deep down, her doubts about their relationship weren't justified and she knew it.

She had to live for Mason, for the Black Knights, and to make a difference in the battle to save humanity.

"Fine," Holly said bitterly. "Let's go."

* * * * *

Mason sat in the bushes, one mile west of Area 51, thinking about Holly, though keenly alert to his surroundings. Something about leaving her had really bothered him. Maybe it was guilt, because he had been holding back information from her. He couldn't quite put his finger on it.

He felt Michael before he saw him, his senses alert and alive like they had never been. The wind shifted, at first slightly. A sudden gush of air produced Michael and two men Mason had never seen.

Mason and Michael made eye contact. To Mason's astonishment, there was a mental awareness between them. He saw understanding in Michael's eyes. Michael stepped forward, motioning for the others to stay where they were. Privacy was an issue with two Arions, who could both be traitors, so near. Options were limited. Mason walked several feet, with Michael following by his side, before he turned to face him. "We have trouble."

"So I guessed," Michael said, his tone calm but his eyes alert.

"Roger was a setup. He's been injected with the first level of enhancements."

Michael frowned. "We knew something was wrong."

Mason's expression was grim. "Yes, but since we killed both Arions, I hoped we had sidestepped whatever it was."

"I won't ask how you know this. I assume you've been thorough. Someone fed me bad information. How far up the chain is the question. Do you have any idea who the traitor is?"

"Besides Roger? No."

"Roger was a willing participant?"

Mason gave a quick nod. "He's lucky to be alive." He nodded toward the other Arions. "I'm reluctant to trust your men."

"These two I have no doubt about. Lucas and Diego are leaders, each with their own teams." Michael sighed. "The problem is, to take over the 51 facility we have to trust their men."

Mason's jaw tensed. "Which is a death sentence."

Michael seemed to contemplate. "Maybe. Maybe not."

Mason's brow inched up. "Meaning?"

"Meaning, my friend, that two can play this game of deceit."

* * * * *

Holly's mind was racing furiously as Roger nudged her forward. Her first step outside the cavern came with an overwhelming sense of finality. As if she would never return to the cavern.

The thought made her insides chill to icy levels. She felt a growing sense of dread, of a forbidding event to come. "Roger—"

Before she could finish the sentence the wind whipped against them, dirt swirling like a mini funnel cloud. Holly knew it was bad news. Roger was no threat. The wind brought the real danger.

She squeezed her eyes shut, focusing on Mason. He said she could communicate with him. Now, she prayed, he was right. With all her strength, she focused on Mason.

Her hair blew around her face, dirt stirring so heavily she could taste its bitterness. And then it was no more. Which could only mean one thing.

They were no longer alone.

Silently, she willed the seemingly impossible, putting her trust in her only hope.

Please hear me, Mason.

Slowly, she opened her eyes, tilting her chin up defiantly as she looked into the blackest eyes she had ever seen. And she knew who she now faced.

He smiled at her but evil lurked in the action. His voice, a deep, sultry tone, held malice he could never hide. "Well, well, Holly Heart. Finally, I meet my brother's mate."

* * * * *

Mason stood with Michael and the two Arion men he had brought with him. Together the men discussed options to deal with their unknown traitor.

Michael was halfway through a sentence when Mason felt Holly's fear. It ripped through his heart like a dagger of death. Her danger was real, the evil near her... Malice was the word that came to mind, clearly, as if Holly had spoken it to him.

David.

"What is it?" Michael asked in a soft, seemingly calm voice but it held an underlying urgency.

"David has Holly."

* * * * *

Mason stepped out of the trees with Michael, Lucas and Diego in position beside and behind him. Holly stood to the right of David, a defiant look in her eyes, and Mason couldn't help but feel a surge of pride. As scared as she had to be, she was not willing to cower to David or anyone, for that matter.

Roger was nowhere in sight. Probably hiding like the coward he was. He was thankful he had gotten to her before she was transported. It would have been harder to free her once David had her within his tightly held world of underground caverns.

David waved him forward, turning his body to face Mason, giving Holly his profile. "So good of you to join us, my dear brother."

Mason took several more steps, not daring to meet Holly's gaze, though the temptation was strong. It was enough to know she was alive and within reach. She stood too close to David for his comfort and Roger held her at gunpoint.

He regretted ever going after that man.

Assessing the situation, he noted five Arions, none of which he knew. They were fairly evenly matched, one thing in their favor, at least.

The two men Michael had brought with him had earned Mason's loyalty. Now that they had exposed themselves to David, they could never go back.

"And Michael," David said. "Always good to do business with you. I see you have recruited a few followers." His eyes brushed Diego and Lucas as he made a tsk sound. "So few of you against so many. What are you thinking, Mason?"

Michael's voice was like a knife slicing through the air. "There are many who will follow us, David."

An evil smile played on his lips. "Everything is not always as it seems, Michael. You of all people should know this."

The wind stirred and from the trees stepped a man. Not just any man. Tad. Arion and dangerous. He walked forward. "Michael," he said with a nod. "I hear you played hardball with my look-alike." He laughed. "Those damn clones really aren't much of a match, are they?"

Mason knew something had been wrong when they managed to kill Tad so easily. "Good thing," Mason said dryly. "I was disappointed I didn't get to kill you myself. Today seems a good day for you to die, Tad."

Tad focused on Mason as a sound, much like a growl, escaped his throat. He took a step forward. David held up a hand, instantly halting Tad's steps.

"Enough," David said, in a voice as deadly and quiet as the slice of a knife.

Mason and David locked gazes. "What game is it you're playing, David? Why involve Holly?"

"I didn't have to involve her," he said with preciseness to each word. "You did a fine job by completing the mating ritual. As your mate, she is a part of what dictates your actions. Perhaps, if I make her see the light, she will make you do so as well."

Mason could feel Holly's eyes on him, sense her confusion, her emotions running wild. Now she knew what he should have already told her. She was his mate. The ritual was complete.

Mason's tone held the threat he intended. "Leave Holly out of this."

"She is in this to stay," David said without hesitation. "Join me and I will ensure her safety. I will pledge to protect her with my life."

"No, Mason," Holly said quietly, but with conviction. "Don't follow him for me."

Mason had no intention of following David but he damn sure wasn't going to let him leave with Holly either. "Give me a week to think."

David smiled. "Of course, Mason."

Mason let out a silent breath of air.

An evil smile twisted David's lips. "But Holly stays with me."

Mason stiffened. "No way."

One of his brows inched upward. "I don't see you having much room to negotiate. Make the decision I want, the one that is your destiny, and she will be fine."

A bullet sound whipped through the air. Tad grabbed his arm, a scowl filling his rigid features. "What the hell?"

"Option number one just arrived." It was Sterling. Mason didn't turn to look. Didn't have to. Sterling, the "Renegade", most certainly was up to something wild and crazy.

And Mason was damn glad.

His guess was Tad just took a tranquilizer.

"You'll pay for that," Tad said, moving toward Sterling.

Sterling laughed and made a come-to-me motion with his hand. "You were always more talk than action."

In a matters of seconds, fighting broke out around them. Mason and David stood staring at one another. The battle was between the others.

"Join me, Mason," David said, in a voice so quiet normal ears would never have heard it over the sounds of battle. But Mason wasn't normal. "Make this nonsense stop."

Mason grimaced. "Be a man and leave Holly out of this. Our battle is just that, between you and me."

They stared at one another, a measure of wills passing between them, a test of who was stronger.

Abruptly, Holly darted forward and, before his eyes, as if in slow motion, Mason saw Roger reach for her. She flung her hands and feet, kicking and hitting him. Mason reached for her mind, trying to calm her, his premonition of disaster suddenly dangerously certain.

But it was too late.

The gunshot rang through the air like a missile seeking its target. Holly screamed. Mason's heart lurched.

And then she crumpled to the ground.

Chapter Twenty-Four

"No!"

Mason's scream reached beyond the ears of those directly around him. His pain, his absolute devastation, echoed through the mountains for miles.

Every muscle in his body was tense, his fists balled at the sides of his thighs. All movement around him simply ceased to exist as if every living creature within hearing range could actually feel his utter anguish.

Moving forward, Mason dropped to his knees. "Holly," he whispered, reaching for her and pulling her in his arms.

Blood oozed from her chest, staining her cotton shirt, representing her pain. His pain. Mason felt her body ache, felt her mind sinking into darkness.

Yanking his shirt over his head, Mason pressed it to the open wound in her chest. The bleeding was extreme, the blood loss too fast.

Holly's lips trembled, so pale, so deathlike, Mason wanted to die himself. "Holly, please don't leave me."

She tried to smile but her lips only trembled harder. Even this near death, he knew she was trying to smile because she wanted to comfort him. But her words held a reality he didn't want to face. Not now. Not ever.

"I...don't fix like you. I'm not sure I can."

He buried his head in her hair. "Don't say it." His voice held desperate denial of her unspoken words. "You can't leave me. I love you, Holly." He breathed in her scent, soaking in her very essence. "I need you."

Near his ear, he heard her whisper. "I...I...love—" Her voice trailed off.

Mason looked down at her, finding her eyes shut. "Holly! Holly, please, no! Don't go."

Tears were streaming down his face. He wasn't aware of when they started, nor did he care. He just wanted Holly, alive and well and by his side. This couldn't happen. Not now, not to Holly. Urgently, he felt for her pulse, desperate to find one, struggling in its absence. Then he found it—weak, slow, nearly gone.

David's voice broke through his torment. "You can save her."

Mason looked at him, still holding Holly close. There was no hesitation in his question. He needed to save Holly. If David knew how, then he had to know.

"How?"

Diego moved forward. Mason's eyes landed on him, stopping him in his tracks with their intensity. And though the young, dark Arion halted his steps, he didn't shy away from his intent. "I'm a doctor. Let me help."

Mason eyed him cautiously. Michael trusted him but it wasn't enough. This was Holly and her life was on the line. With a critical eye and every sense he owned, Mason assessed the man, never forgetting how near David was, observing,

"Yes," David said as if he felt Mason's awareness of his watchful eyes. "Let Diego tell you what we both already know. The answer is not as simple as a medical procedure. Holly is dying. It's too late for anything short of a miracle."

Mason fought the panic growing inside. He was aware of the group of his men, of David's men, gathering around them. But he needed help none of them could offer. Except Diego... Could he help?

With an obvious Hispanic heritage, Diego's dark looks only deepened the impact of his black Arion eyes. He looked the role of a fighter, maybe even mercenary, not doctor. But it was the combination of intellect and kindness he saw in his eyes that won Mason over.

"Yes," he said softly. "Please help if you can."

To Diego's credit, he didn't hesitate and Mason was thankful. Too much time had passed already. Holly needed help now. Seconds later, Diego was kneeling next to her, taking the shirt from Mason's hand. Mason remained by her side, holding her limp, cold hand, not willing to break contact with her.

"Take her to the cave and stabilize her," David said and then snapped his fingers. "Tad."

Mason looked at David, trying to understand why he cared about Holly, what his agenda truly was. Helping was only to benefit his cause. There was no question about it. Still, if he helped save Holly, Mason would accept his efforts.

Sterling stepped forward. "Tad passed out." Sterling looked at Mason. "Holly's idea was brilliant."

Mason nodded his understanding, feeling proud of his mate and praying she would live for him to tell her of her success.

David spoke directly to Sterling, "Help Diego get her to the cave and stabilized. I need a moment with my brother."

Sterling looked at Mason, a question in his eyes. Diego spoke then, his voice soft, lightly accented and deadly serious. "He's right. She won't make it without his help. I can make her comfortable but she won't make it through the night."

"She doesn't have to die," David said quietly, his voice unreadable, as were his eyes.

Mason narrowed his eyes on his brother for a long, tense moment before turning his attention on Holly. Gently he brushed a loose lock of hair from her face. She looked so weak it ripped at his gut, making him tremble from the inside out. Leaning forward, he pressed his lips to her forehead, letting his mouth linger on her skin.

It took effort to pull back from her but he had no choice. His eyes locked with Diego's. "Take her to the cave."

With superhuman will, he released Holly's hand and pushed to his feet. Forcing his spine stiff, he nodded to Sterling. "Stay with her."

* * * * *

As Mason and David both stepped forward, stopping mere inches from touching toe-to-toe, Mason had the eerie feeling of being about to sell his soul to the devil.

"Talk," Mason said in a clipped tone.

David's eyes glinted dangerously in the light of the overhead moon. He looked every bit the madman. "What price are you willing to pay to save your mate?"

"I won't bargain with Holly's life," Mason bit out, silently praying it wouldn't end his hope of saving Holly.

"I'm not asking you to. But there is a price. One that will impact Holly. You, and only you, can decide if you are willing to take the steps to save her despite the repercussions."

"These word games get old," Mason said, eager to get past the puzzles and down to the hard facts. "What do I have to do to save her?"

The corners of David's mouth lifted in a barely concealed smile. "You always were impatient."

"Just spit it out," Mason ground out through clenched teeth.

"All right then," David said in a slow drawl. "The answer is quite simple. Convert her to Arion and she will live."

Mason blinked, David's words barely infiltrating his brain. Convert Holly? No. Never. He couldn't.

When Mason didn't immediately speak, David added, "She is already connected to you, brother. As your mate, she is halfway down the path to conversion. Unlike the steps it would take for another to transition over, the process is quite easy for her."

Mason had a near tornado-like formation of thoughts running through his mind. He didn't know what to do. Would Holly want him to convert her? How could he survive without her? How could he be selfish enough to think of himself?

God.

Without knowing it he had spoken the word out loud.

"Yes," David said. "Let's talk about God. I know how religious you are. Arions are creatures of God as much as humans are. Would you end your mate's life rather than simply finish her conversion? If you believe we are all creatures of God and that God answers your prayers, is this not what you would want? A chance to save your mate?"

Mason laughed bitterly. "You of all people have no room to talk of God and religion."

David smiled but it was not a happy look that filled his face. "God has answered my prayers, brother. He gave me the power, and the word, to lead. Your destiny is by my side. My mate is Arion. Make yours so as well. This will help them help us as we create the New World that is the destiny of earth."

Mason could hardly believe his ears. "You're crazier than I thought. God didn't tell you to take over the world and, no matter what fiction you formulate, I will not be fooled into following you."

David's response was quick. "We shall see, brother, we shall see. Your role is by my side. I know this, and so will you. Together we can create a new world where weakness is no more. I'm going to spare your men tonight as proof I believe in our brotherhood. For now, all you must do is complete the binding of your mate. You need her to be strong. "

Mason ignored everything but the part about saving Holly. David had given him the safety of those around him. In the back of his mind he knew David wasn't as in control as he hoped he was. If he knew the depth of the uprising against him, he'd never free them. "A blood transfer? Intravenously?"

He nodded. "If there is time. The easiest method is more natural, the way of our race. Ask Diego and he will show you." Then he turned, the wind picking up speed, dirt spinning around their feet.

Mason's mind was replaying David's words when David turned back to him. "Acceptance is the only way to use what you are."

David started to turn but hesitated. "Once she is one of us, she will be able to produce a child again. You will want this to carry on our name and our leadership."

"How did you know she couldn't—"

David cut him off. "The same way you can know things. Acceptance, brother. Harness what you have been given. Our power is great. Soon we will show the world. Two brothers with world power."

Mason wanted to tell him to go to hell, but Holly was dying, and his men were weak. He needed to buy time, so he remained silent. The day would indeed come when he and David would be one...in battle. And good would defeat evil.

David smirked. "These few troops you've brought together have nothing to offer. My force is massive because my path is the way of the new day. I know you, brother, and soon you will join me. Together we will dominate."

And then he was gone, leaving Mason wondering just what his words meant. Just what exactly his twin had in mind for humanity. Knowing this battle was far from over. But he had only one real concern at that moment.

Should he convert Holly?

*****

Mason stepped off the elevator to find Michael sitting on the couch waiting for him. The minute he saw Mason, he pushed to his feet and faced him.

Mason felt dread spiral through his gut. He was afraid to ask. Was she dead? "How is she?" he asked, in a choked voice.

Michael's expression was grim, his tone weary. "I won't lie to you. She's not good. What did David say to you?"

Mason watched Michael's expression closely as he spoke. "He said converting her was the only way to save her."

Michael nodded, his lips tightly drawn. "He's right. She won't survive otherwise. You have no option."

Mason ran his hand across his jaw. "It's Holly's choice, not mine."

"She can't make that choice now. Choose life for her, Mason. It's not selfish to want her to live."

Mason's eyes widened, registering his shock at Michael's perceptive abilities. "Isn't it? I want her to live for my reasons. What if she would choose differently? What if she lives and hates me for choosing wrong?"

"She won't. Holly knows you need her and, more importantly, she knows the world needs you. She wants to be there for you."

Mason's voice was hushed, his pain etched in every syllable he spoke, "How can you be sure?"

"I am." The words were spoken with absoluteness.

The door to the bedroom drew their attention. Diego waved at Mason. "Time is short. We must act."

Diego's message was as certain as Michael's words. Holly was about to die. He had to make a decision.

It was now or never.

Did the love of his life live or die?

Chapter Twenty-Five

She looked so pale, so still.

Mason sat on the bed beside Holly and couldn't contain the sorrow and pure pain he felt. Burying his face in her neck, the tears came like water from a faucet.

This was his woman, his life, his mate, and, in as basic a sense as possible, his wife.

"I love you, Holly." He whispered the words over and over, praying she could hear him.

A light touch on his shoulder made him still.

"It's time to make a choice," Michael said quietly. "Will you give her life?"

Mason let out a heavy breath and slowly lifted his head. His eyes lingered on Holly, memorizing every line of her face, dampness clinging to his cheeks.

"Will you give her life?" Michael repeated with the same controlled voice.

Mason touched Holly's hair and mentally he reached out to her, his words spoken silently, to be heard only by the woman he so loved.

"Forgive me, Holly, but I am perhaps more human than I realized. Selfish as it may be, I can't let you leave me."

Then, like a light breeze, he felt a flutter in his mind.

Holly?

Did he dare believe she had just reached for him, that she understood his decision and was okay with it?

Somehow he felt as if he had received some form of acceptance, as if she had blessed his decision. Yet, still, he wasn't sure. Had he really felt her mind connect with his? It had been such a brief contact.

"Mason," Michael said urgently. "I must—"

Mason turned to him, cutting off his words with his own. "She can't die. What do I have to do?"

It was Diego who answered, stepping forward to the other side of the bed. "You must exchange blood with her."

Mason looked at the IV drip beside the bed connected to Holly's arm. It was a clear fluid that dripped into her vein. Not blood. "By IV?"

Mason already knew the answer before Diego spoke. David had already told him the facts. "There's no time," Diego said. "Arion methods are more certain and less time restrictive."

Mason digested the words calmly. "How?"

Diego looked up at Michael and then Sterling. "We need privacy."

Michael and Sterling moved without hesitation, wordlessly accepting and responding to the request. The quiet click of the door shutting sounded before Diego spoke again.

"It is natural for an exchange of blood to occur during the mating ritual and when conceiving a child."

Mason's brow furrowed. He knew Holly bore his mark yet they had exchanged no blood. "But Holly and I never exchanged blood. She bears my mark."

"The ritual can be completed without the blood exchange; however, it is a limited connection at best. With the exchange there are new benefits and abilities made available to both partners."

"Meaning?"

"The two of you will have a mental path of communication; she will share your powers and be better able to protect herself. Those are the critical factors. There are others we don't have time to discuss. For now, we must proceed. She is too weak to wait."

Mason took a deep breath. "How does this exchange occur?"

"The shoulder. At least, that is natural during intimacy. For now, wrist to wrist will do. She will not need a lot of blood," Diego explained. "Arion genes will connect with hers and heal her quickly. With sleep, of course. Just as you require."

Mason willed himself to calm. "Are you saying I have to bite her? Like a damn vampire or something?"

Diego fixed Mason in a steady stare. "It is hardly a vampire-like act. You are not sucking her blood, you are simply exchanging, creating a blood bond. As for the method, you have the ability to sharpen your eyeteeth if you concentrate. I assure you, nature will take over if you focus your mind on what comes natural to our race. She is your mate. You will want this."

Mason couldn't quite fathom the concept of biting Holly and drawing blood. To sink his teeth into her flesh seemed barbaric.

"There is no time to think," Diego warned. "Just do it. Start by biting your own wrist. Gently drip your blood into her mouth. A few drops will be enough. Run your tongue along the wound and it will reseal in a matter of seconds. Then do the same with Holly's wrist. I will leave you alone with her but I will be right outside the door. Simply call my name if you need me."

* * * * *

Mason let Diego's words play in his mind.

Just act, don't think.

Holding Holly's hand in his own, he closed his eyes, willing his mind to the place it needed to be. Holly was his mate. To connect with her felt natural. Reaching for her mind, he searched for a wave of communication.

His breathing slowed until it felt as if it were hers, not his. Thumb over her wrist, he felt her heat beating and it seemed almost to become his own. In his mind, he heard it like a loud beating of a drum, calling him to save her, to make her stronger.

His body responded with an odd surge of adrenaline, much like he felt during battle, only somehow different. It coursed through his veins like a stream of white water, pushing him to a new level of awareness.

His nostrils flared as the scent of Holly invaded his very core. It was as if he could feel her inside him, a part of him. Needing her, he knelt across her body, burying his face in her hair, soaking in her very essence.

Then, without even thinking about his actions, as if he answered a calling of sorts, he sat up and bit his wrist. There was no pain, only hope. His teeth had indeed sharpened. He held his wrist to her mouth and watched as his blood dripped into her parted lips, being careful not to give her too much, fearful she would choke.

When she swallowed, he let out a breath of air, relief inching through his body. This was his only hope of saving her. "That's it, angel, swallow for me." He carefully placed a few more drops in her mouth and then ran his tongue over his wound.

Before he could think twice about his actions, he lifted her wrist to his mouth. It was critical he complete their bond. Her strength to heal would come from the Arion transformation, not the blood. Gently he ran his tongue across her pulse, mentally sending her an apology before he bit down. She didn't so much as flinch.

With care, he let his mouth form a gentle suction, taking in a few drops of her blood before running his tongue across the wound.

He stared down at her, holding her hand in his. "Now it's up to you, Holly." He shut his eyes. "Please don't leave me."

After long moments he let his head drop to her stomach, holding her and praying she would stay with him.

"Mason."

It was Diego. Mason raised his head and turned to face him, answering the unspoken question. "It's done."

Diego nodded. "I'll check her vitals."

"And then?"

Diego's face was wiped of all expression. "We wait. I don't anticipate this being a difficult process. She is partially converted and her body is already in shut down mode. Any trauma she might feel will be shielded by her mind. Your blood will give her renewed power to heal."

* * * * *

Holly blinked.

She remembered everything that had happened to her as if she had watched it through some sort of looking glass. And she knew Mason was worried about her and his decision.

Sensing he was near, she attempted to call his name. "Mason." Her voice was a mere whisper at best.

She heard movement and then he was there, by her side, holding her hand, touching her face. "I'm here, Angel. God, I've been so worried." He called over his shoulder. "Diego!"

"I know," she said as he refocused on her, "but I'm fine." She frowned. "Who's Diego?"

He ignored her question and started to explain his actions. She knew it from his tone, his expression, his focus on her. "Holly—"

It took all of her energy but she reached up and touched his lips with her fingers. "I know. You did the right thing. I would never have wanted to leave you."

A deep voice Holly didn't recognize interrupted. "I need to check her vitals."

Holly raised her head to see, already feeling a bit stronger. "Who are you?"

"Diego. Your doctor."

"Since when?"

Diego laughed and exchanged a look with Mason. "She is feeling better, I see. Already challenging everyone as Sterling said she often does."

"Sterling said that?" Holly demanded.

Mason laughed. "I believe she is indeed improving."

"Twelve hours of sleep works wonders," Diego said as he moved toward Holly.

"Twelve hours!" Holly exclaimed. "I've wasted twelve hours in bed?"

Mason kissed her hand while Diego said, "It was necessary for you to heal properly."

Holly mind raced. "And now? Am I...am I healed?"

Diego stood by her side. "Near so. You know what happened?"

"Yes," Holly said, realizing how impossible that should be, yet it was true. She had seen everything through Mason's eyes.

"Then you know you are now Arion," Mason asked quietly, tensely, from beside her.

She looked at him. "Yes, Mason, I know. You did the right thing." Her eyes softened. "I love you. I could never leave you."

"Oh, Holly," he whispered. "I was so worried you would feel I had stolen your ability to choose."

Diego cleared his throat. "I really need to examine her wound and check her vitals."

Mason sighed. "Do it quick."

Diego smiled despite Mason's stern tone. "Yes, sir. Quick it is."

Holly smiled at Mason. "We have a lifetime, Mason."

"Yes, we do. And I am so damn glad."

* * * * *

Much later that night, after Holly had rested and was feeling well enough to actually move around, Holly lay nuzzled up to Mason's shoulder, propped up in a sitting position against the headboard.

Mason had told her she could have children again and she was still trying to decide how she felt about that. Once, it would have been great news but, in such uncertain times, she wasn't sure she wanted to bring a child into the world.

But maybe the future would be bright enough to allow her the opportunity to be a parent.

With Mason.

For long minutes they sat in quiet comfort together, simply absorbing the good fortune they had to have a second chance.

Mason broke the silence, a hint of torment in his voice. "I should have told you about the mating."

"Yes," Holly said, looking up at him. "You should have. Why didn't you?"

He touched her cheek. "I wanted you to choose to be with me. I didn't want you to feel trapped."

His words touched her deep inside. Her hand went to his. "I am where I want to be, Mason. With you, by your side, and I intend to fight with you. We can win this war. The Arions cannot succeed."

He nodded. "With your mind for science, we have a great edge."

"Yes, but I mean I am going to fight, Mason. Not just with my mind. With my physical skill. I won't get flattened like this again. I want to learn to fight and win."

He frowned. "But you hate fighting and, besides, I don't want you in the line of fire."

"I already am, as we have seen. I need the ability to protect myself. And yes, I hate to fight. I hate war. But I know we have to win this one for the sake of the human race."

"Holly —"

Her eyes danced with challenge. "I want to be by your side. A full partner. Can you deal with that?"

He was silent a moment before breaking out into laughter. Holly glared. "Why are you laughing?"

He pulled her into his arms and kissed her, long and passionately, and with his heart and soul. When he raised his mouth from hers, he said, "My warrior woman. Yes, I can handle it. And I thank God I have you, here, by my side, one hundred percent."

Enjoy this excerpt from
Healer
Underground Guardians
© Copyright Lisa Renee Jones, 2005

Diego's eyes darted behind her towards David. "So he's your bodyguard."

He studied him and then looked back at her. "He wants to fuck you." His eyes held anger and his tone a hint of hostility.

Marcella gasped, shocked at the abruptness of his words. Most people didn't verbalize such thoughts. "He does not!" She was quite certain Diego was a kind and gentle man. Why she didn't know but it was there, a part of him. She always got a sense about a person. With Diego it was more clear than normal but at the same time unlike anything she'd read from another. There was something she didn't understand. It conflicted with the other things she sensed. It was...more animalistic beneath his surface.

His look was a reprimand. "You know I speak the truth. You sense what he feels for you even if you choose to pretend it's something different. Some form of affection not built of lust." He paused. "Besides, he is not capable of protecting you as I am."

She frowned at his arrogance. "He is just as good as you." But she knew he wasn't.

"No." His lips twitched as if he knew she had lied. "He cannot win against the enemy that hunts you."

She didn't like the way he phrased things. It rang so true to her feelings over the past days, it was frightening. "Do you have to use the word *hunt*?" It bothered her. Maybe because it was so true to the dark feelings she had been having. "For all I know, you are the one hunting me. Perhaps you are simply trying to confuse me."

"We both know you can sense my motives. I speak the truth. Nothing less. Nothing more. I am your only hope of survival. You must come with me."

"I'm staying," she responded instantly and then added, "I'm here to heal a child. I will not walk away from her need." Why she felt the need to justify declining to go with him, she didn't know. This man was a stranger.

He took a long time to answer. "When do you see the child?"

Why she told him anything, she didn't know. Something inside her wanted to trust him. And she had been conditioned to let no one into her inner circle. It could get her killed or captured like some animal. "Soon. Tonight. In just a few hours."

His eyes narrowed and she had the distinct feeling he reached for her mind. A whisper of a touch, but it was there. "We leave the instant you have completed your duty."

"Duty?" she asked. "Why did you call it that?"

"Because that is how you see it." There was absoluteness to his words.

He had touched her mind as she had thought. But it had been done with such precision even with her level of skill he had been barely perceivable. "How would you know that?"

Taking her off guard, he pushed off the wall, closing the distance between them. He stood within a breath of touching her. The heat he generated warmed her skin stirring a flutter in her stomach.

"What are you doing?" she demanded, but the words were barely there.

His body was big enough to frame hers, and again, unbidden images flashed in her mind. Him naked. Her naked. Him on top of her, inside her, all around her.

He lowered his head near her ear, his breath trickling along her neck, enticing goose bumps along her skin. "I know you, as you do me." Her mind processed his words, even as her body responded to the deep tone of his voice as if it were a physical caress. Her nipples tingled. Her thighs ached. "I can feel you," he said," as you do me."

She swallowed and pulled raised her eyes to his. "Who are you?"

"Meet me in this exact spot at midnight. If you don't, I'll come for you."

Who did he think he was? He couldn't just order her around. "I won't be here."

His gaze locked with hers, and she heard his voice in her head. *You will.*

Her eyes went wide. She'd never met anyone who could communicate with her telepathically. "Who are you?"

He ignored her question. "Go take care of the child. We don't have much time."

And then his hand slid to the side of her face. The touch was like an electric charge. It, no *he*, ran though her body, touching each and every nerve ending. Her nipples tightened, her heart kicked up a beat, and she had to fight the urge no to reach up and touch his hand. She needed to touch him as he did her. Speaking didn't even seem an option. For the briefest of moments, she was completely lost in this man.

"Marcella!"

David's voice, bellowing through the air, snapped her back into reality. She forced herself to step away from his touch. And it took effort. Lots of it. "I have to go."

"Meet me or I will come for you."

About the author:

Lisa Renee Jones lives in Austin, Texas. She owned and operated a seven-office staffing company for eleven years. She discovered a love for writing in 2003 and sold her business, and now has ten e-published books and a hardback from Five Star/Gale.

Lisa Renee Jones welcomes mail from readers. You can write to her c/o Ellora's Cave Publishing at 1337 Commerce Drive, Suite 13, Stow OH 44224.

Why an electronic book?

We live in the Information Age—an exciting time in the history of human civilization in which technology rules supreme and continues to progress in leaps and bounds every minute of every hour of every day. For a multitude of reasons, more and more avid literary fans are opting to purchase e-books instead of paperbacks. The question to those not yet initiated to the world of electronic reading is simply: *why?*

1. *Price.* An electronic title at Ellora's Cave Publishing and Cerridwen Press runs anywhere from 40-75% less than the cover price of the <u>exact same title</u> in paperback format. Why? Cold mathematics. It is less expensive to publish an e-book than it is to publish a paperback, so the savings are passed along to the consumer.

2. *Space.* Running out of room to house your paperback books? That is one worry you will never have with electronic novels. For a low one-time cost, you can purchase a handheld computer designed specifically for e-reading purposes. Many e-readers are larger than the average handheld, giving you plenty of screen room. Better yet, hundreds of titles can be stored within your new library—a single microchip. (Please note that Ellora's Cave and Cerridwen Press does not endorse any specific brands. You can check our website at www.ellorascave.com or

www.cerridwenpress.com   for   customer
recommendations   we   make   available   to   new
consumers.)

3. *Mobility.* Because your new library now consists of
    only a microchip, your entire cache of books can be
    taken with you wherever you go.

4. *Personal preferences are accounted for.* Are the words you
    are   currently   reading   too   small?   Too   large?
    Too…**ANNOYING**? Paperback books cannot be
    modified according to personal preferences, but e-
    books can.

5. *Instant gratification.* Is it the middle of the night and all
    the bookstores are closed? Are you tired of waiting
    days — sometimes   weeks — for   online   and   offline
    bookstores to ship the novels you bought? Ellora's
    Cave Publishing sells instantaneous downloads 24
    hours a day, 7 days a week, 365 days a year. Our e-
    book delivery system is 100% automated, meaning
    your order is filled as soon as you pay for it.

   Those are a few of the top reasons why electronic
novels are displacing paperbacks for many an avid reader.
As always, Ellora's Cave and Cerridwen Press welcomes
your questions and comments. We invite you to email us
at service@ellorascave.com, service@cerridwenpress.com
or write to us directly at: 1056 Home Ave. Akron OH
44310-3502.

THE
⚱ ELLORA'S CAVE ⚱
LIBRARY

Stay up to date with Ellora's Cave Titles in
Print with our Quarterly Catalog.

TO RECIEVE A CATALOG,
SEND AN EMAIL WITH YOUR NAME
AND MAILING ADDRESS TO:

CATALOG@ELLORASCAVE.COM

OR SEND A LETTER OR POSTCARD
WITH YOUR MAILING ADDRESS TO:

CATALOG REQUEST
c/o ELLORA'S CAVE PUBLISHING, INC.
1056 HOME AVENUE
AKRON, OHIO 44310-3502

Discover for yourself why readers can't get enough of the multiple award-winning publisher Ellora's Cave. Whether you prefer e-books or paperbacks, be sure to visit EC on the web at www.ellorascave.com for an erotic reading experience that will leave you breathless.

www.ellorascave.com

Printed in the United States
56316LVS00001B/9

9 781419 952289